THE WIZARD OF ISLAND HOME

FIRST EDITION, 2025

PUBLISHED BY DICKINSON & COCKCROFT

AN IMPRINT OF FABRICATIONIST BOOKS

ISBN: 979-8-9986819-0-5

BOOK DESIGN BY DIVCON

PRINTED IN THE UNITED STATES

THE WIZARD OF ISLAND HOME

AN AUBREY COCKCROFT KERFUFFLE

G.A. BUNCH

DICKINSON & COCKCROFT

KNOXVILLE

for my parents,
who believe in me,
even when I don't.

to my cats,
Mishka and Dr. Twinkie.
If only we could talk.

for my uncle Aubrey,
a consummate storyteller,
whose photo I took as
a child and rediscovered
thirty years later.

Seeing it again,
the first thought I had was:
*My uncle was a wizard
in the seventies.*

chapter one

We are all fragile –
And need supporting–
If it is done — wrong,
We need saving – But
There are no saviors –
Only witnesses.

— AC

bottle cap magnet obscures my uncle's face on a picture I took with my Kodak Instamatic camera when I was 7, arriving to live with him after my parents died. Like most pictures of the time, it's small and square with rounded edges. Removing the magnet and taking the photo into my hand, I frown a little. His face is irritatingly out of focus, which, in all honesty, is how he would have preferred it. He would have said that it made him look enigmatic. To me, however, it makes him look like a fading memory reflected in the real world. Which, if I'm being honest, is the truth.

Looking down at me, still and patient, while I frame the shot, he's dressed in his favorite shirt. A dark blue polyester long sleeve decorated with white, pink, and orange splattered paint lines, like a Jackson Pollock. It's dark against his exposed arms that cross his chest, the sleeves rolled to the elbow. The line of his mouth is straight, but his right cheekbone is raised, revealing slight amusement. His brown hair hangs on his head, an unashamed mop of bangs. They cascade down before curling like claws grasping at his forehead. On his chin, a beard, between a goatee and a balbo.

There are a few other things stuck to the old Harvest Gold fridge. Some modern take-out menus I don't recognize and a calendar from 1998 on the top freezer door that I do. It's from the year I left and still in July. A black X crosses out the day I walked out. A dense collection of three-dimensional lowercase magnet letters in bright primary and secondary colors cling to the lower door. There's no structure to them now, but there used to be. As a child, this is where I honed my ability to spell. Cooking dinner, he called out words to me, trying to trip me up.

"Poltergeist," he'd say, and I'd touch a letter with my fingers, putting it in play, moving it around on the flat metal surface one letter at a time until I had spelled it.

"Done," I'd call out, stepping away so he could see the fridge door from the stove top that sat perpendicular to it.

"Nice," he'd say when I got it right, or "Close," when I got it wrong.

As I got older, the words became more difficult, pulled from ancient dead languages and obscure occult writings from his library. The library consisted of three five-shelf flat-pack pressboard bookcases set against the wall that delineated the living room from the front bathroom and bedroom. Their shelves kept from warping in the humid Florida air by a yearly chore he called the 'ritual of the sag and hump.' A simple process whereby all the books were removed in order from a shelf, the shelf dusted and replaced upside down so that any sag became a hump. Then the books were returned in order, their weight removing the hump over time, eventually creating the sag once more. The cycle was never-ending, and the ritual was never missed. But, as I look across the kitchen counter at the bookshelves, they're all sagging now and have been for a while.

Crossing the room, I stand before them, pleading for more knowledge—anything to help me understand what I've seen here. For a second, I think I hear his voice.

"Words have power, Aubrey, especially if you put them in the right order and say them with intent."

I learned a lot from those books. I learned even more from him.

Over time, words on the fridge became sentences, and the refrigerator became my blackboard. The kitchen was my schoolroom. With me barely being aware of it, he taught me how to susurrate the Gloam, a particular subset of magic that weaves modifications to reality through word combinations made manifest by their tethering to the Gloam. It sounds like you're mumbling under your breath. I don't use it as much as I used to, but I can still roll a conjuring on my tongue quicker than a Deft can weave a casting. Potions and alchemy are like algebra to me. They're out of reach, with too many variables.

It's just a memory, but it hits me like a finger in the chest. I'm seven again, and he's kneeling down to talk to me.

"A spell is like a lamp, Aubrey. It doesn't do much until you plug it in, allowing the electricity to flow through the wire and excite the filament. The Gloam is the power source you're plugged into. It's energy. It's life." He pokes me in the chest again, his finger pressing just hard enough to make me wince.

"Before you were born, when you were the size of a mouse in your mother's belly, you received your spark. Just enough to get things started. Fueled by our experiences, emotions, and knowledge, that spark grows inside us, our unique life force, our quintessence. No one can ever take that from you."

The last words echo inside my head as I slip the picture into my shirt pocket and turn my attention to the living room, where my uncle, now eighty-three, sits in front of the TV. His once brown hair is now long, white, and patchy. He's sprawled shirtless in his recliner, his mouth open, locked in eternal agony. His eyes are turned violently inward, exposing the milky, glossless sclera. Hemp rope secures his hands and bare feet. It's the nightmare that called me here—the one I had last night, where I killed him—but that's impossible. It took me nine hours to drive here from Knoxville. Nine hours of playing it over in my head, trying to make it stay. A nighttime drive of guilt and a sickening feeling in the pit of my stomach. Standing here, though, I realize I wasted my time trying to keep it from slipping away, because now it's right in front of me.

There's no way to tell when it happened, but it happened long enough ago for the flies to find him. A cesspool of decomposition and septic leak mixes with the perpetual perfume of the nearby paper mill, creating a smell I can already feel clinging to the inside of my nose. On the TV, with the sound muted, a Western—black and white, in both color and morality. Standing in front of the recliner, I try to see it from his perspective, comparing the reality to what's left of the dream.

Knock, knock, knock. He's watching TV. Shifting my eyes to the front door, the killer knocked. In the dream, I knocked. What kind of killer knocks? Someone who wants to be noticed or doesn't care. Looking for the remote, I see it on the counter separating the kitchen from the living room.

So, he heard a knock, muted the TV, and got up. Halfway across the room, he realizes he's still holding the remote and puts it on the nearest surface. Once he's opened the door, he doesn't bother to pick it up again. Why? I close my eyes and try to recall what I did, the killer did, after knocking. It comes back slowly.

"I know who you are," my uncle said, looking at me through the screen door. I know who you are. He knew the killer, and he would have called me by my name or slammed the door in my face. Another bit of proof it wasn't me. But why did he let the killer in? Why didn't he pick up the remote? Why didn't he defend himself?

I don't remember a gun. But I/they had something, a vase? Something with a lid? A jar? I can't remember. My uncle's face. I remember his eyes lingering, then acknowledging something. The killer? The moment? Realizing then he wouldn't be needing the remote anymore. Again, I look around the room. It doesn't look like there was a struggle. Was there a struggle in the dream? Nothing overturned. Nothing was disturbed, other than whoever did this. My uncle let this happen to him. Why?

Turning to my uncle, the smell of the paper mill hits me again. Something's off about it. It takes me a second before it comes to me. They closed the paper mill down. But how long ago? Would the smell linger? If so, for how long? Not for years. Smells don't linger that long. Maybe it's just a sense memory. Maybe I want to smell the paper mill. Go back in time. Make things right. I turn my attention to the horror.

Runes drawn in blood, now dry and brown like mud, decorate the wall behind him and complement the ones carved into his forehead and bare chest. The ones on the wall were painted with someone else's blood. The old woman's blood. I'd been so focused on my uncle that I'd forgotten about the old woman. I killed her first. Not me. Someone else. Somewhere else. A shop basement. I/They drained her blood and removed her eye. Where was that? Shaking my head, I try to focus. Turning to the wall, the runes give me pause.

I'm not entirely sure they're necessarily a part of what happened here. They feel more for show. A set piece for the police, or someone else. Me? Maybe that's why I had the dream, saw all this happen through the killer's eyes. Got to feel all of this happen. I walk around and stand in front of my uncle. The runes on his forehead and chest were deliberate. I step closer, reaching out, but before I touch them, the sensation of carving them myself hits me, and I flinch. It figures I'd remember the parts that fill me full of guilt.

Closing my eyes, I try to recall why this was done. It wasn't part of the ritual; it was something else. Desperation. Then it comes to me, what that smell is, the one I mistook for the paper mill. 'Tar magic,' my uncle called it. Malevolent. A hot, sticky kind of magic that spreads slowly and, if used regularly, can turn a man's heart black or a woman's. No reason to be sexist about it. But, with this realization, more awareness floods back like a tide going out to sea and returning, filling small pools of memory with forgotten knowledge, best left in the deep.

What was done to him is far more horrible than the scene belies. I'm not sure how many people would even know well enough to spot it, but I do. My uncle touched on it a lot, always as a warning. Always as a lesson. Someone ripped his quintessence right out of him, like peeling the skin from a catfish. His eyes rolled into his head as an involuntary response from the brain trying to catch one last glimpse of it before it's gone.

As a kid, my uncle used to talk to me endlessly about what he knew of the nature of quintessence and its connection to the Gloam. The paths it took by force or natural state. He didn't ruminate on its nature, divine or otherwise, but as an element essential to the essence of the human condition.

When you die, your quintessence returns to the universe, fresh potential energy devoid of intent, though some believe we retain consciousness during this time. No one knows for sure but the departed, but they aren't talking. Unfortunately, not everyone departs. Their quintessence gets stuck in one of three known states, some argue there are five.

Eidolons stay tethered to the world, mostly unseen, until reapers find them and tear them apart. Revenants suffer more, their quintessence trapped in their decaying corpses, leading to madness and a hunger for life. Poltergeists are malevolent, broken eidola birthed from the decaying remains of a revenant. My uncle's quintessence didn't move on. Neither eidolon, revenant, poltergeist, or departed. His quintessence was stolen, making him a victim.

* * *

Sirens, in the distance, break me from my fugue. I can't imagine they're headed here. How would they know? But I can't be sure. I mumble under my breath, and the dust motes hanging in front of me slow to a stop, trapped like mosquitoes in the amber rays of the sun. I've temporarily pulled this moment of the trailer's interior into the Veil. It's like taking a super-thin slice out of time. It'll give me room to look around without interruption. But the clock is ticking. The longer I keep the moment here, the more likely it'll attract unwanted attention. Moments that don't belong in the Veil leave a scent like blood in shark-infested waters. On top of that, if I stay too long, I can't ever return to the now. Risky for sure, but like many dangerous things, it also has rewards.

Pulling my cell from my cargo pants, I open the camera settings, switching save to the microSD. It keeps the traces off my phone and is standard practice for me. Each case gets an SD card. This is now a case. We may have been estranged, but he's the only family I had, and I won't be leaving anything behind. We take care of our own.

At the end of the trailer, just past the front door and bathroom, I pause at the closed door in front of me, my hand on the knob. It's been a long time, and I have no idea what to expect. Taking a deep breath, I turn it, open the door, and freeze in the doorway, astonished. Nothing has changed. He kept my bedroom as I left it when I stormed out at nineteen, calling him a hypocrite and a liar and telling him that I hated him. That was over thirty years ago. Thirty years I now regret. I move across the threshold and step back in time, overwhelmed by a deep sense of déjà vu.

The illusion that the room hasn't changed lingers for a few seconds more as I take in the teen boy aesthetic I abandoned here. Above the small desk, the wall is littered with movie ads cut from newspapers. Small black and white movie posters for *Ladyhawke, Labyrinth, Time Bandits, Hawk the Slayer,* and *Krull,* among others. Spiral-bound notebooks left by my hasty departure sit stacked too neatly in a pile on the edge of the desk. Pages and pages of journal entries, stories, and spell ideas, written by a stranger. At some point, he had at least straightened up in here.

The twin bed is made with military precision, the sheets pulled tight beneath the mattress. He'd taught me that too, making my bed first thing. He'd seen it in a movie. They do it in the military to instill discipline and attention to detail. He had me do it for the same reason. It gave a rhythm and routine to the start of the day. I still do it now, but no one inspects it anymore.

Off to the left at the foot of the bed is a TV stand on wheels with a 19" Sony Trinitron color TV on top. The antenna still splayed at the correct angle to pick up all four local channels, but they're all ghosts now—analog bit the dust in 2012, the victim of progress. My heavy six-er Atari 2600, with *Adventure* seated, sits on the bottom shelf. The two black joystick controllers rest on the console's slanted front, their round trigger buttons still a vibrant red.

Phantom pain blossoms in my right hand, a memory of the cramp these joysticks caused. What we used to put up with when it came to new technology amazes me. These days, people complain if the interface on their smartphone changes even a little. Every year, the age to be a curmudgeon decreases.

Beyond the TV is the closet. Opening it, I expect to find the clothes I left, hangers scattered on the floor as I ripped them off and shoved them into a rucksack. But the clothes are all gone, replaced by three war-era metal filing cabinets he got from some surplus sale. They used to be in the living room, where he kept his case files, although he was horrible at the paperwork part of the job. For many years, I was his secretary. I've been good at paperwork ever since. When I remember to do it, that is.

Grabbing the handle of the top drawer of the first cabinet, I give it a tug. Locked. I mumble under my breath, and the lock clicks. If it were anything other than a filing cabinet lock, I'd pick it by hand for the practice, but these are so cheap you can practically talk them into opening themselves, which I kind of just did. Pulling open the drawer, I glimpse a spider web and a few legs frozen in the moment, ready to scuttle to a dark corner. Closing the drawer, I try the next one and the next one.

They're all empty until they're not. An envelope with my name on it sits inside. Picking it up I feel a key at the bottom. Flipping it over to open it, I stop. Scrawled on the back, in what looks like his hand, are two words: 'Not Here.' My head, already spinning, adds another layer of uncertainty. I feel like I'm part of a plan I know nothing about, but I do what the envelope tells me. Then, I stuff it in my pocket.

I forget which drawer I opened last and open the middle one again. Another envelope. Same envelope? I pat my pocket, it's empty. For a second, I had forgotten I'm in a moment. Moments like this are fixed. You can look and touch, but you can't take. Anything I find I'll need to remember to grab once I'm back in the now. For the sake of completion, I finish opening the rest of the drawers. They're all empty, too. Maybe he got rid of the case files, burned them, or called up Iron Mountain. I have no way of knowing, and I'm not sure yet if it even matters.

Turning my back to the closet, I photograph the room. A wide establishing shot first, followed by a multitude of detail shots. I can't imagine anything useful, but I'd hate to miss the opportunity if there is one. It takes a few minutes, and when I'm done, I open the door, stepping out, letting the door settle itself back into place. I kind of want that Atari 2600, but I know in my heart I'd only play it a few times, and then it would become stuff. I have enough stuff.

I quickly pillage the small bathroom across from the front door.

There's nothing there but memories, a thin layer of dust, and small tufts of cat hair on the counter. A tiny stream of water sits frozen in time, so I assume he has a cat, and the sink is its fountain. He had a cat I remember from a long time ago named Arbuckle. In many ways, he was the only friend I ever had here. Taking a couple of photos of the empty bathroom, like ticking off boxes, I document the nothingness.

Putting my back against the front door, I position myself for the establishing shot of the tableau of horror that's been dropped into the middle of the living room. The shot is wide enough to include a portion of the kitchen and dining room area behind and to his left. It's a little ironic, this Frances Glessner Lee diorama of an unexplained death. His diorama, life-size and mysterious. He would have loved it.

He imagined himself the 'Rockford of magic,' and I cringed at it then, as I do now. He had fancied himself a supernatural private investigator for the conjurors of the coastal south. From the 'panhandle to the parish,' it said on his card. For a while, he even drove a 1974 Pontiac Firebird Esprit, which the salty beach air corroded over time in a creeping cancer of rust.

The car was eventually put out of its misery by a small-time drug dealer who dabbled in malison bags, named Angus Donley. He'd shot her right through the engine block with a .300 Win Mag from the window of his trailer after my uncle tracked him down.

A couple of the malison bags Donley had purchased from a third party caused concern when they were discovered at the scene of multiple accidents involving high school kids. The newspapers stirred up some Satanic panic, and the Sheriff of Bay County put it at the top of his list of things to address if reelected. The local coven hired my uncle to see what he could dig up. They were scared it'd turn into open season on witches. 'Florida man channels his Puritan roots and goes hunting.'

I can guarantee one thing—Donley quickly wished he'd shot my uncle and not the car. He gave up his malison bag supplier between bouts of projectile vomiting and explosive diarrhea, a quick and effective curse that wins every time. The coven took care of the rest.

My uncle was a magic prodigy, unlike me. He could do it all. And for that, he was well known, at least regionally, and during the years I was with him, well respected. But I always knew he kept a part of his life private from me, and maybe I can't really blame him for that now that I'm older and like to keep to myself. He hadn't asked for a son, but he'd stepped up when my parents died, and I'm sure that was hard for him. What was hard for me was that he never wanted to talk about them or what had happened. I did because I had no memory of any of it. He'd get mad whenever I asked or brought it up. Whatever had happened had haunted him.

I'm thinking about this as I take his close-ups. Turning the phone to portrait and moving clockwise around his chair, I capture a 360-degree video. After I finish, I walk behind the recliner and position myself to his left. Pushing him forward by the shoulder, I take flash photos of his back, trying not to miss anything. Even at 83, I can't imagine why someone as skilled as he was wouldn't have put up a hell of a fight to stay alive. It doesn't make any sense. He let it happen, but why? Algebra. The last thing I notice is he's sitting on his wallet, and I feel some self-loathing as I hope there's some cash in it.

Grabbing a few good rune-specific shots of the back wall, I run through a list of people I might know who can tell me if they signify anything important. They mean nothing to me. To me, they look like they were copied off an episode of some TV show. Set decoration magic, a made-up language.

The kitchen and dining room are open to—and defined by—the bar jutting perpendicular from the front side of the trailer toward the back wall. A single stretch of counter splits the kitchen from the living room, visually carrying an invisible line that separates the living room from the dining area. There was never a dining room table. We ate in front of the TV, on trays, like normal men left to fend for themselves. We were feral on our best days, and I miss it now. I didn't know how much I had lost until I came back.

Moving past this, I enter the hallway running along the back side of the trailer. On my right is a window and the back door, with a cat flap at the bottom. A stacked washer and dryer are set in an alcove across from it, sharing the plumbing with the master bath. A laundry basket full of folded clothes sits in front of the washer. The master bedroom, his room, is straight ahead. I've never actually been in it before. His personal space, like mine, was for me. I give him credit for that. As far as I'm aware, he never entered my room, except after I left. I wonder how long he waited before he did. Opening the door, I feel guilty even though he's dead.

It's a mess, not how I pictured it. For all the rigors of discipline and tidiness he put me through, I'm disappointed. That is, until I realize it's the only room in the trailer that's been tossed. Someone was looking for something. Racking my brain, I can't remember any ransacking in the dream, but then again, I can't recall most of it anymore.

The bureau drawers are all open. Even the messiest people know you can't open all the drawers together. It's a tipping hazard, and the only reason my uncle's bureau hasn't tipped over is that the drawers are empty. Their contents are in large piles on the floor.

Going through the motions, I do a pick, poke, and lift of everything, generally spreading the piles at the base of the bureau with my foot. Reminding me that a moment isn't a good place to conduct an exhaustive search, I watch it all pile up again. The only thing of note is an empty photo frame. What photograph did it hold? Maybe that's what was taken. What was in the drawers? I have no way of knowing.

Rummaging through his closet is the last thing I do. The shirt from the photo hangs inside, encased in a cheap garment bag. I make a mental note to grab it on my way out. It might be nostalgia, but the feeling is strong. It's not my style, or even close to my size, but I know a lot of work went into it. As a kid, I watched a knife blade shatter against it like a rose petal dipped in liquid nitrogen when a punk at a convenience store tried to stab him for his wallet. My uncle whispered something in his ear that made him slump to the floor in a crying jag while he wet himself. That night was the first time in my life that I stepped over another human being to get where I needed to go.

There's not much left to see after I photograph the bedroom. Tripping over the laundry basket on the way out, I curse under my breath as I catch myself against the wall. The basket makes it halfway over and then returns itself to the moment. My heart is racing a mile a minute from the short burst of adrenaline that kept me from falling on my ass.

Righting myself, I stand for a second to calm down. Once I do, I become aware that I'm staring at the cat door, returning to flush, resetting to the moment. Something disturbed it, but it wasn't me. Nothing could have made the slide into the Veil with me, at least nothing I understood.

Satisfied I've photographed everything I need to, I take the cover off my phone, pop the microSD card out, and put it with the picture in my front shirt pocket, buttoning it shut. Popping open the small compartment on the back of my phone case, I pull another card out and slot it into the phone. I doubt I'll run into anyone while I'm here, but it's best to be safe, and the probability of them checking my shirt pocket for something important is small.

Once, when I was on a case photographing a guy cheating on his wife, I got caught after leaving my hiding place. The husband took my phone in a grand gesture of dominance. I hired someone else to replace me, barely breaking even on the gig. Sure, I could have put some voodoo on him to retrieve it, but it's better when people don't know what you're capable of. And he was the kind of person who had friends. Since then, the card comes out of the phone before I leave my hiding place.

Heading down the hall to the living room, I hear scuttling—like rats on the ceiling. I press my ear to the wall I'd been staring at. Scuttling.

Shit. I've been in the Veil too long.

Stupid. Stupid. Stupid.

How could I have been so stupid? I got distracted by the past, pulled into it—held close while its grip tightened around me, slow enough that I didn't notice. A python's loving embrace.

I mumble under my breath as I run down the hall to the kitchen, but nothing changes. The dust mites laugh at me, still frozen in the sun. For a second, I thought *Frozen in the Sun* would be a great title for a song. The scuttling becomes scratching, and then a chorus of a thousand tiny claws playing dissonate notes on the thin outer shell of the moment fills the trailer. I hear cracking, like the tiny fractures before a glacier calves. It's the sound of instability, a warning. They're getting through. The Skittering is getting through.

"Fuck!"

I say it out loud like it's a spell.

It's not.

Of course, it's not.

If I can't move this moment out of the Veil, maybe I can make a door that will at least let me get through to the now. I hate The Skittering. They're a plague living off the dead skin of time, flaked, sloughed, tossed off, or abandoned between the thin sheets of reality, caught between planes of existence—devouring the universe's glitches. Granted, I made the glitch, but they won't see the difference.

Looking around frantically, it hits me: I can't use a door to the outside—like the front door, back door, or even a window—because they're all connected to the exterior of the trailer, which is still anchored in the now. I'd never be able to push through before the Skittering got to me.

But if I can get inside something still within the moment—both *now* and *here*—that might buy me enough time to stay safe, just long enough to make the slide.

If I can find that, I might make it.

I see it.

Someone—or something—has moved the letters around on the fridge. They swirl and dance in a circle, trying to return to their places but failing. They keep spinning around two words: **IN HERE**.

Pulling open the fridge door, I rake the contents off the top shelf and pull out the wire rack. As I go for the second, the contents on the floor are already reorganizing and creeping toward me. Using the first shelf as a barrier, holding it like a wall, I go for the second.

Behind me, the moment calves with a deafening crack, making me glance over my shoulder—blue light seeps through the doorjamb to what used to be my bedroom. The gap around it flares bright, then fades into thousands of writhing black fingers made of nothing, snuffing it out.

Then the blackness fills with stars.

But the stars are moving—growing—becoming eyes. Swirling fields of radiant blue suns light the way for a million chattering teeth, eager with excitement as they devour the moment and surge toward me.

A wall of death.

I mumble under my breath and place a shield between The Skittering and me.

It's on this side of my uncle, and even though it's only a moment of him that I can see across the kitchen bar, it feels like I'm being stabbed in the chest when they tear him apart.

Screaming in fear and pain, I attack the fridge like a badger digging a hole. Tossing its guts out and away as fast as I can, pushing what's left aside, I cram myself in. All of it trying to escape with me, trying to return to the fridge as The Skittering hit the shield, buckling it. Grabbing the door, *I mumble under my breath.* The words push from my mouth, filling the space like a sonic boom, before I slam the fridge door shut and am knocked unconscious by the impact of the Veil's reaction.

I come to, wet and cold, kicking my feet out and screaming, waking in mid-fight. The fridge door pushes open, and I clamber out, covered in rancid milk and leftovers, standing as quickly as I can, ready to fight. Everything hurts, but I'm back in the now.

"Fuck," I laugh and then vomit all over the kitchen floor.

Breathing heavily, my heart is racing. I hear the sirens again, still the same distance away that they were when I pulled the interior moment into the Veil. Like I said, time works differently there, but now it's time to go. Turning left out of the kitchen, keeping upright by leaning against the wall, I run to the master bedroom. I retrieve the shirt in its hanging bag out of the closet.

Dumping the clothes out of the hamper, I put the garment bag on the bottom. In the kitchen, I scrape all the magnetic letters off the fridge into a grocery bag I find crumpled on the counter. Scouring the floor for the ones that got knocked off, I pick them out of the vomit. I can clean them off later. Like the shirt, it's an impulse. I go through the bookshelves in the living room, taking what I know I don't have and hating to leave the rest. I fill the hamper until I'm afraid the handles will break.

One last time into my bedroom, *I mumble under my breath* and unlock the filing cabinets before I even open the closet doors. Going right to the letter, I grab it, shoving it in my back pocket. On the way to the front door, I keep stopping and stooping down to put the hamper on the floor so I can pick up the lumps of silver he used to make from empty beer cans. He never profited from alchemy, but I have no qualms with it. Times are tough.

The sirens are twice as close as a minute ago. Dropping the hamper at the front door, I walk across the living room to my uncle. Leaning down, I whisper in his ear. I tell him I'm sorry and that I love him. I tell him what I'm going to do next as I cut his feet and hands loose from their bindings to at least make him more comfortable. Remembering the wallet, I pull him forward onto my shoulder. His body, pressed against my face, smells as rancid as I feel, rummaging in his pocket. Pushing him into place, I apologize. Walking to the basket, I drop the wallet on top.

Stepping into the muggy Florida morning, sweat drips from my pores like tears. Securing the hamper in the back of the car, I pause for a split second to breathe—in through the nose and out through the mouth. I clock my breaths and slow my breathing and heart rate before turning to the trailer, a place I first laid eyes on forty-three years ago with a headache and a broken heart.

* * *

The first memory I have after leaving the hospital days after being told my parents were dead is waking to the vibration of a car traveling down a road. The sun pierces the windshield, hitting me in the eyes. I've clinched them shut against the brightness and warmth, which makes my headache worse. I cover my face with my right arm to block the sun so I can concentrate on why I'm here.

"Hey, Tiger. Are you feeling any better? We're almost there. We're almost home." He's trying to sound positive, but it feels forced.

"My head hurts."

"Remember what the doctor said? You hit your head against the boat. You're lucky, you're lucky to be—" I cut him off.

"Alive, I know." It's what everyone has been telling me. Lucky. I'd never see my parents again, and I was lucky. I remember starting to cry again, and my uncle reaching over and squeezing my shoulder.

"Let it all out, Tiger." There isn't any conviction, just weariness.

We finally stop when the sun is almost down, and my headache has calmed a bit. I remember climbing out of the car and staring at the trailer.

It looked small compared to my parents' house.

"Why do we have to live here?"

"Because it's home." That was the last time we discussed it.

Inside smells of cigarettes and stale beer. My uncle shows me where my room will be once we get it cleaned out and tells me I can sleep on the sofa until we do. He gives me an afghan of green and orange that he says my grandmother knitted and a pillow from his room that smells sharply of cologne—which I later learn is called *Hai Karate*. We have scrambled eggs and fried bologna for dinner, then he takes a beer out of the fridge, and I fall asleep on the sofa under the afghan, as he watches a western on the old TV set, a few feet from his recliner. I remember thinking how much it sucked that his TV was black and white.

I wake to something pawing my face and scramble back, forgetting where I am. The smell is wrong, and all the dark blobs I see in the dim light are unfamiliar. But then, I hear strong rhythmic purring, like a heartbeat. Reaching my hand into the darkness, I feel the warm fur of Arbuckle for the first time. I still miss my cats—one black and lean and one grey and strong—but I can't remember their names or what happened to them. The doctor said it would take time for my memory to return.

I had been in a bad boating accident, they'd said. My father had drowned, and my mother was swept away by the current. Somehow, I had clung to the rope from the bow of the boat—a tow line or something. My parents were dead. I was lucky to be alive, they said.

I'd been in the hospital for what felt like forever, but I later learned it was only a few days. When my uncle came for me, I remember feeling relief at the sight of him. I didn't know anyone. The doctors and nurses were nice, but I could see they were talking around me, in hushed tones, feeling sorry for me more than talking to me. I don't remember going boating—just waking up in the hospital, wearing my *Star Wars* pajamas.

I know my uncle loves me, but I felt like a burden on him—something he had never planned for or even wanted—so Arbuckle became my close friend, the one I confided in and went on missions with as we investigated the many curious cases we encountered in the trailer park. Of course, most of them were us overhearing arguments and conversations that we pretended were part of larger stories we made up ourselves, hiding under the trailers, eavesdropping.

In the hot days of summer, when the air conditioner wasn't working well, we'd hide out under the trailer where the sandy soil was always cool and listen to the visitors who came looking for my uncle's help. He didn't like me in the trailer when clients came calling. Sometimes, he even gave me a dollar to see a movie or something when he had a meeting. I'd ride into town on the bike he'd found on the side of the road and repaired for me.

Lying there in the cool dirt, Arbuckle and I would wonder what the words we heard meant—words like lamias, ensorcell, and cantrip. Not long after that, he began teaching me these words and many more after I proved a different kind of burden when I set my right hand on fire.

* * *

The same hand I now clench into a fist, then open slowly, rubbing my middle finger over the scar on my palm. Weaving one of the few castings I know—one of the first ones he ever taught me to control—a green flame appears in my open palm, floating above the scar. Bringing my left hand in, I roll the flame into a ball the size of a grapefruit. I mumble under my breath, bringing it to my lips and giving it purpose so its hunger has focus, keeping it from spreading to the neighboring trailers. It lifts from my hand and passes easily through the screen door, where it settles gently on the carpet and begins to feed.

A second later, something rubs against my leg. It's a cat, a mix of brown, grey, and beige with subtle spots on his back and sides and stripes on his legs. His ears are tipped and colored like smoke stains left on a wall. Picking him up and turning his face to mine, I stare into his gentle bright blue eyes. He chirps at me, and I'm transported back in time. Confusion washes over me, and I quickly check his tail—a half-long thing—a stub barely six inches long. A war wound from a fight for survival with a coyote.

My heart is racing now. How is this possible? I flip his collar around.

It says "Arbuckle". How can this be, Arbuckle? How can this be the same cat from my childhood? I'm not thinking straight. It can't be the same cat, but the memories of him are flooding my head.

Green flame rampages inside the trailer, growing and devouring the horror as I throw the cat into the car and climb in. I can't bring myself to leave him here. Watching the trailer fade in the rearview, I finally drop a tear.

By the time we get to the motel, nothing will be left but memories and ash. A minute later, two cop cars scream past. They'll see the fire and call it in, whether it was their original destination. Watching them recede in the review mirror, I notice a black cloud, tightly bound, of something small. It glides and shifts its shape, floating in the air. I can't tell how far away it is, but I'm guessing it's a flock of starlings spooked by the blaze. Mesmerized—as they paint shapes in the sky—I watch them as something itches the back of my mind. A name. Something I heard in the dream.

Horde.

I forget the name as soon as I think of it because I'm suddenly shaken back to reality by Arbuckle yowling next to me. I look at him and then at the road, where I've drifted into the oncoming lane. Panicking, I yank us back to our side as a horn from a passing car chides me. I jerk the wheel four or five more times to compensate for my first aggressive overreaction. The car settles, and I'm breathing heavily. I quickly check the rearview mirror—the flock is gone.

"Thanks for the save, bud. I owe you one," I say, as the fire engines speed past.

The thought of them trying to put the fire out with water almost makes me laugh. Five minutes later, I pull into the parking lot of a low-slung two-story beach motel.

I mumble under my breath as I park near the office so the clerk can see the car from the window. It's a simple masking spell to make the car look different to everyone who sees it. It'll only attract attention if people who like to point out cars in parking lots argue over what kind it is. Walking behind the car, I take a photo of the license plate with my phone.

The clerk is a young girl, chewing gum and watching something on her phone. She's at least polite enough to have the sound going to a pair of earbuds. She hears the bell over the door go *ding* and looks up, like a dog reacting to a dinner bell, pulling one of the buds out.

"I need a room for tonight," I say, trying to smile.

"Name?"

"Aubrey Cockcroft." She doesn't ask how to spell it, and I don't give her any advice.

Looking over her right shoulder, she pops a bubble at my car. "That your Hyundai?"

"Yes." I'm trying to let her tell me what kind it is.

She talks as she types the car into the computer. "Hyundai Accent," she looks at me, and I nod. She turns and squints at the car again.

"What color is that?"

I look confused and shake my head. "Not sure, maybe a—"

"Beige," she finishes for me. "Year?"

I shrug. "It's a rental."

"2023. License plate?" I hold up my phone so she can see the picture and so she doesn't think I don't have anything concrete to offer about the car. The illusion transfers.

"T-C-D-2-3-8." She calls out the letters and numbers, looking from the photo to the computer as she enters each one.

"That'll be seventy-three plus tax."

Reaching for my wallet, I remember I don't have much money. mild embarrassment on my face, I smile and raise my right index finger.

"I left it in my car. Won't be a minute."

I walk swiftly out the door to the office and over to the car, praying there is money in my uncle's wallet. At least she'll see me accessing it, which gives the illusion more power. I open the back door and grab the wallet. The smell of the vomit from the fridge letters is already beginning to bake in the heat.

Opening it, relief spreads through me warm and invigorating, and I imagine how a junkie feels when they see a fresh bag. Grabbing two hundreds from the modest wad, I toss the wallet into the hamper, shut the door, and lock it. The car barks a short honk of disgust at what I've become.

In the office, I slide over a hundred, and she points at a sign on the counter. 'Twenty-dollar pet fee.' I look out through the window, and Arbuckle is looking at me from the driver's side, his paws on the steering wheel like he just pulled in. I start to say something about how it isn't my cat, but all I do is hang my mouth open and slide the other hundred toward her. Like it or not, he is my cat now.

She gives me my change and a physical key attached to a plastic key chain with the room number printed in flaked gold ink. Putting the change in my pocket, I ask her which side of the building the room is on, but her earbud is back in, and her phone is two feet from her eyes.

Driving slowly around the two-story brick rectangle, trying to read the room numbers takes longer than I want it to. We finally get there, and I park in front of our room. I've only been back in Florida for less than two hours, and I've already covered up a murder, stolen from a corpse, kidnapped a cat, and burned down a trailer.

Florida, man.

∞

chapter two

Old and wise,
The King of cats,
The Lord of Honeysuckle.
The Duke of Treats,
The Mouser Prince,
The Great Cat—Lord Arbuckle.

— ALD
transcribed by AC

P utting the hamper on the floor, I sit hard on the bed. After what I've done today, the man looking at me from the mirror over the dresser is a stranger. We have nothing to say to each other. But truth be told, I need him. I need the man in the mirror to finish what I've started. Grabbing the wallet, I pull the cash out first, then strip it bare and score two points across the room in the trash can. Minus the motel, I still have close to $583.00.

I reach into my pocket and pull out what I have. Flipping the handles of the binder clip up and squeezing them together, releasing the folded bills and cards. A debit card, a credit card I know is at its limit, a punch card one sub short for a free one at a deli that's no longer in business, $11.00. I don't know why I still have the punch card. I've carried it so long that it feels like a part of me. I face the bills, the smallest on top, and clip them together, slipping them into my pocket.

Pocket.

Envelope.

I'd almost forgotten. Pulling it out, I stare at it. The writing is gone now, meaning I can open it. If only I could make my hands move. Magic isn't keeping me from doing it; something else is. Uncertainty? The envelope feels like a contract. Opening it means I'm committing to what's inside. I don't think I'm up to it.

I need structure and a scheduled rhythm to the day to even feel like I can get through it. Everything that's happened since I woke up from the nightmare has been spontaneous, making me feel unsteady and unsure. I already want to go home and be near Em, even if it's in silence. I left her in the driveway last night, watching me pull away in the dark, as she disappeared in the glare of the headlights.

We've been together for a long time, and maybe 'together' isn't the right word—roommates. She needed a safe place to stay, and I had a spare room. She never left, and I never asked her to. She comes and goes as she pleases, and I try not to act like an idiot around her. We've been doing this dance for a long time. To say she keeps me honest is an understatement. I don't know where I'd be without her or even if I'd be. She's never seen the man in the mirror. I'll never burden her with that.

My thumb slides under the flap of the letter, ripping it open. I look at my hands. They've betrayed me, committed me without my consent. Breathing deep, I let it out slowly. A key falls into my hand as I upend the envelope. It's a Master lock, nothing special. I put it in my pocket. Inside is a folded piece of paper. I remove it and open it. A photograph is nestled inside.

The photo is even older than the one from the fridge because my uncle looks twenty. It's rectangular with a frame of unexposed paper, bordered by a thin eighth of an inch bright white outer edge. This outer edge was protected by something. A frame. This is the photo from the frame I found in his bedroom. Maybe he was the one who tore his bedroom apart, running out of time to put this together for me. I can even imagine the key being the thing the drawers were turned inside out for. There's no way for me to know.

Five people, including my uncle. lean against a '69 VW Type 2 van.

A classic hippie mobile, painted with flowers, suns, some occult symbols, and squiggles I couldn't make out. Maybe they're animals, but I can't tell from the photo. And I don't remember it well enough since I only saw it a few times in real life.

Three women, one of whom I recognize, even after all this time, as my mother, and two men including my uncle. My parent's friends, the ones that visited me in the hospital before my uncle took me away. I had met them all before, I think. My memory before the hospital has always been hazy.

I'd even seen a few after, like Pirate Jane on a summer road trip with my uncle. She's the old woman I killed in the dream.

Not me.

They.

They killed.

My eye is drawn to her now, slender and dark-skinned with a free and asymmetrical afro and an eyepatch, black like a pirate. I remember her for sure. And peeking out from beneath the afro, sitting on her shoulder, is a cat. Looks like a calico. But it's hard to tell in a black-and-white photo taken at this distance. It only has one eye, too, but instead of a patch, the location of the missing eye is covered with fur.

That's when I notice they all have cats, either at their feet, on their shoulder, or in one case, flopped over their arm like a winter muff. I flip it over where the names are written on the back. Left to right: Francis Cummings (Alexander), Jane Zuma (Poly), Mia Orton (Saoirse), William Cockcroft (Arbuckle), Olivia Spencer (Pascal), and Johnathan Priest (Augustus). I stare at Olivia Spencer, trying to remember her as my mother, but I can't. I know this is an image of her, but too much time has passed. I recognize the image but not the person. Pascal is familiar too, grey, strong, and thoughtful.

Under their names is written *Autumni lucis defensores*, Defenders of the Autumn Light. The reason I left. The reason I stormed out and never came back. All because he wouldn't let me be a part of his magical order, his family—after I had lost mine. He said it wasn't possible. He said they had disbanded, but I knew that wasn't true. I'd seen letters and had overheard phone calls. They still talked. Often, it sounded like they talked about me.

I hear myself yelling, angry and hurt, rejected.

"Why won't you let me join?"

"Aubrey, it's not what you think," my uncle turning away and loading the van with luggage.

I remember grabbing him by the shoulder and forcing him to turn around, even though I was much smaller. "You think I'm not good enough?"

"That's not it," he replied, exasperated.

"You don't trust me?"

"Aubrey, it's for the best," he'd said, shutting the van's side door and walking around it.

I followed him, continuing to argue, "Whose best? Mine? Yours? What is it that you think I'm not capable of doing? You taught me everything I know."

"And you, you have more raw talent than I ever had. Then any of us have."

"So, why won't you let me help?"

"Because I made a promise."

I watch Arbuckle jump into the van and walk to the passenger side.

"A promise to who?"

"Your parents."

"What was the promise?" I ask, knowing the answer.

"To keep you safe."

He and Arbuckle were gone for a week, leaving me alone. We argued when they returned, and I left a short time later.

Flipping the photo over, I stare at the tiny image of Arbuckle at my uncle's feet, then over to the cat I kidnapped from his trailer. This must be Arbuckle the third, if not the fourth. It's purely coincidental that he's missing a part of his tail.

He's made himself at home on the small round table near the window. His leg is hiked up in an impossible position as he cleans himself. Stopping mid-lick, sensing my gaze, he stares at me, frozen, shifting his expression as if to say, 'Like what you see, pervert?' before returning to the job at hand. Looking away, embarrassed for some reason, I put the photo on the bed next to me and pull the next item from the envelope.

It's a letter, written in my uncle's precise, neat hand. I try to read it, but it makes no sense. It looks like lorem ipsum—filler copy in a newspaper layout. It takes me longer than it should to figure out what he's done, and I rack my brain for a cipher. It rolls on my tongue, soft and sure. *I mumble under my breath*, and the letters dance, rearranging and shifting into legible content.

Finishing it, I flip it over to start again, but the front is now blank. Flipping it back, I'm just in time to see the back page fade, too.

Flopping backward onto the bed, I roll quickly to my side, nearly falling off as I reach for the courtesy notepad and pen on the bedside table. Frantically, I scribble down the address of the storage facility it mentioned before I forget.

The rest of the letter is an apology. I lock it in my heart before the regret and loneliness creep in, spreading across my brain like fog.

Hitching a breath, then another—the third more rapid than the first, uncontrollable, involuntary—I start crying, heaving, gasping for air.

It's part mourning, part anger, a touch of humiliation, with a little relief thrown in.

It's the adrenaline leaving my body. It's sadness, longing, confusion, and fear.

I let out a moan, a howl, a distress call so deep and pained that I feel sorry for whatever creature might be making that sound.

Next door, a fist pounds the wall, and someone screams for me to shut up. My sadness and pain are noise pollution to their ears.

A soft warmth rubs against my arm. Arbuckle is on the bed beside me, doing his best to let me know it'll be OK.

I reach down and give him a scritch on the head, laughing a sad, hiccupped end to my outburst, then lay back on the bed. I wipe my tears with my shirt sleeve.

"Thanks, bud."

Arbuckle gently head-butts me, then makes two small circles and lies down beside me.

I don't know if I'm up for this. I feel overwhelmed and unprepared.

I close my eyes as my breathing slows and my heart rate drops—

catharsis flooding my brain with calming chemicals.

I'm tired.

I'm so fucking tired.

* * *

Waking and rubbing my eyes, I notice that Arbuckle left me at some point to reposition himself back on the table where he's staring out through the crack in the curtains at the setting sun. I must have fallen asleep.

Groggy like I always am after a nap goes sour and lasts too long, I stand up, stripping off my clothes, walking to the bathroom. The hot shower feels good, and I bask in it longer than I should. Stepping out and drying off, I wrap the towel around my waist. As I pass the mirror, I'm horrified at the reality. Nothing humbles a man more than seeing himself in a hotel bathroom mirror.

I don't spend much time looking at myself because, early on, I became disillusioned that I'd never be something worth looking at. But the light is so glaringly bright and the mirror so clean, I can't help it. It makes me look shorter and rounder than my five-foot-six, 200-pound frame.

Sturdy, that's what they called me in my 'husky' sized pants from Sears—never really growing out of it. I look like buttermilk poured into a balloon and set on a two-legged table. I really should lose some weight. Grey hairs have infiltrated my goatee, and the random tufts of brown hair that ring my head look more like a mangy undercoat.

Picking my pants up, I fish in the pocket for the keys, then drop them back onto the floor. In a rare display of confidence or a lack of common sense, I walk outside and pop the trunk on the car wearing only the towel. Retrieving the go bag I'd grabbed before leaving Knoxville, I shut the trunk back.

I stand for a second, secretly hoping someone will see me, standing here, and ask me if I am OK.

No one does.

In the room, vulnerable like a hermit crab, moving from its old shell into its new I dress. Fresh clothes feel good on my skin, like armor. I empty the pockets of the dirty clothes littering the floor, picking up the pieces one by one and stuffing them into the extra trash bag I brought.

Everything goes in its place: Leatherman and sheath on the belt between the first and second loops on the right side, cellphone in pants phone pocket, keys in right front, binder clip wallet in the left, ear plugs in in right cargo pocket, charging cords in left cargo pocket, microSD card and photo into shirt pocket, and microfiber cloth folded over three times and then in half into left back pocket.

Benjamin Franklin knew what was up: "A place for everything and everything in its place."

I fill the bathroom sink with warm water and open two hand towels, laying them on the counter. Grabbing the grocery bag from the laundry basket, I dump the magnetic letters into the sink and scrub them with the washcloth. I've never been one to use a washcloth. Maybe it's generational; I'm not sure, but it's handy now. As I finish each letter, I lay them to dry on the towels.

My stomach grumbles, and I realize I haven't eaten in twelve hours. Considering this my first successful unplanned intermittent fast, I decide it's my last. Arbuckle breaks the silence with a yowl, and I peer out of the bathroom. He's standing at the door, demanding to be let out.

When I do, he walks a few feet, stops at the edge of the walkway, and looks back. He wants me to follow.

Closing the door behind me, I trail after him—just like I used to with the Arbuckle I'd known.

There's a wooded patch behind the motel where I stand guard as he disappears into the bushes. I hear claws scratching through the undergrowth before—somehow—he's suddenly in front of me again.

We walk back, and I let him in.

He must be an in-and-out cat, too. Saves a lot on litter. And unlike a dog, he buries it—so I don't have to play cleanup crew.

"I need something to eat," I say to Arbuckle as he heads for the bed, paying no attention to me.

He stops, looks up to calculate its height, and jumps up, settling in for a nap.

"I'll get you something too," I say, closing the door.

I mumble under my breath and add some security.

There's a chain restaurant within walking distance of the motel. The walk across the parking lot feels nicer than earlier in the day. The light, warm breeze carries the smell of the ocean, which hits me, briny and tepid, like an oyster sitting out too long. Seagulls festoon the light poles like gargoyles from a Jimmy Buffet nightmare. Looking up as I pass under one of the lights, I stare at it. It's enveloped with swarming insects of all shapes and sizes. They move to the rhythm of the light's hum, and I imagine, for a split second, I see a face looking at me.

My mind digs up that name from the nightmare again.

Horde.

At the door to the restaurant, a few tourist families stand outside waiting for their little vibrators to go off so the kids can pick at a fourteen-dollar burger and dad can have a beer. I excuse myself through the small crowd. Pointing toward the bar, I let the hostess know I'm the kind of person who sits at the bar. She smiles like she knows me and nods. It's a simple and elegant transaction.

Settling into a seat near the wall, guaranteeing I'll only sit by one person, I feel relief.

Even alone, I can't stand small talk with strangers. People are my weak spot, to say the least. They require too much energy, and my battery is only half full. All those little social cues you're supposed to be able to interpret and react to appropriately, or even worse, their expectation that you agree that they're interesting.

I suck at all of that 'human' stuff. Everyone is a radio tuned to the same frequency, but my dial is one notch off. The song is the same, but the fidelity isn't.

A few minutes pass before the bartender notices me—another rube come to the circus. He walks toward me, his best sales pitch spreading across his face.

"What can I get you today?"

"Bourbon and branch."

"Branch?" He looks like a confused puppy, his head tilting to the side. He's a young kid, so I'm not surprised.

"Fancy name for water." I stop myself before I explain to him that it's iron-free water fed to distilleries from the rivers that branch from the aquifers of the limestone deposits under Tennessee and Kentucky, which filter the rain and snow melt.

I'm just looking for water to thin the bourbon.

He brings my drink, and I hold his attention with my index finger. Picking up the glass, I empty it into my mouth. I set the glass in front of him like he's made a mistake—which he promptly corrects. We play this game two more times before I order one neat.

"Would you like to order some food?" he says, a bit insistent with a touch of judgment, like we've been dating for a few months, and he's already embarrassed by how much I drink.

"I'll order something to go in a minute," I say, and he nods, wandering off satisfied and victorious.

I watch a cockroach scuttle up onto the bar. It stares at me from just out of reach. It's little feelers making sure no predators are around. I contemplate telling the bartender to get a discount on the food but change my mind. He'd probably kill it discretely with a cocktail napkin or something, and at least for now, the roach hasn't done anything to deserve that. So, I let it watch me, feeling sorry it doesn't have anything better to do.

Someone sits next to me.

I let out an annoyed sigh and rock my chair to the left, but I'm almost touching the wall already. Pulling my phone out, I play with the home screen. I look at the weather like I care, then open a news app and find a long article. I'm not going to read it, it's too loud in the bar for me to even concentrate if I wanted to.

"Sure, was a nice day," the person next to me says, and I know it's aimed at me, so I nod and grunt and don't take my eyes off my phone. "I'm from Ohio. Came down with the wife and kids for a nice vacation."

I let the sentence hang in the air and don't respond. It's a statement. I don't react to statements.

The bartender saves me long enough for me to turn a few degrees away while they're distracted placing their drink order. It's a tactic so they see more of my back when they try to communicate again. It's not as rude as them seeing me turn my back on them.

"You local?" he asks.

I know nothing is going to work, but to be civil and give him short, terse answers, so he gets bored with me and moves on.

"No," I say while tilting my head toward him, so he thinks I'm paying attention. Turning to the article on my phone, I thumb it up like I'm reading.

"Left the fam in the motel. A man's gotta have some time alone with his thoughts," he says, fishing.

"No doubt," I say, my neck hurting from trying to pretend I'm facing two directions at once.

He takes a sip of his drink, and I take it as a sign that I need to settle in or leave. I'm trying not to be rude, but what matter would it make if I were? We'd never see each other again. But it'd make me feel more guilty than I already do for trying to dismiss a person I didn't even know.

I've never understood why some strangers think they can start talking and the world will listen.

"What do you do?" he asks.

I pull my neck toward my shoulders like a turtle trying to hide in his shell. "I'm a private Investigator."

"Man, that sounds fun."

"I guess."

"I bet you have some crazy stories. Am I right?"

"Sure." I signal the bartender to refill my glass. "I have a thousand crazy stories. My cases tend to run along the outer edges of polite society."

Social Anxiety is a weird thing. One minute, it keeps you from saying anything, and in the next, you're hypomanic, talking rapidly, like the words are the only way to make the anxiety go away. I know that's where I'm headed, and the alcohol doesn't help.

"What's the craziest?"

My other weakness is that I can't lie. When someone asks a question, I feel obligated to answer. Simple questions are the worst. They're vague and make me feel a need to explain my answer. *How are you? How are you feeling? What are you doing these days? How have you been? What's the craziest?*

"You look like a parrot guy," I say, settling in.

"A parrot guy?"

"The kind of guy who'd like to hear the story about the parrot."

"Sure," he says, getting the bartender to pour him another.

"I was meeting with the husband of a woman who had gone missing. He'd hired me to find his wife. She'd disappeared after a big fight, and he wanted the police off his back. He was the prime suspect but insisted he hadn't done anything to her. Said he didn't trust the police to find her because they already believed he'd murdered her."

"Had he? Had he killed her?"

I make eye contact to let him know I don't like being interrupted.

He nods slowly, reading the signal correctly.

Sipping my drink, I continue.

"He had two Rottweilers—Jenny and Percival. While we talked, they slept by the fireplace, where he had a fire going. It was early January, and it was below thirty degrees outside. We sat at the kitchen table. In the corner of the kitchen was a large birdcage, and that's where the parrot was. Nice bird. African Grey. The parrot had belonged to his wife, he told me, after I mentioned what a pretty bird it was.

"While he told me where she might have gone, I sipped hot chocolate, and the parrot talked. Normal parrot stuff—catcall whistles and a little profanity. I remember the husband laughing at it, making sure I knew he'd taught the crude stuff to the bird. One of the many reasons his wife was mad at him.

"But then, out of the blue, the parrot said,

"'Stop hitting me—*rawk*—stop hitting me.'

"I tried to keep my composure, looking from my mug of chocolate to the man's face—now filled with anger. He slammed the palm of his hand against the table."

Smack—I hit the bar to punctuate the moment and make my new friend flinch.

"I remember watching warm brown liquid leap out of my mug and race across the table that had tilted, caught by his belt as he stood.

"'You shut your mouth,' he screamed at the parrot.

"Then he looked at me like he wished I hadn't heard it. I was standing too, hot chocolate warming my thigh.

"'It won't shut up,' he said, trying to make me understand.

"It was the last thing he said before walking toward the cage, grabbing a knife from the block on the counter.

"It all happened so fast—I didn't have time to do anything but get out of the way.

"I heard the parrot say, 'Sing us a song,' before whistling.

"I remember being astonished that it could make the sounds it was making. The man reached the cage and jabbed the knife at the parrot, but it flapped its wings, jumped to a higher perch, and kept whistling."

"I drain my glass, waiting for a beat. I can almost hear my new friend's tongue scrape across his dry lips. His eyes squint like he's trying to see if more words are coming. He seems unsure.

"I heard the dog's claws hit the tabletop before I saw it. It went past me in a blur and leaped off the table, latching its jaw onto the back of the man's neck. He screamed, flailing his arms and dropping the knife.

"The other dog—I couldn't tell them apart—had slunk low around the table. As the man fell, the first dog released him, and the second clamped down on his throat. I'm pretty sure it was the windpipe I heard being crushed. The man stopped flailing and went still as the second dog ripped open his abdomen."

"That can't be true," my new friend says, sipping his beer and looking to the bartender for confirmation.

"Scrambling back, I tripped over the chair I'd been sitting in and hit the floor hard."

Smack—I pound the bar again. My new friend flinches.

"I watched them tear him apart through the legs of the table. Then suddenly, the parrot stopped whistling. The dogs froze mid-attack, lifting their bloody muzzles. Their eyes glossed over with confusion. I scrambled up and ran outside, closing the front door behind me as I heard the parrot say,

"'*Rawk*—Who's a good boy?—*rawk*.'

"The police arrived shortly after, and I got hauled into the station for the first time. I spent six hours being asked the same questions.

"The next day, they found the wife at a motel about two hundred miles away. She looked like she'd fallen a lot.

"The dogs were euthanized for rabies testing. The parrot got to stay in its cage. The wife got to go home to a quiet house."

"You're saying the parrot made the dogs kill the man?"

"Technically, the song did. Arguably, a song the wife taught the parrot."

"How can a song do that?" my new friend asks.

"Want me to show you?" I lick my lips, purse them, and whistle a single note.

The man shakes his head. "It's bullshit," is all he says.

Down the bar, a couple leaves, and my new friend gets up and moves without saying a word.

"You should cut him off," I hear him tell the bartender. They start talking about sport ball.

I hesitate but then interrupt them by raising my hand to catch the bartender's eye, then I raise my glass. He brings it as a crowd comes in, using the empty seat next to me as an order hole. Their conversation clashes with the volume of the music, and I get hit quickly by too much information. It's coming from all directions, competing for attention, like children screaming on a playground. It makes the world confusing and puts me off balance. It triggers my fight-or-flight response.

Reaching into my pocket and pulling out the earplugs, I put them in—washing away 26 dB and settling the anxiety building in me. When the bartender brings my last drink, I order a club sandwich to go and a medium rare burger, no bun or condiments, which gets me a look. I settle my tab. My empty glass hits the bar as the food arrives.

Outside, I fiddle with the bag, untying the knot and cracking the foam container to vent the steam so the fries don't go soggy on the walk to the motel. I'd been there a while, so the parking lot is mostly empty now, and the traffic nonexistent.

A shadow flanks me to my right, keeping pace, but never letting me get a good look. I stop in the concession alcove and grab a can of Diet Dr. Pepper, keeping my eye on the shadow as it passes behind me and into the woods across from the motel.

At the room, *I mumble under my breath* before I open the door and do it again as I close and lock it, doubling the protection just in case. It could have been nothing, but it's been one of those days where it was probably something.

Using my Leatherman, I cut the top off the take-out container and then cut the hamburger into small pieces. Arbuckle, who's appeared next to me on the table without me knowing it is already eyeing it. I push it in front of him, and he dives in like it's his last supper.

Grabbing the remote from beside the TV, I sit on the bed. Flipping around, I find an old rerun of *Dr. Who*, where the Doctor and Romana wander around Paris for no reason. They keep repeating moments in time over and over. The episode is *City of Death*, co-written by Douglas Adams. It's horribly boring and deeply comforting.

I start to doze off when Arbuckle yowls me awake. He's standing at the door, needing to go out again. Pushing myself up off the bed, I realize I'm still decently drunk, but the food has certainly taken the edge off. When I open the door, Arbuckle sprints for the woods.

Too slowly, I remember the face in the lamp swarm, the cockroach, and the shadow. I run after him, uncertain of what might be out there. When I get to the curb at the far side of the parking lot, he's nowhere to be seen. The lights at the edge are bright, and as I look up into them, hundreds of moths and other winged insects slam into the hard plastic casing—*tink, tink, tink.*

"Arbuckle?" I whisper-yell, trying to peer into the darkness. "Dude, where did you go?"

The sound of a door slamming turns my attention to the motel. A young woman walks quickly down the outer walkway on the second floor in what can only be a march of anger. She lights a cigarette and hits the stairs, almost running down them.

The door she came out of opens, and a young man steps out in his underwear, smoking. He walks to the edge and looks over the railing at her. He's about to say or yell something, but it's too late. She's already in a car, screeching out of the parking lot. The young man mumbles something and chucks his cigarette butt over the balcony where it hits the concrete sending sparks flying—making a mini fireworks display—a small show at the end of a big moment. The door slams shut, and he's gone. I look to the woods, thinking Arbuckle should have returned by now.

Pressing forward through the trees—which are denser than I would have guessed—I scan around for any sign of him. The ground cover is thin and brittle, littered with large brown leaves, which crunch underfoot. The further I get from the parking lot, the more the light from the lamps fades.

To my left, I hear scraping and head for it. He's probably burying a massive deuce.

"Arbuckle?" I say again, hoping for a meow or something, but I don't get it. With every step, the darkness deepens. Around me, the only light comes from will-o'-the-wisp tufts of silk littering the trees and reflecting the moonlight.

Then, a persistent light breaks through, offering hope. Parting the branches, I find a clearing where a luminous wall collects the moonlight in a way nothing else does. At its center is a darkness that appears, just for a moment, to squirm and adjust itself within the wall.

"Arbuckle?" I say, conjuring the green flame in my right hand, edging forward toward the wall, slowly.

There's something familiar about it, but I'm not sure what, as I reach out my hand and brush my fingers against it. A thick woven sheet pulled taut on a frame—the fibers dense but identifiably delicate against my fingertips. Not silk—the realization hitting me—but spider's web.

Yep, that does it. I pull my hand back quickly and step away. Behind me, the sound of a thousand insects clambering, climbing, scuttling, and crawling crescendos quickly then falls silent as I feel hot breath against my neck.

"Son of a bitch," I say spinning around, my right thigh throbbing with yesterday's effort.

A man stares at me, half his face a smile—wide with teeth the color of my uncle's Harvest Gold fridge. He's between 40 and 60, wearing a tattered jean jacket and sporting a haircut and beard that move in the flickering light of the fireball like a raft of ants. He holds up his hands to let me know that at least for now, there isn't going to be any trouble. Under his skin writhes a chorus of insects, struggling to hold their shape. That's when I notice his jean jacket is also an illusion, shifting in the iridescent shimmer of the green flame, the small beetles shirking away from its luminescence.

He coughs and spits a wad onto the ground, where it explodes in a scurry of activity. He's infested, the poor bastard. It's the kind of curse usually reserved for very bad people, and that's the vibe I'm getting from him. More than a bunch of bugs shaped like a man, he's a weapon, and he's been pointed directly at me.

Horde.

"You found the cat," he says, his smile insincere and off-putting, more a collective sense memory of a thing, no longer fully understood and poorly executed.

"More like he found me," I say, pausing and hoping he'll tell me what's going on.

Instead of a discernable expression or reaction, I see more bugs scampering under the surface of his face. It's a sign that he's nervous. Raising my hand, I set the flame above us, and his face settles, or at least the thousands of things that make it up do.

"I need him," is all he says, flashing that smile again, a drunken dance across his face.

"Want or need?" It's all I can think of until I figure out what's happening here.

"Both," he says, and I feel small pieces of spittle and bug hit my chin below my mouth.

"Desire and survival." Stepping slightly back, I put some distance between us. "Who are you?"

He spreads his arms and laughs like he's gargling rocks. "A man just like you."

"Not like me," I say.

"Oh, come on. Can't we be friends?"

"Why are you following me?"

He shrugs his shoulders. "Maybe I just like you."

"Who do you work for?"

He smiles, "Dark wizard, full of purpose." He says it like he's preaching.

"And who might that be?" I reply, still trying to play the game without knowing the rules.

"Well, if you don't know, then I'm not sayin'." He screams the last few words like he's suddenly become unhinged—but I'm guessing that happened a long time ago.

"That's fair. Doesn't hurt to ask." I feel like this conversation is headed in a direction I'm unprepared for. "What do you want with the cat?" I ask, hoping to learn at least something before he takes a run at me.

"A chat." His smile broadens, trying to do an impression of a smirk. "How 'bout that?"

"With my cat?" I say, unable to stop myself.

"Enough of that," he says, leaning close, a little intense for my taste.

"Honestly, I'm not sure. He's out here poopin' somewhere," I say, gesturing around at our surroundings.

"Call him."

"Call him? You mean, like you call a dog?"

"Yep."

I cup my hands to my mouth and call him. "Arbuckle? Arbuckle? The nice man would like you to come like a good dog." I look around like I expect him to come running and then shrug when he doesn't.

The Infested Man moves quicker than I expect, and he pushes me back with both hands. I hit the wall of web and bounce off slightly. I almost get a nice weave on my tongue before the membrane opens, and a spider the size of a bulldog shoots out and grabs me with its front legs, pinning me against the membrane. It's holding firm, positioning its fangs over my shoulder. I feel their pinch on my skin, just shy of penetration. A subtle reminder that I'm now truly at a disadvantage.

"Friend of yours?" I ask, throwing my right thumb over my shoulder, indicating the spider.

"We have an understanding," he says, closer now so I can smell the stink coming off him like mildewed paper and old garbage.

"So, you don't mind us being this close?"

"She's free to do as she likes," he grins.

"You hear that, sweety? We have his blessing," I say to the spider, looking over my shoulder into all eight of its eyes. I almost pee myself. It's a big spider, and I drank a lot of whisky. It occurs to me that I probably shouldn't have done that.

I give the spider a side eye again. "It's about time you met someone who wasn't so small and unappealing," I say, nodding toward the Infested Man.

"I'm plenty big when I need to be," he says, bristling, growing a bit taller—looming over me like all the insects are now on their tiptoes.

"All this for a cat?"

"The cat's a thief."

"That's a relief."

"Stop rhyming what I say," he says, in an unfriendly tone that makes me want to take my ball and go home.

"OK." I almost immediately regret it as the fangs press even deeper into my skin.

"He stole the vital essence, the once proud presence, of the old dead wizard man," he says calmly, twisting his head side to side.

"So, the cat stole that?"

He's angry now or frustrated by my antics and lets out a small scream of impatience, pacing and slapping himself in the head with his hands. Each slap is in rhythm to the beat of his words. Walking in circles, talking to himself, and killing himself, little pieces at a time. Piles of insects fall off with each strike.

"Why won't he listen? I'm saying everything plain. He won't stop, what do I do?"

"You alright?" I ask, and this is the final straw because he's on me, in my face, spitting bugs and lord knows what else onto me as he yells.

"He killed him. He should have the essence. But it ran, it ran to the cat. I want the cat. I need the cat. Where is the cat?"

I let his last words hang in the air for a beat or two, hoping he'd calm down. "How should I know? He's not my cat."

"I saw him with you. He was in your room."

"You win. He's my cat," I reply, and he gives me a nasty look. I feel the spider's fangs getting antsy on my shoulder.

He clears his throat again and spits another writhing wad onto the ground.

"I'd tell you where he was, but I'm not sure you're in any position to make demands," I say, looking for a reaction that isn't an outburst of instability. "The only thing keeping you together is the curse. Your consciousness has already been split into who knows how many smaller pieces. There's no Humpty Dumpty movement for you. And whoever it is that did this to you can't undo it, but if you tell me what this Master of yours wants with my cat, I'll kill you quick," I tell him.

"He said I wouldn't like you. He was right."

"So, he knows me?"

"Oh, he knows you."

"What does he want with the quintessence of the people he's killing?"

"Revenge," he says it like he wants it too.

"I asked what, not why?"

"One is 'for', and one is 'to take'. The answer applies to both."

"Gotcha. Kind of a twofer there. Very clever."

That smile again, but this time conceited.

"Well, if Arbuckle does have my uncle's quintessence, he's not going to give it to you, and neither am I."

Concentration crosses his brow, and his entire body moves like bug-shaped pixels on a screen. In no time, I'm staring at myself in more frightening detail than I'd guessed he was capable of.

"How about yours then?" he says, stepping very close this time, inches away. The only difference between us is his eyes, which squirm like maggots in a soap bubble.

"You can't have the cat," I say and mumble under my—instead I feel two fangs the size of tiger's claws piercing my shoulder. "Motherfu—" is all I get out before the spider drags me into its burrow, but not before I flick my wrist and send the fireball directly into my stupid bug face.

"Here, kitty, kitty, kitty," is the last thing I hear, mixed with the smell of burning insects.

* * *

My shoulder throbs in rhythm to my beating heart, which is a surprisingly positive thing after everything that's happened. I can also feel my thigh, but it's throbbing to a different beat. Opening my eyes offers nothing but darkness. Lifting my arm, I brush into something, feeling the floor beneath me telegraph the response. The spider scuttles toward me, fangs bared, her hairy legs bristling in the moonlight. Each time they touch, I feel the vibration in my gut. *I mumble under my breath* a transmutation spell, and all the spider silk turns to water. We both go crashing to the sandy ground.

What's left of the fireball is fading fast, but it's enough light to see the spider struggling to attack me. The spell transmuted the silk in its glands too, which wreaks havoc with its general ability to function. It keeps squirting water onto the sand, where it does nothing but make a mess. It's funny at first and then a bit sad.

I mumble under my breath, applying the only antivenom spell I know, hoping it's not too late to counteract whatever that spider injected into me. Then I look around for something large and heavy. A tree branch as thick as my arm. I bring it down hard onto the spider's head. It pops like a water balloon. A spider this big doesn't belong, even in Florida.

Feeling my way across the ground, the light from the fireball dying behind me—and with considerable effort—I make it to the edge of the woods and into the yellow pallor of the parking lot lamps. A littered trail of charred carapaces, wings, and tiny legs winds across the lot toward the swimming pool. Following it, hoping to get some explanation from what's left of the Infested Man, I get to the pool, and the only thing left is a raft of bugs floating in the center. I have no way of knowing which parts survived.

Looking over at the room, the door still wide open, I run for it, down the pool's length, out the gate, and across the lot. I grab the complimentary shampoo from the bathroom and jog back. The raft is close to the edge. A few bugs have even made it onto the deck, where Arbuckle has magically reappeared and is playing a fun game of leg and wing pull, chasing the survivors in a frenzy of excitement. I walk around until I'm near the raft.

"Who sent you?" I ask it.

The center of the raft stirs, but all it says in a chorus of chirps, buzzes, and clicks is, "Here, kitty, kitty, kitty."

I pour the shampoo into the water and watch the raft slowly submerge—the surface tension broken by the soap spreading across it. Behind me, I hear a tiny scream and turn to see Arbuckle, a large beetle in his mouth, most of the legs ripped off. And it's pleading for help in a tiny voice like Andre Delambre at the end of *The Fly*. It sounds almost human.

"Thanks for all the help," I say sarcastically to Arbuckle.

Arbuckle drops the beetle in the pool, and I watch it sink. He pads across the concrete, through the fence, heading for the room.

"Shoulda put a box on the ground," I say to the black dots littering the bottom of the pool. Rubbing my shoulder, I follow Arbuckle.

In the room, I lock the door. I mumble under my breath, applying the security spell.

Arbuckle's already curled up on the bed near the pillows. I sit on the edge and lean back, falling asleep before my head hits the mattress.

* * *

I wake to feral growling, lying next to cold fries and what remains of last night's dinner. Arbuckle is meticulously picking what meat is left out of the club sandwich.

While I was sleeping, someone replaced my brain with cotton. My feet hurt when they hit the floor, and I learned to walk again, heading for the bathroom.

The coffee station sits on a brown cafeteria tray on this side of the counter. I go for a cup and step on something hard and sharp. I yelp and grab my foot, feeling whatever it is fall away. Hearing it hit the floor, a dull pain shoots up my left side. Falling against the wall, I slide down, unable to catch myself.

The bathroom floor is peppered with plastic letters from the counter. There's no way to know exactly which one I've stepped on. I wonder how long Arbuckle sat up here last night, knocking them onto the floor.

"Dammit Arbuckle," I call out hoping he understands how angry I am.

Pushing off the wall, I roll over on all fours. Like an old man, I grunt as I collect them, turning them all upright. My hands move them around like I did as a child until I've spelled out: **HELLO AUBREY**.

I stare at it for a split second, mesmerized.

"Got your message." I mockingly yell from the bathroom. "Next time, try and deliver it without almost killing me."

Arbuckle stares at me until I'm uncomfortable enough to turn away.

"I guess that was you in the trailer telling me to use the fridge to escape as well?"

Arbuckle raises his paw to his mouth, licks it, and rubs it over his ear. He does this a few times before looking at me again. He winks.

"Oh no. No. No. No." I say it loud as a thought creeps into my head.

Arbuckle has done this on purpose. He sent me a message. Opened the lines of communication. But that's ridiculous, my brain saw what it wanted to see. Shaking my head, I let out a weak, frightened laugh and scoop up the letters, dumping them overhead into a pile on top of the others, before pulling myself up into a standing position using the counter.

Ripping a cup from its protective cocoon, I fill it with tap water and pour three-quarters of it into the coffee maker. The rest dribbles down the side and onto the counter. Struggling to extricate the coffee bag from its mylar prison, I frustratingly resort to using my teeth.

The disk of filter and coffee pops free, flying up, a newly hatched bird that catapults across the counter where I try and catch it. I fail as I slap it hard, and it hits the mirror and drops into the sink. I pick it up, convincing myself that the steam of the coffee maker will kill anything that might be on it now. Placing it in the filter basket, I check twice that the light is on before taking a long, gratifying pee.

Stripping off my t-shirt and underwear, I stumble into the shower. I let the water run cold to wake me up and clear the whiskey and venom from my brain. Shivering, I step out, the cotton in my head melting away like candy floss. Drying off, I realize how much my hip hurts and look down. A bruise the size of a whole in bag brisket blooms on my right side where I sat in the fridge. I finish toweling off and wrap it around my waist.

Pulling the coffee cup from the machine, I hold it up. "Cheers," I say to the hairless Shar Pei in the mirror and think about what lies ahead— whatever is coming is going to hurt. Limping into the main room, I stare at Arbuckle, who's back on the table. A small ray of morning sun gives him a little key light as he regally sits on his haunches, staring at me.

Feeling less like gum pulled from the bottom of an unsuspecting shoe and more like a half-eaten Twinkie thrown from a car window onto the side of the road—lighter and less worked over—I get dressed.

Then I make a loop around the room, looking for anything I might wish hadn't left here. Pulling the liner from the ice bucket, I fill it with the plastic letters off the counter and drop the bag into the hamper.

Hamper in hand, I open the door as Arbuckle shoots out for the woods, while I hiss at the sun hitting me like an icepick behind my eyes. Chucking the hamper into the trunk, I grab the go bag and the trash bag full of dirty clothes from the room. Putting them next to the hamper, I close the trunk.

Walking to the hotel office to turn in the key, I find the same girl at the counter. I don't know if it's the time of day or good peripheral vision that gives my intent away, but without looking up, she points at the empty thirty-two-ounce pickle jar on the counter with 'Keys' hand-written on an index card strapped to it with packing tape. I drop in the key and walk out.

At the car, Arbuckle waits patiently for me to open the door. As soon as I do, he jumps in and promptly crosses to the passenger seat, where he sits expectantly as I climb in. Shutting the door, I put the key in the ignition and hesitated. I turn to Arbuckle, who's already looking at me, and we stare at each other for a few seconds. It feels weird when you think your cat is trying to tell you something, but I can't shake the feeling that the letters weren't a fluke. That's the thing about magic. Once you know it exists, anything is possible.

"Well, here we go. you and me."

Arbuckle lets out a quick, snappish chirp as if to say, 'Let's get this show on the road.' I start the car, and we pull out onto East Fifth Street.

* * *

The storage facility is off MLK Blvd, down and across the street from Denny's. It's a single-story non-climate-controlled type with an onsite apartment connected to the office. I mumble under my breath as we approach the gate. Any surveillance should pause for about an hour, locking onto the last image before I drove up. There isn't as much technomage weave in my head as I would like, but this one is a modified camouflage spell from thirteenth-century Japan. Those Samurai mages were one focused group.

I'd bought it from a street magician in Okinawa. He said he got it from a librarian at the Ordo Templi Orientis, who has a side hustle in selling secrets from their special collections. I had it modified by a tech-nomage I know in Oneida, Tennessee, who spends all his time in a se-cluded cabin watching twenty-seven televisions broadcasting news from around the world over IPTV. He's waiting for the end of the End Times, but if you bring him a carton of Virginia Slims and a case of Zima, he'll update just about any weaving you could think of to affect the modern.

He never lets me watch him work, but I saw him typing the original spell into an old Commodore 64. You get a nice dot matrix printout of the modified spell when he's done. You memorize it while sitting on his front porch and then drop the piece of paper into an old beat-up number sixteen Bush bean can. He hits it with lighter fluid and throws in a match.

"Anti-virus," he says every time, as you both watch it burn.

The four-digit code from the letter works like a charm. The front gate rolls open with the pulley chains sounding loose and barely capable of opening the door. Eventually, it hits the far side with a clang, and the chain rattles into silence. I don't care if someone thinks my uncle visited here; I'd prefer they didn't know it was me.

Thirty seconds after I've crossed beyond it, it trundles back, leaving me locked inside with a sea of orange doors receding into the distance down aisles listed in alphabetical order. I wonder why I never knew about this place. Remembering how much time has passed, I realize I now know less about him than I ever did.

Turning down aisle D, I park just past door fourteen in case I need to load anything I find inside into my trunk. It's still early, but the sun is creeping up, squeezing the air for all the moisture it can call up to the heavens. As usual, I'm already sweating. Seventy-two degrees is my breakpoint for dripping, and it's already seventy-six. I hold the door open long enough for Arbuckle to jump out. As soon as he does, he's stalking a bug along the building's front.

"Save room for lunch," I call after him, as his quest draws him further and further away down the aisle.

The lock is pristine, and the smell of WD-40 hangs lightly in the air. My uncle, or someone else, has been here recently, maybe even in the last few days. The thought makes me nervous. After the Infested Man, I've started to think I'm being watched. Scanning the area to ensure no one is there, I slide the key into the lock. It goes in smoothly, and the lock pops with barely any pressure. I remove it and stop. It can't be this easy. Placing the lock on the ground, I step back, and I mumble under my breath.

The runes on the door flash bright, like I flipped a switch. I recognize the design. It's one he'd made me memorize early on. A kind of rune password that triggers an action once solved. Stepping closer, I rework the runes on the door, like the plastic letters on the fridge. They flare at a light touch, letting me know they're in play. Moving them one at a time, I reorder them into the correct sequence. Satisfied, I reach down and grab the door handle. I practically strain my shoulder as the pain of the spider bite and the throb of the bruised hip cause me to grit my teeth as the door slides up.

The first thing that hits me is the smell of stale bong water and patchouli, so now the smorgasbord in my nose is something close to dead hippies. Staring me in the face is the '69 Volks Wagon Type 2. It's straight from the photograph, looking practically new, the paint barely faded. Around it is a small garage worth of tools. I'm awestruck as I step over the threshold; the black and white photograph didn't do it justice, nor did my limited memory of it.

Reaching the driver-side door, I swing it open, not even wondering why it's unlocked. Planting my foot on the step-up, I lift myself into the driver's seat. Arbuckle, returned from his quest, jumps up, lands in my lap, and transitions to the passenger side. Technically, it's all one seat since a bench seat runs across the entire front. Reflexively, I reach up and pull down the sun visor, and the keys fall into my hand.

I look over at Arbuckle. "You think she still runs?"

He responds by continuing to stare at me before blinking his eyes once. I close the driver-side door and put the key in the ignition. Taking a breath, I push down the clutch and turn the key. The van comes to life, growling, settling into a low-key Model T purr. It's got a full tank, and the dash even has a GPS screen. I laugh.

I turn her off and look over at Arbuckle. "I don't know where to go next. I'm not even sure why my uncle left me this van."

Arbuckle makes a coughing sound and gives a wheeze. He licks his nose, smacking his muzzle together in a wet staccato that lasts a second or so before he begins to yowl a low, distressing sound. I don't know what to do. Reaching for him, he suddenly vomits a hairball onto the passenger-side floor mat.

"You alright?"

Arbuckle composes himself, turns to me, and says, "Sorry about that. It's been inevitable for a few days now."

You know that expression, 'I almost shit myself?' Well, I almost shit myself.

"How is this happening? Why is this happening?" I say, looking a bit scared.

"It's the van," Arbuckle says, his little cat lips moving impossibly. "It's connected to the Gloam."

Closing my mouth, I shake my head and go with it. What can I do?

"Do all cats talk?" I ask, thinking this is a valid question, having never met a talking cat before.

"Don't be absurd. I'm not a cat," he says, licking his paw before raking it over his right ear.

"You sure look like a cat, specifically like a cat I grew up with, which would make you more than forty years old."

"See, there you go. The average life span for a cat is only fifteen, and I'm much older."

"How much?" I ask, not sure I want to know the answer.

"Depends on which me we're talking about," he says as he turns around a few times and settles onto the seat.

"Which you?"

"There was me before," he nods his head to the left, "and me after," he says, and then nods to the right, emphasizing the difference.

"After what?" I ask, feeling like at some point he'll tell me everything and we can wrap up what's going to be a hundred questions.

"After being brought here."

"OK, how old are you, after being brought here?"

"Fifty-six, give or take. It took a few years to learn English, so I wouldn't have been able to read a calendar, but it was a few years before you were born."

"And before you were brought here?"

"I don't remember," he says, then bobs his head to the left and the right, thinking about it. "I think I've always existed, just in a different form."

"What form would that be?"

He hesitates, "Something different than this."

"You're from the Gloam?"

"Of the Gloam, but yes. Given this form by your uncle."

"And the other cats in the photo?"

"My brothers and sisters, for lack of a better term."

"Yesterday, in the Veil, I saw the cat door returning to the moment. Was that you?"

"Yes. I thought it silly after everything for you to die like that."

"Thanks."

"No problem," he says, then pauses. He tilts his head and continues. "And before you ask, you were right in the hotel room. Thank goodness we finally got here. It would have taken forever to get you up to speed if I had to do it by knocking letters off a table."

I imagine us sitting in a room with a large table full of letters and me transcribing each letter as he bats it off and onto the floor. I laugh at the image in my head until I notice Arbuckle glaring at me from the passenger seat.

"So, what now?" I ask him.

"Moving lips or resting cat face? Either is fine with me."

"They're both weird, but I think moving lips. I'll let you know if I change my mind."

"OK. First, I recommend we swap your ugly car for the van. Then we should probably go somewhere we can sit for a while undisturbed. It'll take a bit to catch you up to speed."

"I think I know a place," I say.

∞

chapter three

Grey and Sleek,
The Stalwart Boy,
The Proponent of Morale.
The Eyes of Night,
The Twilight Sheen,
The Forever Lost—Pascal.

—ALD
transcribed by AC

T he Walmart parking lot is relatively quiet. I park the van
in the far northwest corner at W23rd. A small greenway
separates it from the road. There aren't any other cars
near us, except for a tractor-trailer taking up seven spots
twenty yards away. Climbing out and walking around to
the side of the van, I open the door, climb in, and shut it behind me.
Arbuckle is already on the small bench seat, having climbed over. I'm
across from him, with the fold-out table between us. I start fixing lunch.

Before leaving the storage unit, I had backed my car in and resecured
the lock. I'd transferred the stuff from the trunk to the van's under-seat
storage. We'd stopped at a jewelry store that advertised buying silver,
and I'd offloaded the nuggets from my uncle's trailer for about $1200,
making us flush. So, I'd run into Walmart to get a few things before
we parked.

Pulling the lid off some solid white albacore tuna, I extricate a fork from a wrapped to-go set of plasticware and flake it onto a paper plate.

"What exactly did the bug man want?" Arbuckle asks, jumping onto the table.

"You, for stealing my uncle's quintessence from his Master."

"Rescued, more like," he says, then dives into the tuna.

"He was telling the truth. It's inside you?"

Arbuckle pauses, tuna hanging from his mouth. He gives me a sideways glance. "Didn't I tell you? I thought I told you."

"When would you have told me?"

"I meant to," he says earnestly before diving back into the tuna.

"You still haven't."

"Right," he says and looks up mid-chew. "He's inside me."

"How's that possible?"

"Does it matter?"

"Does it matter that my uncle's literal life essence is in a cat? Yes, it kind of matters."

"Not a cat."

"Not the point."

Arbuckle finishes eating before he responds. "Look. You're upset, but my being a vessel for your uncle isn't the big issue right now. Let's try and figure out who the killer is first."

"Fine," I say, pointing my finger at him again. "But we're not done here."

Arbuckle sits on his haunches. "This is what we know. Bugman works for the killer."

"Why are we calling him Bugman?"

"He was made of bugs."

"Infested. We should be calling him The Infested Man, or maybe Horde. I think that was his name from the dream."

"How about Karl. Can we call him Karl?" Arbuckle asks, frustrated.

"I'm good with Karl," I say, his frustration satisfying.

"Karl works for the killer. The killer knows I have your uncle's quintessence. Karl can't extract your uncle from me, but the killer can or at least thinks he can."

"He may just want to kill you at this point," I say.

"Why would he do that?"

"At the end of the nightmare, there was a calico. The killer got angry when they saw it, and I remember them thinking, 'All the cats must die.'"

"Why didn't you tell me that before?"

"I meant to," I say, unable to keep the smile off my face.

Pulling a ready-made sandwich half from its plastic tomb and sniffing it for freshness, I take a bite. Chicken salad probably wasn't the best idea, but it was the sandwich with the furthest out best-by date. It's two pieces of white bread with lumpy mayonnaise in between them. I drop it in the container and open my Diet Dr. Pepper.

Arbuckle is staring out the window. "Maybe the killer wanted to see what kind of a threat you were before engaging."

I open a bag of chips and dump some onto my plate, remembering I'd gotten water for Arbuckle. So, I pull it out of the bag next to me and pour some into a small bowl I'd found.

"How did Karl find us?" I say, trying to eat the chips one at a time to make them last.

Arbuckle laps from the bowl, then jumps onto the bench seat. "Thanks," he says, licking his paws and cleaning his muzzle. He suddenly stops and looks at me.

"When we left the trailer park, you were distracted. What did you see?"

"Flock of starlings," I say, trying to remember. "Maybe something smaller. Hard to say. A black cloud of something."

"Insects, maybe?"

"Could have been. So, if Karl was already at the trailer park, why wait to engage?"

"Maybe he was just there to see who showed up. I don't think he knew I was there."

"But then you came out of hiding and rubbed against my leg."

"He'd just watched you set the trailer on fire."

"Bugs hate fire."

"So, he followed us until he could gain an advantage."

"The larger question is when did the killer decide I was important?"

Arbuckle says, holding my gaze for a second, then continuing to clean himself.

"The runes," I say, pointing my finger at Arbuckle. "He painted them with Jane's blood. He…" I shake my head, closing my eyes. "He cut her arm…after he killed her. Didn't get much. Her heart wasn't pumping. Used a mason jar." I take a breath and a sip of soda. I can't tell if it's the sandwich or the dream making me feel sick. "He cut out her eye after he couldn't get her quintessence. Put it on a table in the main showroom."

"William wasn't the first," he says.

"Jane was, and he didn't get her quintessence either," I say, racking my brain for specifics and wishing I'd recorded it on my phone while it was still fresh.

"He must have used the eye as a scryer," Arbuckle says.

"The calico?"

"Poly. He must have seen Poly after he left and after Karl told him about me. How did he piece it together? How did he know about the pact?"

"Pact?" I say, getting a little confused.

"I may know who the killer is. We need to find Poly."

"I need to understand what's going on first," I say. "I can't just go poking around. It's too dangerous. I'm a mediocre wizard at best."

Arbuckle's demeanor changes. He shakes his head, then goes stiff. His voice changes. It's lower, gruff. "You were a prodigy, the best I'd ever seen."

"You're not Arbuckle." I try moving away, but there's nowhere to go.

"So much promise, and you threw it away."

It sounds like my uncle. His quintessence forced its way to the surface, overriding Arbuckle.

I revert to eighteen almost immediately, defiant and angry again.

"You think that just because someone is good at something, they'll achieve greatness and live up to expectations. I learned that was bullshit a long time ago. Expectations have weight. Not everyone is born to bear that weight," I say.

"You ran away," he says.

"I escaped. You let me."

"It was the only way to protect you."

"By pushing me away?"

"By cutting ties, letting you go."

"Then why call me back now? Why put me in danger now?"

"Because you're the only one who can stop him now."

"Who? Stop who?"

Arbuckle lets out a low growl that grows into a yowl.

He screams, "You're hurting me, William. I can't sustain it. It's too painful. We have to find another way." Arbuckle shakes it off and licks his nose.

"You alright?"

"I will be."

"Was that him?"

"Yes. William was trying to take over my body, use it as a conduit to communicate with you. Maybe if I was human, but he'll end up killing us both if he keeps it up. But, I think I have a handle on him now. We'll just have to find another way for him to tell you what he wants to tell you."

"Without the sanctimony, hopefully," I say, feeling worked up and ready to argue. "Why were you conjured?"

Arbuckle shrugs, although I had never seen a cat shrug before. He could have been stretching. "Why do humans do anything?" he says, curling up on the bench.

Shrugging back, uncertain, I say what I'm thinking anyway, "Because they can?"

Because they can," he says in a singsong tone, making me feel guilty. "It turns out we were conjured for no particular purpose—at least not at first. They learned how to do it from your Great-aunt Miriam after she conjured Monvoisin.

"My what?"

"Your great-aunt," he says, pausing, waiting for me to respond.

But I don't.

"Your father's mother's sister," he chides.

"I know what a great-aunt is. I just didn't know I had one."

"Your uncle didn't exactly get along with Miriam, but it wasn't entirely her fault."

"Why didn't he want me to know about her?"

"Because—" Arbuckle catches himself and shakes his head. "He was afraid you would try and find her."

"Exposing my location."

"And she might tell you everything."

"Like everything I've been trying to ply out of you for the last thirty minutes?" I say a little too pointedly, my frustration level hitting its peak.

"It isn't easy, Aubrey. Mistakes were made. Time. So much time has passed. I didn't ask for this job. I didn't ask to be brought here or made a vessel for your uncle's quintessence. I didn't ask to be the keeper of secrets," he says, his irritation rising too.

"Ok, I'm sorry," I say, holding up my hands, unsure why I'm the one having to de-escalate this situation. "Let's both take a breath."

"Yes, a breath would be nice."

Reaching over, I open the side door, and we're hit with a warm breeze. I step out, stretch my legs, and roll my neck. The seats aren't very comfortable. Looking back, I see Arbuckle stretching too, hindquarters in the air and paws out low on the table. He pulls himself up and sits on his haunches. Taking a moment, I close my eyes and tilt my face into the sun's warmth. My heart slowed to a more acceptable rate—I climb into the van.

"What could be worse than what's happened so far," I say, holding my hands out to encourage Arbuckle to talk. "Huh? I'm a grown man. I can take it. Just lay it on me. Start wherever you want." I take a sip of soda.

"You don't know the truth about how your parents died," he says.

I almost spit the warm soda out. Instead, I reflexively hitch a breath and suck it into my sinuses, where it comes out my nose. I scramble for some paper towels to mop it up, then try and clear it out with a couple of powerful blows. The top back of my throat burns right before I sneeze. Finished, I pull myself together, I look over at Arbuckle like he'd taken a shit on the floor.

"You could have buried the lead," I say.

"Maybe," he says, "But we're just getting started."

"So, if it wasn't a boating accident, how did they die?"

"Let me give you some context first," Arbuckle says, getting comfortable. "Thursday, September 22, 1977, the autumnal equinox, and the order had gathered at your parents' house for dinner at your father's request. They were still very close. They'd all met at the University of Tennessee a decade earlier. Only your parents had married. You were the only child. The Adults were in the dining room, and we lounged in the living room, except for Alexander. He's an orange tabby, a beggar, who spent most of the meal trying to get table scraps.

"Sometime after eight, your mother had you say goodnight. She took you upstairs to brush your teeth. They had dessert and coffee, and we got treats."

Arbuckle pauses, lost in thought.

"They've perfected those things, you know. They're so much better now. I'm not sure what they put in 'em," he says, licking his nose, then smacking his mouth like he's eating one. "Man, they're good," he says, looking at me. "You mind picking some up? The catnip kind with the crunchy outer shell and soft interior? Holy smokes."

I stop Arbuckle here. "I'll get you some treats."

"Great," he says. "Where was I?"

"The Equinox. I remember, playing on the stairs, a slinky, the metal kind. I'd start it at the top of the stairs, and it would go down step by step, making that metallic *slink*. You guys showed up to investigate, and by the time we were done, you had all positioned yourselves along the sides of the stairs to watch it go down. Our cats," I realize I can't remember their names.

"Silas and Pascal," Arbuckle chimes in.

"Yeah. Silas and Pascal sitting at the top with me, grey and sleek and black and strong," I say, locked in the memory, trying to recall more, but all I hear is *slink, slink, slink* as it tumbles down the stairs, marking time, like a metronome, until it turns into the *beep, beep, beep* of the monitor I woke to in the hospital, my world in a million pieces.

"I've never been able to remember what happened," I say.

"They thought it was best," he says, looking away now.

"What do you mean, they?"

Arbuckle looks tired, the weight of something pulling on him.

"The ones who survived."

"Survived what?"

"What happened next," he says, reluctant, as though thinking about it now is painful. "I want to give you access to your uncle. I don't know another way. I'm incompatible with his quintessence. Holding it, containing it, is one thing. Allowing it to overtake me is another."

"How do we do that?"

"I think we can use the van's link to the Gloam to push his memories to you."

"What memories?"

"The ones he needs you to see. The ones from that night."

"How do we do that?"

Arbuckle jumps up onto the table and walks toward me.

"Do you trust me?"

"Do I have a choice?" I say.

"Lean forward," he says.

I shift in my seat, making sure I'm settled and comfortable for whatever comes next, and then I lean my head forward.

Arbuckle bonks me in the head, hard.

* * *

I try to rub my forehead and tell Arbuckle how much that hurt, but I'm not in the van anymore. I'm in my childhood home, where I live now, but this is the past. This is the night my life takes a turn I can never undo. I'm not in control of this body. I hear it talking, like words through a paper towel roll. I have to concentrate to understand. I'm my uncle, and this is his memory.

I'm sitting at a table across from my mother, in her late twenties, and she's laughing at what I am—what my uncle is saying. Her smile is full and broad, and her eyes are bright. To her right is my father, who is laughing too, before turning and looking away. My mother follows his gaze. So, do I. And I see myself, seven years old, in my favorite pajamas, the yellow arms and dark blue cuffs looking large on my frame. R2-D2 and C-3PO stand on the sands of Tatooine with a blue sky broken by X-Wings careening upward, breaking out of the yellow and black circular border. A red Star Wars logo under it all. This body laughs and turns its head, and I see everyone else.

Mia, face scrunched, smiling. *You are so cute, Aubrey,* I hear her saying. She looks at Jane, who nods in agreement, squinting her one good eye as she mouths the words. *Oh, my God.*

Johnathan is giving seven-year-old me the thumbs up, smiling too. He claps his hands and says *Epic.*

Francis claps too, as everyone enjoys either my outfit or my discomfort being assessed in it.

My mother gets up, takes my small hand, and says, *Tell everyone goodnight.* I watch myself wave halfheartedly like it's something I've been taught to do. She leaves the dining room with me, and I turn to the table, where my father looks grim, his smile faded.

I watch him closely as he looks at each person at the table, his eyes settling on me. *We need your help,* he says, not just to me, but to everyone.

I feel myself speaking, the words are distant. *What's happened, Xavier?*

Olivia's dreams, my father says, pausing, trying to find his way to continue.

The ones about the second child? I ask.

They're getting worse.

Have you taken her to see someone? Jane asks.

One gifted with the touch.

What did they say?

That they aren't dreams or visions but memories. He pauses, looking for the right word- *Crumbs of memories. A trail was left behind when they were taken.* I watch my father shake his head like he still isn't sure he can believe it.

I don't understand, Jane says. *There's another child?*

Yes, one we don't remember, taken from us at birth, and all memory of it erased.

Who would do such a thing? asks Johnathan.

My father looks up, his eyes awash with tears and anger. *We have no idea. It was Aubrey's brother, a twin.*

I feel overwhelmed, right before I'm flooded with a sense of nausea.

* * *

I snap back to the van's interior and barely make it outside before I throw up.

Turning to Arbuckle, who watches me from the table. "Why did I snap out? I need to get back in, now," I say, grabbing his bottle of water—to rinse my mouth out—before climbing into the van.

"I think you need to take it slowly," he says.

"Why?"

"You threw up. It's disorienting, you need to go slow and acclimate."

"Fine, then let me acclimate."

Arbuckle does the cat shrug, and I take a deep breath and settle myself again. lean my head forward.

Arbuckle gives me a bonk.

* * *

I'm in a basement now, yelling. pulling against something as I lean forward. The floor comes into view, and I look side-to-side, but I can't see my arms. I feel the tension of the stance release, and my right wrist comes into view, bound by a cuff of dark metal, attached to a short chain. I pull against it, then look to my left, where my other wrist is likewise bound. I'm chained to something. A wall? A post? I can't tell.

Something draws my eyes to the center of the room, where a dais rises above the concrete floor. Two metal posts, ten feet apart, hold metal clamps whose fingers hold open the chest of the world. A rift of some kind, spills pallid green light into the room, deadening the color of reality. For a second, I stare into the rift. Breaking my gaze away I see her.

To the left of the rift stands my Great-aunt Miriam. I know this because my uncle knows it. She's in her seventies or eighties, outfitted modestly in a knee-length floral dress and low-heeled pumps. Over her dress, an apron is tied. It's as though she were interrupted while baking cookies. Her hair, a short bob, highlights her small stud earrings. At her feet is a large Maine Coon, with silver points sitting patiently, waiting. She catches me looking and smiles sadly, never moving her hands, which are cupped formally in front of her.

Finally, my uncle takes in the rest of the basement. There's the dais in the middle, the rift at its center, and around it five posts. I assume there are seven, with two hidden behind the rift. Like me, the other members of the order are each chained to a post, and in front of them is a holding circle. In each holding circle, their cat, unconscious but breathing.

I don't know what happened between now and the previous memory of us all in the house. How did we get here? My father said something about another child, my brother, and that someone had taken him, but for what purpose, and why were we all chained?

My uncle's head jerks to the left, his eyes landing on wooden stairs leading to the structure above. I get nauseous again but push it down. I need to know what's going on here.

The door at the top of the stairs opens. That's when I see myself again as a young boy. I appear to be alone, but I swear there's something else there or someone. It's like seeing something from the corner of your eye. You know it's there, but when you turn to look, it's gone. It's like watching a video that's been doctored as though someone has erased part of this memory.

I'm still dressed in pajamas, my hair mussed like I just woke up, but my eyes are wide open, and there's a grin on my face. My pajamas are more conventional, with drawstring pants and a matching long-sleeved collared button-up shirt, both with French stripes. My uncle's eyes follow me as I step off the last stair and walk barefoot across the concrete floor to the dais, then up to the rift.

My uncle turns his head, and I see my mother, face agog with confusion. She's screaming something I can't understand, garbled by sadness and muffled by the others. Everyone is yelling at once, including my uncle, drowning out my ability to understand what anyone is saying.

It's impossible to pick out a single word until I hear, *Silence!*

We settle on Miriam, who holds a finger to her lips, looking at each chained member of the order, including those blocked by the rift.

I won't say it again, she says, now that everyone is quiet.

She looks pleased with her handiwork. Then, her attention is drawn to someone or something off to the side. I can't tell what or who. The anomaly on the stairs? It must be saying something because she's listening intently and nodding. Abruptly, her gaze lands on my uncle, on me, and she tilts her head like a dog who thinks it hears something.

Stepping off the dais, she approaches, Monovision trailing behind until she's there, in the periphery of our vision. I hear *tsk, tsk, tsk* as something scrapes across the floor. And then Great-aunt Miriam is right there, stepping into my uncle's line of sight. Her face looms in front of us. She squints, looking for something deep beyond my uncle's eyes. That's when I heard her say, *You don't belong here.*

* * *

I don't make it out of the van this time before I vomit, but luckily, it's mostly water. My head feels like I got hit with brass knuckles right between the eyes. I sit down hard on the warm concrete and hold my head in my hands.

"I was in a memory; how did she know I was there?" I say, hoping Arbuckle can hear me. Maybe he knows the answer, but I'll have to get in the van to hear it. Right now, I don't feel like getting in the van. I feel like lying on the warm concrete until the bells stop ringing. "Someone tampered with the memory. It's been doctored somehow to remove someone."

Twenty minutes or so pass as I wait for my head to settle. I still feel a little nauseous as I roll over and push myself to standing, where I wobble in the sun. Arbuckle has laid down on the table but still watches me from the van, unsure how long it will take for me to recover. It's not like he could do anything to help. I stumble back and grab his water bottle again. I rinse my mouth out and drink the rest.

"I've gotta go to the bathroom, and then I'm going to grab some stuff and clear my head. When I return, I'm going in," I say.

He puts his head down onto his paws to take a nap. I close the side door and start the long walk across the parking lot.

I'm not going to lie, the air conditioning feels great as I walk through the sliding doors of Walmart, stopping at the restroom first. When I'm done, I walk over to the pharmacy aisles. I pick up some bismuth subsalicylate and a small bottle of Ibuprofen, grabbing a couple bottles of grape electrolyte solution as I do. Grabbing two large bottles of water from the cooler near the register, I begrudgingly head to the van.

Along my walk, I take six Ibuprofen and drink the entire bottle of BS. It probably won't help, but it sure couldn't hurt. When I open the side door, Arbuckle raises his head but doesn't move. I get in and shut the door behind me.

"I'm ready to go," I say.

"I'm not," he replies.

"How did she know I was in there?"

"She didn't," he says, putting his head down onto his paws. "Not really. She or someone else must have put a worm in the memories to keep people from prying. If they were tampered with anyway, it would make sense. Now let me sleep."

Folding down the bench, I curl up on the makeshift bed, taking a nap, too. When I finally drift off, I'm somehow in the memory again.

* * *

It's the same memory I was in last, but there's been a short time jump forward. Now there are two of me on the dais: one—dressed the same as before in the French stripes—and the other me, from the house, in my Star Wars pajamas. That version of me is crying like any scared, kidnapped seven-year-old would. But, of course, there aren't two of me standing there on the dais. French Stripes is my brother—the brother someone stole and erased.

Miriam stands silently to the side while Monvoisin makes the rounds, stopping at each bound cat and inspecting their cages. Miriam's hands are still cupped in front of her, her smile unchanged as she looks upon French Stripes with a mother's pride and a soldier's bearing. I wonder if she will see me this time. So far, so good. I concentrate on hearing what is happening. French Stripes is speaking, and though the voice sounds right for his age, the words seem too mature and knowledgeable.

Once we are finished here, brother, you will understand and take your rightful place at my side, he says to the room, like a King speaking to his court, then turns to the other me, anger rising in his voice. *Why are you crying?* He yells. *When we are done, we will be kings here, you and me.*

Shaking me in frustration, he slaps me down to my knees. My instinct is to go to my younger self, to help him, save him from this bully— the anger welling up in me. Feelings of shame, frustration, and humiliation as I'm bombarded with the remembering of all the times I was bullied as a child. But I can't move; I can't help this younger me. All I can do is watch.

I'll do it alone then, he says, turning to Miriam, *Mother, he won't stop crying.*

Miriam crosses the dais, standing me up by the wrist, keeping my arm high enough that my feet are lifted but still touching the floor with my toes. She marches me awkwardly to the other side of the dais, where she has me stand next to her. I can see on my face that she's hurting me.

Let him go, my mother screams, rattling her chains in anguish.

French Stripes steps off the dais, crossing to confront her. Stepping around Pascal as my mother strains against the chains. He stops just short. One more step, and she could have him in her teeth.

I dreamed I'd lost a son, but now I know I've found a demon, she says and spits into his face.

Wiping the spittle away with his sleeve, his face resets from anger to a salesman's smile. *You'll feel better once we've replaced your quintessence. It's done wonders for me. Only seven, and look at what I have accomplished.* He waves his arms around, again showing off the room to no one but the captives. *Of course, I was blessed with shadow energy from the start, so you'll be a bit less,* he says, before turning to address the room.

Everyone, he says, raising his arms and climbing onto the dais. *Let's begin.*

Frantically, my uncle looks around the room, landing on the ceiling. Unfamiliar runes are spread across it. The room must be shielded like a Faraday cage, cutting them off from their magics. But then I realize they aren't unfamiliar. I have seen them before. My uncle's trailer. Whoever created these runes killed my uncle.

French Stripes is gleeful, reveling in the torment as green tendrils flow from the rift at his feet, snaking toward each cat. The cats attempt to flee, pulling against invisible restraints. They twist and contort until the tendril finds them, and the cats go rigid as though shocked by a current. Their tiny muscles flex rapidly beneath their skin.

To my astonishment, I see black electric phantom shapes spark forth from the cats. These shapes writhe with silent screams, their teeth-filled beaks pushing forth from the folds of their faces. These new forms, the size of bears, flutter in and out like cut-paper silhouettes caught in a strobe light. Is this what they look like? Is this really what Arbuckle is?

I don't have long to contemplate as thick, dark shadows shaped like slugs emerge from the rift, snaking toward each of the order.

Jane writhes and rattles against her chains, then screams when the shadow hits her, and so do all the rest. I brace myself against the one that strikes now, its circular mouth chittering at my uncle's face. Of course, I feel nothing, as the vision through my uncle's eyes goes blurry and then dark.

* * *

I wake up but don't feel nauseous this time. Arbuckle is standing on the table, looking down at me.

"You alright?" he asks.

"I think so. I was back in the memory, like it's inside me now."

"Not impossible. This is all new territory. Maybe once a memory is transferred, it resonates for a bit."

"So why can't I access it right now?"

"I don't know. I'm not a neuroscientist," he says.

"That's fair," I reply. "Why did they take these memories from me?"

"You cried hysterically for days and refused to eat. They were afraid you'd be traumatized."

"I'm not sure that removing the memories removes the trauma," I say, feeling like I'd spent a lifetime looking for a reason why I was the way I was and not feeling any relief that this might be it.

I look at my watch. It's already past four in the afternoon. We'd already spent most of the day in this parking lot, and I still didn't know everything. What I do know is I have an evil twin, my great-aunt was a bitch, you could alter memories like video clips, and generic Pepto tastes nothing like bubble gum, especially when you burp.

I should probably care more about the evil twin brother than I do, but at my age, I'd prefer to leave him alone if I could—assuming he's still alive. I hadn't seen how the memory ended, so maybe he was dead or the killer after all, seeking revenge for something the order did to him as a kid. Possibly, after he tried to do whatever it was in the memory he was trying to do. Something about shadow energy, whatever that was. I mean, it couldn't be good. It had the word 'shadow' in it.

"What do you know about my brother?" I ask outright.

Arbuckle takes a deep breath like he's been hoping this moment would never come. "His name is Alistair."

"My father mentioned my mother dreaming of him."

"She spent a year having visions of him, but no one remembered her having twins. The hospital records didn't even support it."

"So, what happened that night? The night I've been seeing?"

I don't know everything you've seen, but the night the order reunited, Mia did a Tarot reading for your mother. They wanted to see if the cards could reveal more.

"Did they?"

Bonk.

* * *

I watch Mia spread the deck of cards onto the table before collecting them, shuffling them seven times. Tarot isn't something I have much experience with. I've had a few readings but don't have the gift of divination or second sight, which is why my having dreamt of murdering Jane and my uncle doesn't make any sense.

Sitting across from Mia as she shuffles the cards is my mother—everyone else settled quietly at the far end of the table. I'm looking at her, she notices, and smiles. My uncle closes his eyes, and I listen to Mia's reading in the dark.

Do I have another child? my mother asks.

Slap—a card is laid on the table.

Yes.

Is he alive?

Paper against paper as a second card is drawn.

Yes.

I hear my father intake a breath, and I feel my uncle reach to his left and grip my father's arm to calm him.

Is he close? my mother asks.

Very, Mia replies, after the sound of a card being turned over.

Where is he? my father yells, and my uncle's eyes snap open.

My father is standing, angry, and we rise to meet him.

Mia turns to look at him while flipping over another card and laying it in the spread.

Your child is with family.

What family? my father says, confused.

My mother looks up at him as if she knows. *There is only Miriam left,* she says.

My father screams, slamming his fist onto the table. The force is enough to disturb the cards.

We're done here, Mia says, collecting her cards into a stack.

My uncle is trying to calm my father, but it isn't working. My father breaks free, pushing my uncle, and storms toward the door.

I'm going to get my son, he says, before slamming the front door behind him.

We need to go after him, my mother says.

Headlights glare through the front window, fading with the screeching of tires.

Do you think he'll hurt Miriam? my uncle says.

My mother locks eyes with us. *I'm more worried about what she'll do to him.*

We need to back him up. He can't go in there alone, Johnathan says. looking at Mia. *How certain are you? How accurate are the cards?*

I'd bet my life on them.

We should call the police, Jane says, garnering everyone's attention. *She kidnapped your child seven years ago. Do you think barging in there, powers raging, will make what's about to happen any less scary for him?*

This is family business, my mother says. *Magic answers to magic.*

We need a plan. Time to think this through, Mia says.

We need to get to Xavier before he makes a mess of things, my uncle says.

Turning toward the front door, I see all the cats waiting, including Silas, who my father left behind.

Johnathan opens the door, and I watch the cats scurry to their respective cars. It feels like a cartoon. I have no control as we drive toward what I already know is a bad idea.

Then it's over.

* * *

"Why do I keep getting thrown out of the memories?" I'm asking the universe more than Arbuckle since he's already told me he doesn't know. But I also kind of am since he's the one who came up with the idea. The process is frustrating, and I know I'm being a jerk, but it's the space I'm in right now, so I own it.

"Is there anything in common with the points you get thrown from?" he asks.

"What do you mean?"

"Walk me through what you saw before you got kicked out each time."

"The first time was right after I found out I had a brother."

"Ok, one for shock," Arbuckle says, pawing a one in the air.

"The second was the worm. Miriam discovering me there."

"One for worm," Arbuckle says in a tone of interest. He also marks this one in the air with his paw.

"The third time was when the shadow thingy struck at my uncle."

"Shock and attack."

"This one just faded out. We were in the car driving, and I woke up out of it.

"Boredom."

"I don't know that I'd call it boredom, but yeah, it lacked forward momentum."

"Let me think," Arbuckle says, pacing in a circle on the small table. "Shock, worm, shock, attack, boredom." He repeats the words a few more times, then suddenly, he stares at me, his mouth open.

"You got it? You know why?" I say, looking at his face and knowing the answer will be good.

"Because you're an idiot," Arbuckle says, shaking his head. "Of course, I don't have it. I told you I didn't know how it worked when we started. I told you at the beginning of this that it was an unknown," he says, still looking at me.

"You're right. I am an idiot. I should have known better than to trust a cat, or whatever you are." I regret it as I'm saying it, but I'm still up and headed out of the van.

"I'm doing the best I can here," he yells.

As I exit, he jumps off the table onto the back of the front seat, then into the cab.

I'm angry at myself, but humans are weird and stubborn. We like to make others feel guilty for our feelings, even if it isn't their fault. We don't like being alone with our own emotions. Right now, I feel stupid. Stupid, I don't know how to stay in the memories and that I got dragged into this thing in the first place.

I feel alone, exposed, in over my head. Pulling my cell out, I try to think of anyone I can call. As I scroll through my contacts list, the names feel distant. I don't even know who half of them are. Former clients? My plumber? I think I recognize a few who used to be friends. I doubted they were more than acquaintances now. I sit on the curb, realizing I don't have anyone to call. I wish I could talk to Em.

I watch Arbuckle come over the seat to sit on the running board, staring at me. I hold up my phone. "You'll be happy to know I don't have any friends but you, I guess," I say, pushing myself up off the curb and walking to the van. "I'm sorry about what I said. I need to know how my parents died."

"Maybe you're the reason you're getting thrown out. A subconscious defense against being hurt by the truth," Arbuckle says.

Maybe he's right. Picking up Arbuckle, I put him on my lap. It's weird handling him like a cat when I know he's something more, but he seems alright with it. I lean back, and he stands, front paws braced on my chest. He rubs his muzzle against my chin and whispers, "I'm sorry too, Aubrey. I shouldn't have said you were stupid. This is frustrating for both of us."

"What do we need to do?" I ask, petting him down his back.

"Hold still," he says, stretching up and placing his front paws on my shoulders before leaning his face toward mine. "I'm also sorry—" Arbuckle pauses.

"Why?"

"Because this one's going to hurt." Instead of his usual bonk, he gently lays his forehead against mine.

* * *

It's chaos, and it takes me a second to get my bearings. My uncle is no longer in chains, I know this because we're dodging hexes from Miriam. I see one break like black fractal lightning against the shield we're holding in front of us

Like listening through a can tied to a string, I hear my uncle yell, *No*, as he watches my father fall, right near Alistair's feet. Pushing forward, more hexes hit, each one more powerful than the last.

My younger self crawls to my father, crying. My father reaches up, touching his face, and mouths the word, *Run!* But he stays. I stay.

Suddenly, the hexes stop as Miriam flies back, as though jerked by an invisible cable. She lands hard against the wall, dropping to the concrete floor. We follow the line of attack, and I see my mother, standing guard over my father and me. Her hands are poised to strike again. Pascal bravely at her side.

We turn to the sound of Alistair laughing as he moves toward Mia, who is still unconscious and hanging from her chains. He rolls a hex between his hands, a coward preparing to strike a defenseless foe.

We raise our hands, and I hear the words echo down the tunnel to my ears. The shield drops as we take the words, giving them direction and purpose, pushing the spell, aimed true at Alistair. We unleash it, and I watch as my mother, unaware, moves across the dais against her stolen child, who dives away from her advance.

The force of the spell hits my mother instead. She and Pascal are lifted into the air. My mind slows the memory down like moving a moment into the Veil. I watch as surprise spreads across my mother's face as she's thrown back, disappearing into the rift, which wraps around her and Pascal, embracing them like they've dropped into a lake of bloomed green algae. And then they are gone. like that, in the blink of an eye. Lost forever.

I see my younger self screaming in pain and confusion. One arm reaches toward the space where my mother used to be, and the other around my father's neck as Silas approaches.

Alistair is on the ground, pushing himself up. He looks toward us and laughs, pointing, mocking, and taunting us in our moment of humiliation. My uncle's cry of grief rumbles through me like bass from a subwoofer.

My perspective drops as my uncle crumples to his knees. We watch as Alistair steps down from the dais and walks toward us, weaving a hex of black lightning in his hands. We remain still as he chides us for defying him, calling my uncle a mongrel—a seven-year-old bully lording over his playground.

Looking down at Arbuckle—crouched before us, scared but loyal and alive—our eyes lock, caught in shared grief that courses through my body, so overwhelming that, for a moment, I fear it will stop my heart. Drunk with sadness, my head lifts to Alistair, who readies a hex—I want to die this way. I need this punishment.

As I wait longingly for it, Alistair is engulfed in a swirling amber light that solidifies around him, then fades with his laughter—freezing him inside the newly formed crystalline prison. Behind him, the order, or at least what is left of them: Jane, Mia, Johnathan, and Francis. They've used the distraction of the tragedy to regroup and defeat Alistair.

They approach as we stand, and I think this must be the end, struggling to remove myself from the memory—it's been too much.

But then I am running, as my uncle's eyes catch sight of the distortion again, the erasure from these memories. It makes for the stairs, and we follow quickly—up and through the kitchen, down the hall, and out the back.

Stopping, we scan the backyard. But whoever it was is gone. There is nothing here but a large oak tree, its branches gently lit by the waxing gibbous moon.

* * *

If I didn't have trauma before, I sure do now. Watching through my uncle's eyes and seeing my mother die at his hands wasn't as helpful as I thought it would be. She's still dead, and now I get to live with a piece of the guilt of killing her—like I was the one who miscalculated and missed the mark. I feel like I've been doing that all my life. At least now I know why they took my memories, because I would do anything to give this one back. It's even worse than the one they erased—how could it not be?

I sit quietly, wondering what it all means, if anything.

An hour passes, maybe more, and I drop out of my haze to the sun pressing down on the tops of the trees. All the contemplation has led me to only one question.

"After all of that, why did he teach me how to susurrate the Gloam?" I ask Arbuckle, who's waited patiently for me to pop out of my stupor.

"He wasn't going to at first, but then one day you saw him conjure the flame in his hand, and you—"

"Tried it myself." Reflexively, I caress the scar on my right hand with my middle finger.

"You did it without formal training or even specific knowledge."

Looking at my scarred hand, I laugh, the memory clear and vibrant.

I'm watching my uncle from the cracked door to my room as he lights a cigarette from the flame in his palm. I remember holding out my hand and wishing I could do it, too. And then it was there, a small green flame dancing in my hand. I was ecstatic at first, but then it felt hot and began to burn. Panicking, I screamed, running to the bathroom, shoving my hand under the tap as I turned the water on. I watched in horror as the water poured over the flame, unable to extinguish it.

Then my uncle appeared behind me, mumbling under his breath, putting out the flame with fear on his face—fear of me.

"I burned myself pretty good," I say.

"Which is why he trained you. It was too dangerous for him to let you discover it yourself."

"What happened to the order?"

"They disbanded. They all felt complicit in following your father that night and guilty for what happened."

"But they saved me and defeated Alistair."

"If they'd only waited. A little more time, a little more planning. Seven years had passed since your brother had been taken. A few more days, or even weeks, to plan their response could have made all the difference. Alistair used their impulsiveness against them. It was obvious he was prepared."

"Why did my uncle transfer his quintessence to you?"

"It was the pact we made after that night. A way of making sure that if Alistair ever broke free, there'd be enough power to fight him. But the binding held, and everyone got old and drifted apart. We all forgot, or at least became complacent," he says, looking out the window, not paying attention to me. "I cared for William, you know. Even though he had taken me away from my life, whatever it was, I cared for him. He was the only family I had, too. He's the one who taught me to read. I used to—"

"You used to pace along the counter behind me as he taught—" I say, before he finishes my thought.

"To spell, to read, to think. Yes, I learned along with you. When you left, it was just the two of us. No one came around, he had no friends. His interest in helping others slowly faded, too. I got bored, and when I wasn't outside stalking and killing small mammals and birds for fun, I was inside, pulling the books off the lower shelves and reading them.

"He caught me one day, but instead of stopping me, he encouraged me. We still didn't have a way to communicate, but I could use the letters on the fridge to pass along simple thoughts or answers to questions. He eventually figured out how to connect a small space to the Gloam. The trailer was too large to sustain, but the inside of this van was manageable.

"I'll never forget the day he did it. He came running into the trailer happier than I had seen him in a long time. He scooped me up, took me outside, and threw me into the front seat. He got in and shut the door. He was laughing, tears streaming down his face, as I went on and on about how rude it was for him to scoop me up and take me wherever he wanted like I was some toy. But then I realized that he understood me, and he apologized, and I forgave him, and we talked. We stayed in the van until the sun slipped quietly away without us noticing.

"After that, we would go for drives. Short ones in the beginning. He'd take me on errands to keep him company. This led to longer trips to see Jane in New Orleans or to hunt for some obscure tome. Sometimes, we'd be gone for weeks, staying in campgrounds and sleeping in the van.

"He thought of reaching out to you many times but always stopped short of doing it. His justification, he'd say, was that you deserved to live your own life. We even drove by your house on a couple of occasions. He'd idle the van across the street. We even saw you once, leaving the house and walking in the snow down the boulevard."

"I never knew." I rubbed my shoulder where the spider had bitten me and stretched my bruised leg under the table. "What now?"

"We need to find everyone that's left and make sure whoever is doing this is stopped."

"How do we find them, and how useful are they going to be? Everyone is in their eighties."

"Power and knowledge are not bound by age." Arbuckle nods his head toward the Garmin. "Their locations are in the GPS. Your uncle always made sure he knew, as best he could, where everyone was." Arbuckle pauses. "Except for Johnathan. Johnathan is always moving—sometimes on other planes. Maybe one of the others knows where he is."

"Can't we call them first, to warn them?"

"Do you have their numbers?"

"Don't you?"

"I'm a cat—where would I keep them?"

"Did my uncle have a cell phone?"

"Yes"

"Where is it?"

"I assume in that pile of ash you left behind."

"Dmmit," I say, trying to remember. Pulling mine out, I pick the microSD card from my pocket and swap it back into my phone. I open the photo gallery and flip through the photos.

"What are you doing?" Arbuckle asks, jumping onto the table and coming around to look at my phone.

"I photographed everything before I torched the place. I don't remember seeing a cell phone or a wall phone, for that matter. So, I'm looking to see if I missed anything." My bedroom flashes by quickly, then the bathroom, and the wide of the living room. Then into the close-ups.

"Hold on, go back one."

I flip back to a semi-wide shot of my uncle sitting in the chair. "What is it?"

"Those runes."

"What about them?"

"I've seen them before."

"Where?"

"That night, on the basement ceiling. Not the same configuration, but the same syllabary."

"I thought the same thing when I saw them in the memory. So, it's Alistair. He must be the killer."

"Maybe, but I don't know for certain he was the one that put them on the ceiling. It could have been Miriam or our phantom stranger."

"Do you remember anything from when my uncle was killed? Any detail that might help?"

"No. I was outside hunting when it happened. Your uncle was day-drinking, watching westerns. Never a nice Nat Geo special about big cats or something interesting—like a good bird video," he says, his voice filling with disgust. "Dirty, dirty birds."

He catches me looking at him with what I hope is a face that conveys my concern.

He shakes his head as if waking from a dream. "Sorry, back on track. I was out hunting near the fence when it happened. It was over before I even knew what was going on. I remember being mid-jump, chasing a grasshopper, when your uncle's quintessence entered me, knocking me to the ground, where I lay for a good while, overwhelmed. I heard cursing, screaming, and something shattering."

"It was a clay pot," I blurt out, suddenly remembering that part of the dream. "The killer threw it against the trailer when he couldn't get the quintessence. It was the vessel he'd brought to capture it in."

"Interesting," Arbuckle says. "Anyway, I crawled under Ms. Standish's trailer after regaining my strength. I lay there on the cool sand, hidden behind the back support, concealed by the skirting. His quintessence swirled in my head before I passed out. The next thing I knew, it was morning. Climbing through the cat door, I knew it was too late.

"Then your uncle spoke to me like a whisper in a dream. We somehow pushed into the moment you were in. He had me work the letters on the fridge, then we ported back to the present using the cat door."

"How did you use the cat door? It was connected to the exterior of the trailer, which was still anchored in the now. It shouldn't have been possible. It's why I had to use the fridge and not any of the actual entrances."

"Cat doors are very special things," is all he says. "Anyway, I eventually, snuck around front, and there you were, leaving the trailer. It had been a long time, but I knew it was you. In that moment, I knew I was safe."

"And that's when you rubbed against my leg."

"I was very happy to see you." Suddenly, Arbuckle's leg is in the air, pulled by some invisible string, and he's cleaning himself.

"Do you have to do that here?"

Arbuckle stops and makes brief eye contact. "No," and continues with it anyway.

I get up, open the side door to the van, and step out for another break. The wet staccato-smacking sounds of him cleaning himself follow me. So, I headed toward Walmart.

I'm not entirely sure what it is about fluorescent lights, but they calm me, and I was definitely in need of some calming. Wandering through the produce section, I picked up a couple of apples and a banana. After that, I went down every grocery aisle, looking mindlessly at everything, letting it wash over me—a large pocket of normalcy, a warehouse of the mundane. In here, no one was trying to kill me. There were no talking cats, and best of all, there were cookies. I love cookies.

While wandering, I grabbed a couple of Cliff bars and canned items, like Arbuckle's tuna and some more bottled water. What if we get stuck here? What if the van breaks down? I had my car still, but Arbuckle couldn't talk to me in my car. My brain shifts to survival mode, and I compulsively put together a survival food store in my arms just in case something happens.

Next thing I know, I've grabbed a cart.

In sporting goods, I get a flashlight, some windproof matches, a two-pack of propane, and a mini propane grill. You never know. A small cooler.

I should probably get some steaks. Arbuckle likes steaks, right? Everybody likes steak.

In the pet aisle. I grab leashes, harnesses, a disposable litter box, and a cardboard scratcher. I get some balls with bells in them, a laser pointer, the catnip treats he wanted, and anything else I think I might need. I've never owned a cat before.

On the grocery side, I get a two-pack of chuck-eye, dried mashed potatoes since I'm not making fresh mashed potatoes on this propane grill, and steak needs mashed potatoes.

When I finally leave, the sun is headed to set. At the van, Arbuckle gives me the side eye. I unpack the groceries and curb the cart since there is no way I'm walking that far again to put it in a cart rack. Arbuckle jumps in, and I close the side door and walk to the driver's side.

"Why did you buy all that crap?" Is the first thing out of his mouth.

"I don't know," is the only thing I can think to say as I climb in and shut the door.

It's the truth. I have no idea why I bought this stuff. All I can figure is my desire to return to the normalcy of two days ago was so strong it overrode my common sense.

"I mean, it is almost dinner time, and I did get some steaks, and I bet you like steak. We can find somewhere to set up the grill and make dinner."

"We don't have time for that," Arbuckle says, staring intently at me, possibly frowning.

"Why not?"

"Because it's almost twilight."

"What happens at twilight?"

"We go looking for the members of the order. We start with Jane because you said she was already dead, and Poly is alone." Arbuckle paws the GPS, and the screen comes alive. It's a map of New Orleans with a small, blinking red dot.

"That's a five-hour drive even if traffic is good."

"We can be there in less than fifteen minutes."

"How?

"We drive the van through the Gloam—all we need to do is wait for twilight."

chapter four

Strict and quick,
The First of Smack,
The Matriarch of Folly.
The Coat of Splotch,
The Missing Eye,
The Pirate Queen—Miss Poly.

—ALD
transcribed by AC

We're idling in the Walmart delivery bay, hidden by two parked semi-trailers. Being here is Arbuckle's idea. He doesn't know what people see when the van enters the Gloam, only what it looks like riding through it. My seat belt is on, and my hands are gripping the wheel like I'm driving through Dallas. Arbuckle showed me the harnesses my uncle stored in the glovebox. The one he's wearing now hooks around him, attaching to the seatbelt drawn across him and the seat. I wish I had known about them before I bought the others.

Around us, the sky is shifting to what cinematographers call the 'magic hour.' Twilight is when the sun moves below the horizon, but its light still illuminates us. This is when the membrane between us and the Gloam is thinnest and more easily penetrated, or so I've been told. It's beautiful behind the shopping center, now bathed in rich, warm colors.

Prying my right hand off the wheel, I tap the screen on the GPS, which blinks to life. The address in New Orleans is still up. It shows the entire route. I tap it again, and it pushes in until it's us—an arrow pointing West.

"You sure this is going to work?" I ask, staring down at Arbuckle and wishing I had a small pair of aviator goggles I could put on his head.

"No." He replies, then eyes me like he knows what I'm thinking.

"What do you mean, 'No'?"

"Well, I've only done it once or twice with your uncle, so I know it works, but I can't guarantee it still works."

"Why are you telling me this now?"

"Because you asked. Now remember. Hit 'GO' on the GPS, then get up to speed. At sixty miles an hour, pull the big red control cable, there to your right."

"What does that do?"

"I'm not sure, but it's vital."

"How do you know it's vital?"

"Because it activates the mechanism your uncle put in place to pierce the membrane between here and the Gloam."

"What if it doesn't work?"

"Then we drive there normally. Now quit stalling. Let's go."

"Fine. If we die, it's your fault."

"That's fair," he says, which doesn't give me any comfort at all.

I take a deep breath, then hit 'GO' on the GPS. The voice tells me my next turn, but I'm not listening because I've got my foot on the gas, and we're picking up speed as best as the van can. We're bouncing down the long narrow area behind the shopping center. We pass the last Walmart loading dock, hitting thirty. I push the pedal to the floor, and the engine complains like a pack of whipped mules. I lean on the pedal like there's a landmine under it, and I heard a *click*—lifting my foot will kill us both. I look over at Arbuckle, who appears to be smiling.

We hit forty, passing the back edge of T.J. Maxx, the van shaking a little.

"This isn't exactly a Porsche. We may run out of road before we hit sixty," I say, as we hit fifty.

It takes all I can muster to keep from hitting the rough to my left behind Big Lots as the path veers to the right. I'm afraid the whole van is going to shake apart. I can see the end of the road, and my eyes keep jumping from it to the speedometer. My right hand leaves the wheel to hover over the red knob. Keeping the van steady with one hand, which is considerably difficult, takes all my concentration.

Fifty-six, fifty-seven, fifty-eight—it stops at fifty-eight—my eyes go wide. "It's stopped at fifty-eight. We aren't going to hit sixty," I scream over the putter of the engine.

"Close enough," Arbuckle screams.

I pull the red lever as we hit the curb and head into the trees. My hands instinctively leave the wheel, my feet leave the peddles. I cover my face and scream. But we never hit anything. So, I lower my arms, and we're now in darkness, except for faint shimmering light outside the windows. Curtains of colored lights, like the Aurora Borealis, surround us.

I'm laughing, filled with childlike joy I haven't felt for a long time.

I look over at Arbuckle, who screams, "Hands on the wheel and eyes on the road."

"What—" I feel the van's tires hit hard, and I grab the wheel. All I see are trees. I'm screaming again until I realize we're on a narrow, garbage littered road. Grass tufts up from the center, with trees on either side. But we're still going fifty-three, so I tap the breaks, slowing down, worried we might tip if I slam them on. We come to a stop about ten yards from a cross street.

I'm breathing heavily. I look over at Arbuckle. "You, OK?"

"It could have been smoother," is all he says.

I'm about to say something when the woman's voice from the GPS butts in. "Recalibrating," she says. "Turn left on Behrman Hwy."

New Orleans blooms like a field of wildflowers before us as we drive into the old part of town. Magic hour, indeed. We find a parking spot a couple blocks from Jane's store. I feed the meter as Arbuckle wrestles out of his harness and jumps down. Shutting the front door, I run my hand along the Van's side, and I mumble under my breath, giving it a small measure of security. I'd hate for it to get stolen now.

Jane's Apothecary is right where it should be. The closed sign is turned out. I cup my hands and look through the window. It appears no one's discovered her yet. I ease down the alley next to the store and wind my way to the back door.

I mumble under my breath, a reveal spell like I did at the storage facility. Best practices. Always know what's on the other side of a door before you open it. The one time you don't, you'll step into a binding trap, or a pit viper comes flying at your face. Maybe you just get blown across the alley by the old string-on-a-shotgun chestnut. The spell pings clear, so I pull out my kit to pick the lock.

Lockpicking is a hobby I'm pretty good at, so I never learned many complex knocking spells. I prefer the feel of the pick and turning hook in my hand and the subtle *click* of the pins as you work your way down the tumbler. The lock is a Master Lock Pro Series 6321, a simple five-pin. The hole where the deadbolt used to be is covered by a steel plate screwed into the door from the inside. The lock secures two halves of a stainless-steel hasp and staple.

Looking down at Arbuckle waiting behind me on the stairs, I retrieve a prybar and pick.

"Pick along with me," I say, knowing he can't respond and I'm about to annoy him with my lock-pick commentary.

I pick it from the bottom using top-of-the-keyway tension.

"One is binding, a click there went into a false set. A little counter rotation on two, click out of three, nothing else there, four, gives some counter rotation, counter rotation on five, then back to one and nothing, two a click, and three," the tension rod spins down, and the lock clicks open.

I remove it from the staple gate and return it once I open the hasp. I start to pick the core in the door handle, but when I grab the knob, it turns.

"Magic," I say to Arbuckle, who's not impressed.

The door creaks slightly as it swings out, so I push myself right. Listening, I don't hear anything. Arbuckle and I step inside the windowless back office. It's dark, damp and smells of mildew spiced with cumin, garlic, and death. Moving forward, I shuffle, arms outreached, until I find the desk with my knee and say a few words under my breath that aren't very magical at all. Pulling out my cell, I fumble around trying to find the flashlight app. I don't want to use magic in here unless I have to.

The flashlight from my phone is brighter than I thought it would be. It reminds me that I bought a flashlight at Walmart but forgot to bring it. Waving the phone around the room more to navigate than investigate, I land on Arbuckle's eyes and almost give myself a heart attack. He's sitting in front of me on the desk, waiting for me to stop being an idiot again. I can see it in his eyes.

The office is a cluttered mess, so I keep the phone pointed at the floor. Even with the phone, it's still mostly shuffling as I cross the small room to the door on the other side. It empties into a dimly lit hallway. To the right is a beaded curtain leading to the store, and to the left are two doors.

Suddenly the curtain tinkles and jangles and I whip pan the light around just in time to see Arbuckle's ass move through it. I whisper-yell, "Asshole," at Arbuckle heads down the hallway.

On the right is a bathroom. I flip the switch to light up the hallway. The other door leads to the basement, and I notice it has a cat door cut into it. Opening it, I feel a tinge of déjà vu before I pull the string in front of my face. The bare bulb fills the stairwell and basement with shadows. This is where I watched her die, where the killer pushed her down the stairs. The song he sang returns to me, low and guttural, like throat singing, calling to her quintessence as it rose from her body.

The stairs are unfinished wood, colored by stains left from spills and probably a few leaks over the years. Easing my way down, I pretend it's not my weight causing them to creak and moan as they strain. At the bottom, the air is cool and wet, and the cumin and garlic are gone, replaced by copper and the sweet tones of sandalwood.

I find Pirate Jane, missing both eyes now. Her skin pulled lightly against her skull. I see the cuts on the arms. Bits of the dream come back to me. The bloodletting. The eye extraction. The Mason jar. I close my eyes and take a breath.

Leaving Jane where I find her, I head back up. I'll call in an anonymous tip once I'm on the road. I tug the light off at the top of the stairs and shut the door. I pull the microfiber cloth I clean my glasses with from my pocket and wipe down the door handle. I won't be burning this place down, so it's better if my prints aren't found.

Down the hall, I part the beaded curtain into the apothecary proper. Here, what's left of twilight falls through the windows, highlighting the dust in the air. I turn the flashlight off and slip my phone into my pocket. Outside, people pass back and forth in front of the store. Their shadows—taking shape from the light of the streetlamps—dance across the floor, bringing movement and life to the room.

Something squishes underfoot as I step forward. It lets out a series of cracking sounds. Looking down, I lift my shoe, and what's left of a mouse carcass slowly peels away. Kicking it aside, I look across the floor and count six or seven more. It's a good indication that Poly's still alive. I hear a bell, tingling lightly, combined with the song of plastic rolling across the floor, followed by scampering, claws clattering across the hardwood.

Stepping out from behind the counter, my eyes adjusting to the darkness, I see two cats playing in the open area of the sales floor. Seeing me, one of them shoots away, and the other turns and walks toward me. It's Arbuckle looking disappointed as he jumps up onto the counter. I step toward him, forgetting we can't communicate in here. Before I have time to react, he baps me on the face twice in quick succession with his paw.

"Hey!" I back up, holding my face with my hand, while he jumps off the counter without responding. I follow him. "What was that for?" I ask, staying a few steps behind him, as I guess it was him expressing his displeasure with me scaring Poly.

We could communicate after all.

A short search later, we find Poly in the basement, hunched up against Jane's body, hissing. Arbuckle walks over and sits in front of her. I hold my hands up as I step off the last stair and back away as far as I can across the concrete floor. I sit down cross-legged, placing my hands palm down on my knees. I pause for a minute, unsure what to do.

"Poly," I say out loud, assuming if Arbuckle can understand me, she can, too.

It gets her attention, and she stops hissing and looks at me with her one good eye, head craned to look around Arbuckle.

"I'm sorry I scared you. I'm Aubrey Cockcroft. You may remember me as the kid in the *Star Wars* pajamas or the awkward fourteen-year-old who dropped by one summer afternoon almost forty years ago. Like Jane, my uncle's dead too, and Arbuckle and I are trying to find anyone left of the order. We're not sure who, but someone is hunting you guys, and they'd have their quintessence, too, if not for this pact that was made. I'm not here to hurt you, and there is nothing we can do for Jane now, so I recommend you come with us."

There's a momentary pause, and then Poly steps around Arbuckle and slowly walks across the concrete floor toward me, sizing me up. Even in the harsh yellow light of the exposed bulb, I can see that she's a beautiful calico with a predominantly white coat covered with a large portion of orange and black splotches. Her face is split between the two colors, encircling a white nose and muzzle. Her left eye is a deep yellow-green. The pupil, large in the dim light, takes me in. It's balanced on the right by a fluffy patch of black fur, the eye having never existed.

I stay still and let her come as close as she wants, which is closer than I thought she would. Slowly, I lift my right hand and extend it, positioning it low. She moves in and sniffs, then rubs her head under my hand. I bring my fingers in and scratch her lightly around the ears. Détente achieved, I rise as Arbuckle bolts up the stairs, and Poly follows, pausing one last time in front of Jane to climb on her lap and give her one last head rub across her face.

Following them through the beaded curtain, I stop on the main apothecary sales floor. Twilight has come and gone. This lack of natural light has enhanced the streetlights' intensity, giving the shadows on the floor of the apothecary clean sharp edges. As they pass, the once whimsical headlights disrupt and aggravate the shadows, giving rise to manic writhing shadows that scurry across the floor.

Poly jumps up on the main counter, Arbuckle watching from the floor. She walks to the side of the cash register and baps it with her paw. The cash draw opens. She turns and looks at me.

I feel uncomfortable taking the money, but arguably, the quintessence of the owner is in Poly, and the cat did offer it to me. It's not much, but everything helps. There's also a skeleton key that Poly baps the drawer for me to take, and I do. Calicos really like bapping things. Closing the drawer spurs Poly to jump down.

Walking out, I remember the eye—the one the killer removed from Jane and placed on the table here. I can't leave it. I find it on a table in the middle of the sales floor, surrounded by the oddities. A shrunken head made from an apple, common and obscure tarot cards, a brass compass with seventy-two points, its needle made of silver and suspended in an amber liquid, numerous corked jars of withered plants and small dead animals, and a stuffed monkey's paw. Jane's eye is positioned to look toward the beaded curtain.

Knocking it on the floor, I step on it, nausea washing over me as I feel it pop. Jane doesn't need it anymore, and whoever did this doesn't need to see us here. Heading toward the curtain, I see Arbuckle and Poly half in and half out of the beads, waiting for me.

"I'm coming," I say, before I go down hard—my legs pulled out from under me.

I look toward my feet, where shadows wrap around my body, while more break from the floor, wrapping me up tight like a pharaoh. I should have figured there'd be a trap here. Whoever is doing this wants the quintessence. When they killed Jane, they didn't know it transferred to Poly. They went to see my uncle soon after. Not knowing to look for Arbuckle. I should have remembered the eye sooner. I should have dealt with it first. They were smart to rig this place in case they missed something, and now they know I'm involved, and they know the cats are here. It looks like I'm about to find out who's behind this.

The green light is blindingly bright as it streams through a gash being cut into thin air right in front of me. It's the same color as the portal from my uncle's memories. Something is coming through to this side from the Gloam. I can't tell who or what is doing the cutting until the gash reaches the floor and two hands split it apart. Opening further and further, the rift finally gives birth to a dark, hooded thing. It's close to six feet tall, with spindly fingers like spider legs that end in needles, one of which is tipped with a silver adornment, kept in place with a harness made of webbing, spun from the same material.

That was in my dream, too. The killer had used it to cut a rift, just like the one I see opening now. The killer had stepped through it, and we'd come out right in front of my uncle's trailer. But what is coming through this rift can't be the killer. This thing isn't even close to being human.

As it steps through, the wall between planes wobbles like it's made of rubber—the Gloam on one side and the inside of the apothecary on the other. The gash closes behind the figure as it pushes through, but it doesn't seal. There's just enough left for the light to trickle in, a glowing scar in the darkness.

Moving slowly, it comes at me as I struggle against the shadows. My mouth is covered, and my hands are bound. The figure glitches and spasms like it isn't yet fully formed. I wonder if only part of it can cross because behind it is a matte black trail of viscus, tar-like mucus.

In no time at all, it's upon me. The flowing inkblot of a hood pushes forth its face, a blurry spiral of teeth like a lamprey. It hovers a moment above me, emitting squeaks, ticks, and clicks of excitement—the sound of hunger in sight of a meal. The lamprey mouth wavers and shakes above me, the proboscis of a horrid butterfly come to drain my nectar. It emits one last giddy chitter of excitement, which turns into a high-pitched thrum, and I feel the muscles in my body go rigid. It's painful, like being hit with a taser—electricity exciting all the pathways—paralyzing me. And then I feel it, the essence of me drawing up and pulling away. My quintessence, being vibrated free from every cell of my body, excited electrons being removed from the atoms that form me.

The urine spreading beneath me is warm and oddly comforting. Tears roll down my cheeks, but I cannot wipe them away. And as the thing above me continues to drink, I begin to lose sight of it as my eyes roll back involuntarily in mourning of the end of me, and I think about how silly all of this has been, my life. One failure after another.

* * *

I guess I'm dead. I'm standing on a mesa, looking across the arid ground toward something huge. A giant moving city. Parts of it are turning and thrusting, not like wheels and pistons but more organic, like organs and muscles. The wind carries its sound to my ears, wet and embryotic. It crackles like a live wire hitting a puddle after a storm, sparking, smoking, boiling, and screaming. It's all bathed in green and black tints, a duotone photograph of a beached alien whale.

"You're not him," she says behind me.

Startled, I turn to see a hooded figure standing within hearing distance. Her face is covered by a scarf, as though she never knows exactly when the winds here will blow hard enough to lift the grit from the ground. At her side is a large thing, the same creature I saw in my uncle's memory, that sparked like an electric shadow from the cats. It rubs against her side like a nervous bear. She calms it with her hand.

"Where am I?" I shout a little over the drone of the city machine in the distance.

"The Gloam. The Shade brought you here. Brought your quintessence."

"Why? Why did it attack me?"

"It thought you were someone else," she says, stepping closer, studying me for a moment.

"Who does it think I am?"

"It thinks you are the shadow child."

"Well, I'm not."

"I can see that."

"By Shadow child, you mean my brother, don't you? You mean Alistair." I feel like I'm shouting louder than I need to.

"Yes."

"How do you know him?"

"I used to watch over him," she says, pointing to the thing in the distance. "He used to hang against the tower, encased in his crystal. Sometimes, it would catch the light just so, and I would see him looking at me."

I turn to the distance, to the city.

"It is the Perpetuation, but you won't remember that," she says.

"Why not?"

"Because it doesn't want you to."

"The city doesn't want me to? It's alive?"

"It is life," she says before turning her back on me. "Return him to me," she calls over her shoulder.

"Wait!" I shout, the winds picking up and the grit pelting my skin. I look down for a second, wondering how I can feel it, and when I look up, she is almost gone into the coming storm. "Who are you? How do I get out of here?" I yell as she and the beast disappear into a wall of dust.

"Same way as you got here," I hear her say, her voice echoing around me.

I try to go after her because I don't know what that means. I don't want to be left here. Even if it is the source of my power. But then I hear it, over the din and drone of the living city she calls life. A cacophony of discordant yowling pierces the air, visceral and violent. Spinning, trying to pinpoint where it's coming from, I see the rift. I also see the long slug trail of a shadow that leads to it. Looking down, I'm standing in it.

Suddenly, I feel myself being pulled down. The black shadow is thick, and I'm being dragged into its tub of nothingness. Everything goes dark as I struggle to keep my head above it, but the current is too strong. Everything fades into blackness around me, and I'm falling, deep into never-ending darkness.

* * *

I wake, my back against the wooden floor washed in pale green light. I feel weak and tired, the sensation of cool wetness beneath me. I turn my head to the sound of hissing and spitting and see Arbuckle and Poly, tails puffed and low, backs hunched, driving the thing into the rift. It chitters and squeaks as it retreats.

Then car lights pass and wash across the room. My eyes follow the light, and once it has passed, I see the shadows of the cats cast by the illumination of the Gloam. Their shadows are the same as the strobing black silhouettes from my uncle's memory and the beast who strode beside the woman. Feral and dark, they continue to advance, pushing the thing that came for me through the rift until it is gone.

Soon, the green light fades and I feel Arbuckle rubbing against me, he begins to purr, and I flinch, pull myself up and scooch and scramble on my ass across the floor the best I can, bumping into the front wall. Their shadow beasts are fresh in my mind. But now, through the dim and hazy air, fresh with a smell like ozone, Arbuckle and Poly come cautiously toward me, tails up, and all I see are cats again.

I wobble as I stand, trying to speak, but the sound I utter is weaker and more unsure than I had hoped. "Let's get the hell out of here."

They both run in front as I old man it across the room.

I had forgotten about the skeleton key until I passed through the office and decided to use the light switch this time. After the thing from the rift, I doubted anything worse could happen. Flipping it on, the low hum of fluorescents kicks in, and a few seconds later, the lights flick on.

Arbuckle is standing in front of the exit, but Poly isn't. She's sitting on a safe, obscured by stacks of paper and a chair. I walk over and clear everything out of the way. Inserting the key into the lock, I turn it, then crank down on the door's handle. It pushes down, and I pull. The heavy door swings open, its hinges well-greased. Inside is empty.

I look at Poly, who sits on top, staring over the edge and into the safe. She jumps down and climbs in. She baps her paw on the back of the safe in a rhythm of taps, and there's a *click*, and it opens. I reach in as she moves out of the way. Pulling the panel toward me, I find a small spiral-bound pocket notebook in the void. It has a worn, mottled green pressboard cover. Grabbing it, I don't even look inside. I've had enough for the night.

We walk to the van in silence. When we reach it, I mumble under my breath and dry my pants and shirt. Then, I remove the security before unlocking the driver-side door. Arbuckle jumps in first, followed by Poly, before I pull myself up and in. Poly explores by jumping over the driver seat and onto the small counter space behind the cabin.

Arbuckle settles in the passenger side and says, "Well, that was a shitshow."

"Can we save it until we find a hotel or something?" I say, cranking up the Van and pulling out onto the street. "When's the next time we can take this van through the Gloam?" I ask as we head down Canal toward I-90.

"Sunrise, why? You should probably rest before we go to the next location. You almost died back there."

"What the Hell was that thing?" I ask.

"I'm not sure," answers Arbuckle.

"What about you, Poly? Know what that thing was?" I ask, looking at her through the rear-view mirror.

She looks at me, confused.

"The van. It's connected to the Gloam. It should let you speak to me—or whatever it is that Arbuckle does."

From the back, I hear Poly for the first time, her voice small but confident. "You mean you can hear me?"

"Yeah," I say, smiling. "I can hear you."

Poly's posture changes, and she stands up straighter, more confidently. "I think it was a shade."

"That's what the woman I saw called it. But what is it?"

"They're like enforcers for the Gloam or something. Jonathan would know more. He was the Gloam scholar."

"What did it want with you?" Arbuckle asks.

"It thought I was Alistair," I say.

"How do you know?"

I hesitated before telling him what I had seen.

"She asked me to bring him to her, so I guess he did get out somehow. Evidently 'eternally bound' doesn't mean what they thought it meant."

"So where are we going at sunrise?" asks Poly from the back seat, her voice light and unsure.

I look at Arbuckle, but he's already curled up and sleeping. "Home," I say. "I need to go home, Poly."

* * *

The sun hints at the kind of day it will be as we load out of the motel room and into the van. After we'd grilled some steaks in the parking lot, I'd gotten about five hours of sleep, which was more than I expected. Arbuckle and Poly had stayed up all night seeing who could keep me awake the longest. For a couple of cats that weren't cats, they had the schtick down.

Switching on the GPS, I add a new entry to the list—my home

address. I'm not exactly sure where we'll land, as getting to New Orleans was pretty much Walmart to Walmart, and I didn't want to do that again. Instead, I figured it was early enough that all I needed to do was find a long strip of quiet roadway where I could push the van to sixty, or fifty-eight, and pull the knob. So, I headed for I-10 and hoped it was early enough.

The fog was low and rolled with us down the interstate. About two miles from Irish Bayou, I announced my intention to jump to the rest of the van. My foot was already on the floor, keeping us from being hit on the 70 mph road. So, technically, we could punch it at any time. Again, the van felt like it would rattle apart, so what did we have to lose? Ahead of us, another bank of fog rolled across the road, giving us cover.

Bringing up my address, I hit 'GO' and pulled the red lever as the voice from the GPS told us the route. This time, I don't flinch, and I see the iridescent curtain part before me once more—a breathtaking light display. As quick as that, we come out on a long, open stretch of road on the other side.

Traversing the Gloam is beginning to feel like riding a bike. Only two times so far, but it now feels normal. I suspect that a few more times, it'll be old hat. Looking out the window, I have no idea where I am at first. It takes a moment to orient myself. We're on the DKX runway. It's a small local airport near my house. Luckily, it's still early, before civil twilight, so only a few lights are on in the buildings. I know it doesn't open until seven, but I have no idea if people are here before that.

I immediately shut off the headlights and veer toward the exit.

"We've gotta see if we can get more accuracy out of this thing," I say to Arbuckle.

"Do I look like an engineer?" he says, a new note of sarcasm in his voice.

Heading toward the gates, I mumble under my breath and use the same technomage spell I used at the storage facility to mess up the security cameras. Then I toss off another spell to open the electric gate before slowing down to accommodate its speed. I hit the gas once we're through. I keep it at a comfortable pace. I don't think I've ever been more excited to be home.

Not far past Island Home Blvd, I take a right onto a small access road and pull directly into my backyard. I leave the front door open as I hit the grass with both feet. I forgot to mow it before I left, and it's getting out of hand. The dew clings to my boots as I walk across the lawn.

I'm up the few steps onto the small back porch and through the screen door seconds later. It's never locked because what's the point? You could cut through the screen with a pocketknife and be in faster than using a credit card to jimmy the gate hook, which I only use if the wind picks up to keep the door from blowing open and slamming against its hinges.

All the locks on the house, including the back door, are keyless and tied to my phrasing. I mumble under my breath and push through the door into the small hallway that leads past the bathroom into the kitchen.

I don't know why my heart is racing a mile a minute, but I've got a sick feeling something's happened to Em.

"Em," I call her name out, wait less than a minute, and call it again. "Em!"

Through the empty kitchen and down the hallway—created by the stairs on my left and the outside wall of the office on my right—I barely pause, grabbing the office doorjamb to peer in quickly. She isn't here either.

"Em?" Like a mantra, I can't stop calling her name.

The living room is empty as well.

Where could she be?

I take the stairs two at a time—not a great idea, considering I haven't exerted myself this much in a long time. I'm breathing heavily by the time I reach the top. I open every door as I go down the hall, all but one—still, no Em.

Again, I call out, "Em?" stopping at the end of the hallway. Only one room left to check. I try to calm myself, to be rational. She's not a prisoner here; maybe she left—went for a walk or up to the house on the hill—even though she hasn't left since the night we met.

It's not working, trying to rationalize where she could be other than here. I check the rooms again before pausing at the door to hers.

"Em? Are you in there?"

No response. I turn the knob and throw open the door.

The room is empty.

Before I have time to think, I step across the threshold—violating my promise to her.

Nothing has changed since I gave her the space. What could she even do to it? Eidola don't leave impressions—not like that. No dip in the bed or mussed sheets. No litter on the floor, no fingerprints.

A panic rushes over me, followed by a wave of sadness and longing. It's silly—I try to push it down—but for all my gruffness, ever since we met, I've needed Em. She keeps the loneliness and self-doubt at bay. Around her, the voice in my head telling me I'm worthless and meaningless goes quiet. I'm not sure anymore what I'd do without her.

And then I see her—out the window, sitting on the roof. Shimmering in the morning sun as it begins to rise through the trees.

I walk across the room and open the window, raising it so I can step through. Her pale, ephemeral head turns toward me as the sun passes through it, and she smiles.

"You're back."

"Mind if I join you?" I ask, motioning to the roof.

"Not at all. I was watching the sunrise."

I step through the window. It's a bit of a strain to get out, but I manage without too much groaning and creaking from my joints. Then I'm beside her, sitting.

She looks at me again, and I smile for the first time in days. My heart slows, and I breathe a heavy sigh—part relief, part effort to push down the emotion.

"How was your trip? You left in quite a hurry the other day."

"It was OK. My uncle's dead."

"I'm sorry to hear that."

"Thanks. We weren't close."

"I'm sorry to hear that, too."

"Yeah. Oh—I brought back two cats."

"I like cats."

"Me too."

Over the next half hour, the sun climbs higher into the sky, which turns a brilliant, clear blue.

We sit, watching the world shift from darkness to light.

I'm comfortable and content in her presence, my mind drifting back to the day we met.

* * *

I'm standing on the bank of the Tennessee River before sunset—or at least as close as I can get, here in the park. I walk here most days for an hour or so, to relax and let the day wash off me. It isn't a large park, but it's a short walk from the home my parents left me when they died.

It's spring, and I can hear a mockingbird nearby, making a ruckus. The river is brown with sediment that never settles. It's full of mercury and other crap not fit for consumption. There's a song about it—*Tennessee River*, by a band called Alabama, themselves named after one of the four states it runs through. But the river begins here in Knoxville, formed at the confluence of the Holston and French Broad rivers. I wouldn't swim in it or eat a fish from it, but I like watching it flow.

Today, I also like watching the woman standing even closer to the bank. She's practically in it. At first, I thought she might be part of a local reenactment group—or maybe out on a stroll after a performance nearby, possibly at the Ijams Nature Center or over the fence at the East Tennessee School for the Deaf.

I think this because she's clothed modestly, in what looks to be a dress from the late 1800s—assuming I know my periods well enough from years of watching *Masterpiece*. The dress is light in color, with simple lace atop her shoulders. Her back is to me as she hovers her right foot above the river's surface, holding up the bulk of her lower dress with considerable effort. It's as though she's taunting the river to take her, whisking her away to somewhere else. Her chestnut hair is pulled back and secured in a loose bun that sits low against her neck. She's small—or at least smaller than me.

Stepping forward, as the mockingbird takes wing, I land in her sightline when she turns to watch it fly past. Her face is delicate and chiseled, eyes the color of sherry. She appears to be somewhere between thirty and fifty, her skin smooth and her features plain. Straightening up and away from the water's edge—quickly, as though caught in the act of something untoward—she brushes down her dress to let it hang again above the ground. She continues to stare as I follow her movements.

"I didn't mean to startle you. I apologize," I say, holding up my hands.

She looks around, trying to figure out who I'm talking to, and realizes there's no one else here.

"You can see me?" she replies, breathless. "Am I real to you?" she continues, more curious than frightened.

"I can see you, yes. Should I not be able to?"

"Well… I'm not sure," she replies. "Are you a medium?"

"More like a large," I say, but the joke falls flat as she continues to stare.

"I'm not sure I understand."

"Not worth explaining. I assume you mean—am I a seer?"

"That *was* what I meant. I used to hold séances when I was younger. I never expected to be on this side."

"You're an eidolon, then. It all makes more sense now. Twilight. The river. You were thinking about ending it all over again, weren't you?"

"It was a thought I had."

"Well, the river will certainly do that. Drag you off for good—which would be a shame," I say.

"I don't know where I am, Mr.—?"

"You're in Knoxville, Tennessee. Island Home neighborhood. Island Home Park, specifically. That's the Tennessee River you almost stuck your foot in," I say, stepping forward. "I'm Aubrey Cockcroft. I'm a—local."

"Tennessee. I had wondered where I might end up."

"What brings you here, Ms.—?" I pause, hoping she'll offer her name.

"Em is fine."

"What brings you here, Em? Usually, eidola are tethered to a place. But this isn't your place, is it?"

"It's where I ended up."

"You're a Death Runner."

"Death did not stop for me," she mumbles lightly, and I almost don't catch it.

"And you did not stop for Death," I reply, the phrase feeling familiar somehow, though I can't place it.

"Something like that."

"Where are you from?"

"Massachusetts."

"Nice place?"

"Lived there all my life—until two days ago."

"What happened? Reapers?"

"They swarmed the house, clawing and screeching," she says, looking out toward the river again. "If that's what you call them."

"It is indeed," I reply, suddenly feeling exposed out here in the open. "You want to come with me, Em? Back to my house? I think it might be safer there."

"We've just met. How do I know I can trust you?"

"Well, you can't. But on the bright side—you're already dead, so what's the worst that can happen?" I punctuate the line with what I hope is a charming, not creepy, smile.

"That's a good point."

We walk slowly east, leaving the riverbank along the Will Skelton Greenway. Eventually, we turn right, keeping to the roadside along the fence that borders the School for the Deaf. There isn't much discussion along our walk, but with twilight fading, so does the color from Em.

By the time she points out the house on the hill to me, she's become a well-defined, hazy misty green.

* * *

"Aubrey, those aren't cats," Em says, knocking me out of the memory.

She's looking down across the lawn at Arbuckle and Poly enjoying the grass. Poly is rolling in it while Arbuckle eats it.

"At least not like any cat I've ever seen."

I turn to Em, both excited and a little uncertain. "So, you can see their true forms?"

Em turns to me and looks me directly in the eyes. "Unfortunately."

"What do they look like?" I say as we both turn our heads to look.

Arbuckle is vomiting up the grass he ate, and Poly, now broken away from her revelry, has walked over to sniff it out of concern.

"It isn't easy to describe. They are large and shift like shadows, free from the light that created them. They have a form, but it is never still enough to capture," Em says, then turns to me. "Can I go down and meet them?"

"Of course," I say as I get up and wedge myself back through the window. Behind me, Em steps off the roof's edge and floats down to meet them.

Stepping out the back door, as Em walks toward them, I watch them size her up as she approaches. Em's head is focused upward, not on the cats I see on the ground, as though she were approaching a horse. She stops a foot or so from them and reaches out her hand. She tentatively pets the air, and I see Arbuckle react like he's being scratched behind the ear.

I shake my head and walk across the grass to the van. I open the side door and turn to Em and the cats.

"Alright, family meeting. Everybody in the van."

For reasons I am unsure about, this causes Em to smile, clap her hands, run across the lawn, and climb in. The cats are more skeptical, and it takes a few minutes for them to finally wander over and jump in, which gives me time to walk around and shut the driver's side door. Finally, I get in myself, closing the side door.

Em sits on the short bench that butts against the driver's cabin, and I sit across from her. Arbuckle and Poly are on the table. Arbuckle is looking out the window while Poly, half lying down, cleans the dew off her legs with her tongue.

"OK, I called this meeting because I need everyone on the same page. And right now, everyone but me seems to be on that page."

I reach out a finger and lightly poke Arbuckle on the shoulder to get his attention. He turns to me, annoyed as he has been eyeing a chipmunk and chittering in anticipation of the kill.

"Can't this wait? That little fur clown needs to be taught a lesson," Arbuckle says crankily.

"No, it can't, and I like chipmunks, so please try not to kill all of them or any of them."

"No promises," he replies as he slumps onto the table, bored now.

"Can both of you see Em?" I ask the cats.

"Yes," they both reply.

"And Em, you can see them, but they don't look like cats to you, correct?"

"Well, outside they didn't look like cats, but in here they appear to be cats."

"OK, well, that's one more wrinkle than I expected, but let's keep on track. I can see Em, and the both of you, but you look like cats to me, both in the van and outside. Except when you're exposed to light from the Gloam. So, who wants to tell me what's going on? I saw your shadows in my uncle's memories and at Jane's when I came to, and I almost pissed myself."

"I'm pretty sure I smelled urine well before that," Arbuckle chimes in.

"I did too," says Poly.

"You had already pissed yourself," Arbuckle says, as he looks at Poly, and they both nod their heads in agreement.

"Can we move on?"

"When you saw us illuminated by the Gloam, for a split second, we existed in both of our states," Arbuckle says.

"Em is an eidolon," Poly says, examining her. "She has some residual Gloam energies on her. I can see them."

I squint but can't see anything different.

"So, I guess she has traveled by Gloam," Poly continues. "Is this correct?"

"Is that where I went when I escaped the reapers?" Em asks, turning to me.

"Most likely," says Arbuckle. "Eidola can pass across the barrier between here and The Gloam."

"Gloamtrotting," I say with a certain amount of pride.

Arbuckle's ears slowly scrunch against the top of his head, and he glowers at me. "Please, no," he says.

"Fine, we won't call it—Gloamtrotting—again," I say deliberately, pausing for effect. I watch his ears go down again. "Last time. Promise," I say, smiling.

Arbuckle sighs with relief and straightens his ears up. "Your uncle mentioned the van travels similarly," Arbuckle adds.

"Good to know," I say, not sure I care.

"Now that you've seen us as cats, you should be able to choose how you see us," Poly adds, looking at Em.

"That's good," she says. "No offense, but you are more pleasing as cats."

"OK. Family meeting over," I say as I check my phone. "We have about twelve hours until we can travel again, so I suggest we all eat something and maybe take a nap, agreed?"

"That sounds very reasonable, Aubrey," Em says, trying to boost my confidence.

I grab the handle of the door and slide it open. When I do, Arbuckle and Poly are out like they'd never been here, and Em, not needing to mimic every single step, is across the lawn on the porch. I grab a can of tuna out of the under-seat storage and shut the side door to the van.

In the kitchen, I see what there is to eat. Not much. All I find is six eggs, half a pack of bacon, some oat milk, yogurt, salami, and cheese. Breakfast for lunch it is. I make two eggs over easy and two slices of bacon. I find a loaf end of bread in the panty and put it in the toaster.

Done eating, I pop the top on the tuna and portion it onto two plates. I take them outside onto the deck off the kitchen and put them down. Looking around, I don't see Arbuckle or Poly.

"Lunch," I call out and head inside.

Just as the screen door closes, I hear a chipmunk scream.

"Dammit. Nobody even listens to me," I say under my breath, to no one in particular, and close the door to the kitchen behind me.

* * *

I'd be lying if I said I understood everything in the notebook I retrieved from the safe at Pirate Jane's. Like many things over the past few days, I haven't flexed these muscles in a long time. I was never a theoretical magician or a scholar of either the history or the science of magic, and yes, there is a science of magic.

I was taught how to do it. I do it. I collect what I need when I need it and often forget things when I don't use them often enough. I am, if there is such a thing, a practical wizard, and you notice I don't capitalize the word 'wizard'. So, you get my point. I'd like to think I'm altruistic in my use of it, but I am not. Life requires money, and money requires compromise.

Em enters the kitchen while I pour over the notebook and sits across from me. Since she doesn't sleep, it's fortunate that her curiosity is never-ending. She can't press flowers anymore or even write poetry like she used to, but she and I have worked out a reciprocal relationship. Symbiotic to a degree. I transcribe her poetry onto whatever is lying around, and she keeps an eye on things and me centered.

When I'm away or asleep, she keeps an eye out. You'd be surprised in my line of work how many people want to kill, threaten, or intimidate you. Most of them are too dumb to pull off the killing bit, but occasionally, there's one, and you only need one.

"What's that?" Em asks, pointing to the notebook.

"My father's old notebook."

"Your father? The one that died in the accident?"

"It wasn't an accident, at least not in the way I thought it was."

"You've had a long two days."

"I have," I say, wanting to change the subject. "You come up with any new poems while I was gone?"

"I did, as a matter of fact."

"You want to get them down? I need a distraction."

"Absolutely."

We head down the hall to the office, and I sit at the desk. I open the shoe box, grabbing a stack of paper that I fan out like a deck of cards. Em, sitting next to me, concentrates on them before reaching out and gently grabbing the one she wants. Her gentle tug moves it slightly. Her face scrunches to concentrate her focus, and she tries again. I loosen my grip, and she pulls it out but loses her hold on it so that it drops to the desk.

"You're getting better," I say.

"Lots of time to practice," she says, happy to have connected for a moment with this plane.

I put the rest back in the box, take the one she selected, and peel it apart until it's flat. I rub my hands across it to remove as many creases from the folds as possible. Grabbing the quill box from the top of the desk, I remove the ink bottle and quill. Unscrewing the cap from the ink, I dip the nib in delicately and scrape it against the glass ridge of the bottle's opening.

I look at Em, and she looks at me. I wait. I wait for the words that roll from her tongue like a conjuring and put them down onto the envelope, leaving spaces between the words the way she taught me. I write at a measured pace. Her voice is always calm and matter-of-fact, never excited. She tells me when to add dashes and when to capitalize a word. She tells me when the poem is finished, and I place a small hyphen and her name after it. '-Em'. I don't know much about poetry, but I know power when I read it, and some of Em's poems contain power—some even make me jealous.

"Let me see."

I hold it up for her and keep it steady as she reads it to herself, her head bobbing and lips moving in silent cadence to her thoughts.

"Thank you. It's finished."

I open the top drawer of the desk and lay the paper inside. It winks out of sight. A portal spell transports it to the bottom drawer of the chifforobe in her room. I see her hand on my shoulder from the corner of my eye and wish I could feel it.

Putting Em's words down and taking a moment is a simple act that helps me forget about my problems and focus on what needs to be done.

"I'm leaving again later today," I say. "We still have three people and three cats we need to check on: Francis and Alexander, Mia and Saoirse, and Johnathan and Augustus."

"I understand," she says. "Just promise me you'll be safe."

"I'll do my best. I'm worried we may not find any of them alive."

"Why is someone doing this?"

"I'm not entirely sure," I say. "But I'm going to find out."

Pulling more papers out for Em to choose from, I help her transcribe four more poems, which takes about an hour because Em also spends a little time attempting to hold the pen herself. She does alright and gets two words roughly written out, but she's not quite there yet.

When we're done, my previously clenched muscles have loosened, and calmness has settled in my head. It's a form of meditation for me, this collaboration where I let myself succumb to Em's words. They soothe me like a balm and let my mind take refuge from the self-doubt and ridicule it bombards on me.

The attempts to connect to this plane tire Em, so she excuses herself and heads upstairs to her room. I have no idea how taxing it is on her, but I know she's been working to be able to interact for a long time. There are a couple of small items in the living room she works with on nights when I'm watching something on TV she isn't interested in, which is often.

She's gotten pretty good at pushing the small golf ball around on the floor and stopping it. It's the delicate things that are giving her issues. I know her goal is to one day be able to write again.

We still have time to kill, so I pull out my father's notebook. It's in surprisingly good condition for being over fifty years old. I open it up, and on the first page is his name and what looks to be the date he began writing it, April 1, 1970, the day I was born. That's right, I'm an April Fool's baby. How's that for the universe getting its kicks?

The first few pages are generic thoughts on new fatherhood, questions to ask the doctor, and a list of things he wants to teach me as I grow up. I pause on the list for a minute and see how many he accomplished before he died. The items are simple: To laugh, read, question, reason, persevere, protect, be honest, loyal, loving, and kind.

I'd had to learn most of them on my own, and a few of them I never mastered. I keep flipping through, and the notebook shifts away from me and onto Alistair, or at least onto visions my mother was having, and the research he was doing to try and get to the bottom of it. He isn't subtle about words or phrases that he thinks have meaning, like 'Doppelgänger' and 'Shadow Energy!' Under this is a piece cut from a xerox of a page, the tape brittle and yellowed.

"For every spark of life sent forth to man, its equal in shadow is left behind, carved into the Gloam forever."

There is also a summoning for things called 'Caretakers' and their 'Shades,' like Poly had said. There's a timeline of his attempts to bring them forth from the Gloam. Two pages are dedicated to the intricate sacred pattern one draws upon the floor. It's not the same as the one from my uncle's memory, but it is similar in its geometry. I wonder where he did these experiments and figure it must have been here, with my mother and me in the house, or maybe he only did them when we were away.

Without realizing it, I'm staring at the door across from me, the one leading to the basement. Standing up, I take my father's notebook and cross the kitchen to the door. Opening it, I descend the wooden stairs into the basement. I don't know what I'm looking for, but everything seems to happen in basements. So, I wonder if there's anything down here in mine. There's a switch near the railing at the bottom of the staircase, and I flick it on, expecting to see something different than I did last week when I was doing laundry.

Before recently, it was just a room, a bare concrete floor with a drain in the middle of it. The cinderblock walls are sealed but exposed. The damp smell of earth from the encapsulated portion of crawlspace that sits behind the partial wall at the front of the house permeates the room. It's highlighted by the smell of coal emanating from the non-functional chute and bin—lying half-full beside the crawl space. It's a surprisingly large room for not being finished, but I wonder why my parents never did. Then I wonder why, other than having the crawlspace encapsulated years ago to keep the moisture levels down, I didn't either.

A washer and dryer sit a few feet from the bottom of the staircase, and the water heater is in the space under the stairs. The rest of the room is empty, and I can't remember if I ever really stepped beyond the small laundry area much before. Why would I? All I ever came down here to do was wash my clothes.

I imagine my father down here, beseeching someone or something to help him understand the visions that plague his wife and cause such uncertainty in his heart.

Opening his notebook, I flip to the page where he wrote down a spell I haven't seen before but wished I had. It would have come in handy only a few days ago. Closing my eyes. *I mumble under my breath* before opening them again. The spell is a type of scrying that uses the residual energy left behind in a room to recall what happened.

We tend not to think about how much energy remains after we impact a space. Some of it gets left behind, whether it's emotional, kinetic, potential, magical, or intentional energy. After almost fifty years, I'm hoping there's still enough lingering to see and understand what my father found, if anything.

Slowly turning my hand, I reverse the flow of time. I see myself walking backward up the stairs from when I entered the space just now. Then, I increase the speed, incrementally at first. It's me doing laundry, one mundane day after the next until I am a blur, as the little bit of light through the small window strobes with the passing of the days. Speeding it up still, moving back through the residual energy, like rewinding a videotape, I watch my life in reverse.

Occasionally, there are blips of Em, popping in and out like a lightning bug blinking in the nighttime. Then my new washing machine and dryer were gone. The space is now empty as it was when I arrived in my early twenties, claiming my inheritance. This empty rental home whose mortgage had been paid off over the twelve years I spent with my uncle. Another gift I never thanked him for. Then, in that space, the avocado Maytags of my childhood appear.

I slow the speed down to watch my mother descend the steps. She's as young as she was in my uncle's memories. Backward still, I pause at her looking toward me, then put it into normal speed, and I hear her say my name.

"Aubrey," my mother calls to me.

For a second, I forget my purpose and almost speak, as my young self runs to her, passing through me.

She leans down and hugs me. "You're getting too big for me to carry," she says, smiling. I watch as I take my mother's hand, climbing ahead of her up the stairs.

I stop. Stepping back, I look across the empty expanse of the room. I should be able to find my father here. I'm close to it now timewise. I turn my wrist more delicately until I catch a blip of him. I dial it in until

I see him, his back to me and a small rift to the Gloam before him.

Stepping up to look my father in the eyes, I'm too short. I look for something to stand on and find a small bucket under the stairs. I carry it over and place it at his feet, then awkwardly step up on it. It's not the steadiest thing I could have chosen, but it gets me where I want to be.

"Why is all this happening now?" I ask him, but he has nothing to say. Stepping off the bucket, I sit down and flip through the notebook, looking for anything that will help me make sense of everything. Why was their memory of Alistair erased? Why did my aunt have him? Who had my aunt been talking to? And if it was him, why was my brother trying to kill everyone again?

From the corner of my eye, I catch movement on the stairs. Arbuckle and Poly survey me through the railing from halfway down. After a second, they continue to the bottom.

"What are you looking for, Aubrey?" Arbuckle asks, and I'm surprised to hear him speaking to me in the house.

"I can understand you here."

"The entire house is steeped in residual energy from the Gloam," he says, nudging his head toward the small portal. "Possibly from the rifts your father opened, even after all these years."

"That's great. No more meetings in that van."

"It also means the barrier here is weak. Weak enough for something to cross," Poly says.

"That's not as good, but I should be able to fortify it. Until I was transported there, I thought the Gloam was just an energy source. It's a whole other world."

"A world populated by many different beings, like here. But there, the purpose of every being is singular. Keep the Perpetuation running and producing energy," Poly adds.

"What happens if it stops?" I ask.

"Stops?" Arbuckle says. "Aubrey, if the Perpetuation stops, then there is no more energy to power new life."

"You mean new life here, right?"

"Yes," Arbuckle says. "And your magic would simply become words, mumbled by a madman," he adds.

I remember the living city, screaming and pulsing in the distance. The woman had said it wouldn't let me remember, but I did. Why?

I stand up and pace in circles, trying to work some things out.

"This quote," I say, pointing to the paper taped into the notebook. "If what it says is true—and all life energy is counterbalanced by shadow energy in the Gloam—then Alistair was somehow sparked from my shadow energy. Which means there was a puppeteer before there was a puppet." I point to my father. "He was trying to figure out why. I only need to figure out who. So what you're telling me is this—" I hold up the notebook, "is a dead end."

"Only for now," Arbuckle says, walking across the floor to me. "Because something does not contain the answers you need today doesn't mean it won't be useful tomorrow."

"You're right," I say and flip the notebook closed. I stuff it into my pocket.

I mumble under my breath, and my father disappears.

"Who's next on the list?" I ask.

"Francis and Alexander."

∞

chapter five

Fat and kind,
The Lord of Loaf,
The Beggar and Demander.
The Scab of Mooch,
The Belly Pouch,
The Bum King—Alexander.

—ALD
transcribed by AC

e drop out of the Gloam in Bricktown, near Skinny
Slims in Oklahoma City. The sun is falling below the
Mickey Mantle overpass as we roll under. Correct-
ing for our new location, the GPS reroutes. It's a short
four-minute drive. The building is a low three-story senior
apartment complex called The Township. I park in front, to the right
of the entrance. As I do, I mumble under my breath and lock the security system
into a loop.

"You both wait here. I'll see if I can find Francis and Alexander," I say,
looking over my shoulder at Arbuckle and Poly, who've settled on the
far back cushion.

"Be careful," Arbuckle calls out.

"Thanks, Mom," I say before I shut the door.

I'm unfamiliar with Oklahoma City, so I assume we're in a rough part of town. Despite the woman across the street walking her dog and talking on her cell phone in front of the Episcopal Diocese, all the windows on this building have iron bars bolted over them on the outside. On the ground level, they're boarded up with plywood that no one bothered to paint.

Maybe it gives the tenants a sense of security. Either way, I mumble under my breath and give the van a quick lockdown. I've left it running so Arbuckle and Poly can have some A/C. Taking a quick look over my shoulder, I notice Arbuckle is now watching me from the counter behind the passenger side. I give him a nod, turning to the complex.

The entrance is small, only three steps up with a ramp to the left. An older couple sits on the black wire bench, watching the sunset. They look happy, holding hands, his head nuzzled into her neck. I notice the metal chain attached to the bench running under his jacket. It's none of my business, but it seems an odd policy. Maybe he has dementia and wanders off. Maybe he likes being chained up. It's got nothing to do with me.

I climb the stairs to the thick sliding entrance. It takes a minute to realize I need to be buzzed in. I've already put the security feed on a loop, so no one knows I'm standing here. Even worse is if I press the bell, and their camera shows no one is out here. I mumble under my breath, and the buzzer goes off, the door slides open, and I pass through. I'm working on the premise that more than one person can buzz me in, so walking in like this won't raise any alarms.

Inside, the tiny vestibule is big enough for a wheelchair and maybe two other people, with a push bar door into the lobby. The lobby is decorated like the common room at a mid-level university dorm or a motel from the 1980s that you find on a back road trying to avoid the interstate.

Stepping up to the receptionist's desk, I stare at an empty chair. Looking around to verify that no one is watching, I slide behind the desk. The computer is on, and the directory is open, making it easy to search for Francis Cummings.

He's on the third floor in apartment 317. Closing the search brings the directory to the homepage. I've barely gotten out from behind the desk when an unkind-looking woman in scrubs rounds the corner and stares at me like I'm getting ready to pee on the floor.

"Can I help you, Sir?"

"I'm here to visit Francis Cummings in 317. Didn't know if I needed to sign in or anything."

"Is he expecting you?"

"It's a surprise."

"We don't do surprises. This is a secure building. I'll call and make sure he's up to having a visitor. He'll escort you if he is.

"OK," I say, unsure what to do if he doesn't remember me. For all I know, he could have dementia.

She looks him up on the computer and then gives me a serving of side-eye like she knows I was in her computer mucking about—but she doesn't say anything. She punches in his number, and I can hear the ring on the other end get nervous when I don't hear anyone pick up.

But before she can hang up, there's a mild, "Yes?" Over the receiver.

"Mr. Cummings, I have a—" she takes the receiver off her ear, cups her hand over the mouthpiece, and looks at me without saying anything.

"Aubrey Cockcroft," I reply, feeling like I'm in trouble again for something I haven't done yet.

"A Mr. Cockcroft is here to see you," she says.

Another long pause I hear, "Right down," and then the click of the other end being hung up.

"He'll be right down," she says, pointing to the book on the desk. "You can sign in now," she says, rotating the ledger to face me.

Stepping forward and picking up the pen, I write the date, check my watch, write the time, and sign my name.

She's been watching me the entire time, and as soon as I'm done, she rotates the book toward herself. "You can wait over there," she says, pointing to the ugly furniture across the room.

"Thanks," I say and walk across, shoulders slumped, feeling her watching me the entire way.

I choose one of the hardback chairs instead of the love seat, convincing myself that it has probably had less use over the years and is less likely to smell. I'm wrong. Sitting, the aroma wafts up: baby powder, Gold Bond, and something close to rotting meat. I comically spring up like I sat on hot coals.

While I wait, I look around, trying not to look at the receptionist. I know if I do, I'll get that side-eye again. I've seen curses with less side-eye. Focusing on my limited surroundings reveals details most people would probably miss. Some of the furniture cushions and pillows have small tears, like claw marks, that have been sewn by hand, and a lot of the wood surfaces, including the coffee table, show extensive scratching, some of it hidden by the piles of old *Field and Stream* magazines.

Pushing a small stack of magazines with the back of my hand reveals dark brown scratch marks. Blood? Maybe. Hard to say, but I'm betting it is when I notice a torn fingernail caught in the carpet fibers at my feet. Looking up at the reception desk, I'm thankful she's distracted by a phone call. I'd missed the break-the-glass emergency box on the wall behind her, which contains an axe and a riot shotgun. Before I can put these things together, I hear the elevator *ding* in the distance.

Turning, I see Francis, in his mid-80s, unkempt gossamer wisps of white hair clinging in desperation to his head, round the corner. He's walking with a cane, followed closely by a large orange tabby, which can only be Alexander. Small round framed glasses with dark lenses sit on his nose. He's dressed in a loose white muslin shirt and pants with white Vans, making him look like a beach prophet. Stepping toward them to meet them halfway, I'm stopped by the sound of a throat clearing. The woman behind the reception desk is shaking her head.

Frances slows as he approaches to size me up, extending his hand and smiling.

"Aubrey, is that really you? All grown up?"

"Grown old."

"Haven't we all," he laughs lightly, his grip surprisingly firm. "How's your uncle?"

"He's dead, and so is Jane."

A frown sets across his face, triggering his forehead to make a beachfront of worry lines.

Leaning in, he whispers, "Let's talk upstairs," and then signals for me to go ahead of him, which is good because whatever cologne he's wearing makes my eyes water and almost makes me gag. It's that same smell from the furniture.

He waves to the woman behind the desk. "Thank you, Bernice."

I'm only a few steps out of the sitting area when he calls out, "Alexander! We're leaving."

I hear a small, sad *yowl* as Alexander breaks from where he was attempting to access the trashcan and then plods over to Francis's side. I hadn't noticed or paid much attention, but Alexander is not a happy cat. His body is low to the floor, and his ears are pulled back in vigilant alert. His tail is swishing rapidly, sometimes even smacking the ground. He moves slowly but purposefully, like he could be attacked at any moment.

"He really will eat anything," Francis confides while scanning his badge and punching the button for the third floor.

"Lot of security for a retirement home," I say.

"Well, you can never be too sure. The world is a dangerous place," Francis says, smiling as he steps into the elevator, and I watch Alexander follow.

I hop onboard, and the doors close behind me. The ride is short, and there isn't much to say. There's a sound, too—constant—beneath the hum of the elevator and the light, jazzy refrain of the Muzak: howling and screaming, muffled and filtered by concrete.

When we get off on the third floor, Francis leads us a short way down the hall to 317, which he also unlocks with his pass card.

The apartment is a 700 square foot one-bedroom, the front door opening into the living room, There's a tiny kitchen off to the right. The living room has a loveseat just inside the door with a TV opposite. A chair sits against the wall across from the front door. Even though it's dark outside, I can see the one window through the open bedroom door—small and south facing—so it gets some light all day. A street-light across the street gives the room a yellow glow.

Francis shuts the door behind us and moves to the kitchenette. "Cup of coffee?"

"Sure," I say. I could use the caffeine.

I watch Alexander make himself at home on the sofa, almost disappearing as he squishes himself into the corner. When Francis brings the coffee out, I sit in the single seat while he takes half of the loveseat Alexander has left for him.

"The last time I saw you," he says, sipping the coffee.

"Was when I was holding my father's head in my lap screaming as I watched my mother being blown through a rift into the Gloam."

Francis almost drops his cup. "How do you know that? We took those—" He catches himself, shaking his head. "We took those memories to spare you the—you were so young."

"I still don't remember. My uncle showed me, or Arbuckle did. Still not sure how it worked." I blow on the top of the mug out of habit and take a sip.

"So, it worked, the pact?"

"You mean do Arbuckle and Poly now carry their quintessence?"

"Yes."

"It worked."

"How are they?"

"The cats are safe. Outside actually. They came with me. They're in the van."

"You have the van?"

"I do."

He nods, contemplating something. "Tell me how they died."

I put my cup down on the small table. "My uncle had his quintessence forcibly removed, and Jane I found with a broken neck in the cellar of her apothecary in New Orleans."

Francis nods and then looks at Alexander. Reaching out to pet him, Alexander pushes himself deeper into the sofa, letting out a low growl. He hisses and strikes out at Francis, scared and angry. Sadness fills Francis's face.

"He won't let me touch him anymore, not since—" Francis's voice trails off again, and he turns toward me. He looks smaller than he had moments ago. "Will you take Alexander?"

"Of course. You can come too. It will be safer for you both."

"He's been such a good boy. He doesn't deserve to see me go this way—to be here while I devolve and deteriorate. He needs to be with his kind. And there's nothing that can be done to free my quintessence. We've tried it all. I even tried to remove it myself with tar magic, but my connection to it is too weak," he says, pausing to collect his thoughts.

I get a sick feeling. The old man chained out front. Bars on the windows. Tears and scratches in the furniture.

The shotgun on the wall behind Bernice.

The smell.

"This is a revenant hospice." I'm not sure if I meant to say it out loud or not.

Looking down, all strength and stability gone, Francis says, "I'd called 911. I was having chest pains. By the time they arrived, I was gone. They knew the signs—lifeless but living. They put me on a gurney. I kept asking if I could make a phone call, something to find Alexander a home, but they strapped me down. Alexander jumped onto the gurney and clung to me. Dug his claws in. They tried to pry him off, but he wouldn't let go. It's not the first time an animal companion has been allowed here, so they've let it go—for now."

Francis sighs, looking over at Alexander, crouched and afraid, but staying as close as instincts will allow him.

"I even put a portal spell in that box on the floor there," he says, and I follow his finger to the shoebox his Vans came in. "He could go wherever he wants, but he refuses. He refuses to leave me. He's scared—you can see he's scared. Once I get to stage four, I won't even be able to stop myself from trying to kill him, and still, he won't go."

Francis pulls off his glasses and meets my eyes, and I know it's true. His eyes are matte—gloss and life all gone. He's a revenant, alright, and this complicates things.

Revenants are people who die, but whose quintessence doesn't separate upon death. So, Francis is still trapped inside what is now a slowly rotting corpse. Because of this, the quintessence enters a phase of entropy at an ever-increasing rate since it's no longer part of a closed system. It's being dispersed slowly. Eventually, it will all be gone.

That's why Alexander is scared. He doesn't know how to get the quintessence out. He feels the obligation of the pact but can't fulfill it. All he gets to do is watch his friend die—as the very thing that makes him who he is drains away to nothing.

"How long do you have before you turn?"

"A few days, maybe a week. I'm stage one, which is the only reason you were allowed to see me. It happens rapidly. The time between stages halves with each one, and I've been in stage one for a few weeks now."

"How did my uncle know you were here?"

"I called him to see if he could help. When Bernice called, I thought he'd sent you to help."

"In a way, he did. There's got to be something I can do." I say it knowing it's probably not true.

I'm up and pacing in the small space as Alexander and Francis look on.

"I'm a zombie, Aubrey, and unless you know someone who can perform some pretty sick shit on me, I'm going to be put down like a dog and everything that made me who I am will be lost."

"Step one is to get you out of here," I say, firm in my conviction.

"That's too dangerous. There's no telling what I might do once I reach stage two. I've seen stage twos go after relatives, even with the plexiglass between them."

"We'll take it as it comes. How do we get you out?"

"You can't. I'm registered. I die here."

"What about the guy out front chained to the bench? Can I take you for a walk or something?"

"That's a stage one sunsetting. Relatives can sit with you one last time before you enter for good. When it's nice outside, they let it happen on the benches. Usually, it's in a room off reception with a projector that plays a tape of a sunset on the wall.

"There's no way to get me out. No one's risking losing sight of a revenant they already have in custody. I'm fortunate there's a Humane Sunsetting law in Oklahoma. Who would have thought? In most places, the coroner would have put me down with a captive bolt pistol. Get Alexander out. Walk out with him."

"I can walk out with Alexander?"

"No one is going to stop you from carrying a cat. Picking him up is a different story."

"What if I wasn't carrying the cat?"

"What else would you be carrying?"

* * *

I don't have much core strength. However, I do have a low center of gravity and balance. So, I'm walking toward the elevator, Francis in my arms—having locked a glamour around him to make it appear I'm carrying Alexander. Reaching the elevator, Francis hits the panel with his card, my arms trembling from his weight. Luckily, Alexander is a big cat, so maybe it'll look like I'm so out of shape I'm struggling to carry his fat ass outside. Waiting for the elevator to arrive, I hear those screams and howls again, echoing up the shaft.

"Subbasement six," Francis says, seeing the worry on my face.

"What's down there?"

"Poltergeists," he says. "Five percent of Stage 4 release what's left of their quintessence."

I shiver. "I hate Poltergeists."

"Me too," he says, smiling.

The elevator arrives, and I push forward, almost hitting the young woman who steps out.

"He's a big boy," she says, looking more hungry than complimentary. She reaches out and pets Francis on the head, and I pray I used the correct glamour. The one that also covers incursions into the illusion.

"He sure is," I gasp, distracted, and step in. Francis's head hits the door frame, bouncing his head back. Luckily, the woman has continued down the hall.

"Sorry about that," I say, as he punches the button for the lobby.

"Oh, don't worry about it. I can't feel anything anymore."

We hit the first floor. The door opens, and I stumble out with Francis, losing strength and balance. As I round the corner, the lobby stretches in front of me. The distance from the elevator to the front door expands from thirty feet to 300 yards. Anxiety, my old friend, never misses an opportunity to drop by. Putting one foot in front of the other, I walk toward the entrance, trying to look normal. As we pass the reception desk, I can't help but glance sideways at Bernice, who's staring at me.

"Sir?" she says, trying to grab my attention. "Sir!" she gives it a little more oomph. "Mr. Cockcroft!" she says, standing now.

I turn and look at her, trying to look as casual as possible. "Yes, Bernice."

She points to the book on the desk. "You'll need to sign the cat out."

I look at Francis and mouth, "Sorry," as I lay him on the floor and walk over to the reception desk. Bernice pulls out a smaller ledger and lays it on the desk. This one asks for my home address, so I write down the address for Ijams Nature Center instead and misspell my name as Audrey Camshaft. Bernice scans it for completion rather than accuracy and smiles the kind of smile only a woman capable of working around zombies all day can.

Across the room, I squat and wonder what it looks like as I gather Francis in my arms and lift him up. I should have put him on the sofa. Francis reaches out slowly, knowing that the one thing that breaks a glamour quicker than any other is moving too fast for it to compensate. He wraps his arms around my neck, which helps considerably as I lift with my legs. My back screams, and I grunt, but I make it up.

"That cat must really like you," Bernice says behind us, laughing. "Cat hugging a man like that," I hear her say to herself.

The door buzzes, and I try to keep my cool as Francis grabs the handle. I step back so we can open the door. We pass into the vestibule and hear Bernice call out behind us.

"Visiting Hours end at eight."

"Sounds good," I yell over my shoulder as the door closes behind us, and we wait for the last buzz that will slide open the outside door.

Staring ahead, the light from the lobby pushing past us into the night. The cat I'm carrying is reflected in the glass, and I watch it grow back into the shape of a man just before the buzz and the door slides open. For a split second, I think about attempting to reinforce the glamour, but then we are out, in the night air, and I can see Arbuckle and Poly looking at me from the van.

I almost trip because I'm moving too fast—before catching my balance again. Putting Francis down, I mumble under my breath, removing the security and opening the van's side door so he can climb in.

Shutting it, I walk to the driver's side and get in.

"Where's Alexander?" Francis says, looking furiously around.

"He isn't here," Arbuckle says.

"But he agreed to come," Francis sighs.

I look at my watch. "It's 8:03 PM. Visiting hours are over," I say. "Not sure how we can get back in tonight.

"Portal the sink there," Arbuckle says, gesturing to the small stainless-steel sink on the counter.

"What for?" I say.

"I'll use it to get to the room. I persuade Alexander to return with me."

"That might work," Francis says. "He'd probably listen to you."

"I don't know," I reply, feeling like everyone's dad. "It's a revenant hospice. If you come out in the wrong place."

"Francis should be able to link it precisely to his room. His residual energy should be sufficient to bind the connection."

"Yes, that's right." Francis pulls his wand from his shirt sleeve.

"You can still do it?"

"Usually, until stage two," he says, running his wand along the edge of the sink, making sure not to remove it while he speaks the spell in low chanting tones.

I can tell it isn't working almost immediately. "You must be close, then."

"It's hard to connect to my quintessence. Making the body move is still relatively easy," he replies, not breaking the rhythm.

"Put your hand on me," Poly says, jumping onto the table and edging close to Francis.

"I'll help, too," replies Arbuckle.

Francis continues running the wand along the circumference of the sink. As he reaches out his hand, touching Poly on the head, Arbuckle pushes in, giving his hand a side rub.

Poly closes her eyes, and I watch the wispy hairs on the back of Francis' arm stand up, signaling the energy running through him. It continues down his arm, and suddenly, the tip of his wand goes bright, and the sink fills with a swirl of phosphorescent smoke.

"It's working," he cries out, then immediately returns to his chant.

Soon, the phosphorescence fades, and the sink appears normal again.

"Done," Francis says proudly.

"How was Alexander getting out originally?" Arbuckle asks.

"Showbox on the floor. It's a portal of intent, so you'll need to be specific for it to work properly," replies Francis. "Alexander may still be hiding. He might be squashed into the sofa."

"Got it," Arbuckle says.

"You're going to need to wear this," I say, pulling a harness with a camera on the collar and a small GPS tracker in a pocket on the back from the glovebox. My uncle had made a couple of custom harnesses for him, and I had tinkered with this one at the house, testing and charging it before we made the trip.

"You've got to be kidding me. I hate that one," is all Arbuckle can say.

"No way I'm losing you. If something goes wrong, we need to know where you are so we can pick you up."

Arbuckle contemplates this for a second and nods, "OK, but if it hinders me in any way, I'm ditching it."

"I'm betting my uncle paid a lot of for this."

"Money means nothing to me," Arbuckle replies as he jumps into the front and comes close enough for me to pick him up.

I put the vest-style harness on him and connect the two belts, one around his abdomen and the other around his neck.

"How does it feel?" I ask as I situate the camera under his neck.

"Like I'm a pack animal."

"Sorry," I shrug. "You look good, though."

Arbuckle jumps onto the counter, checking the weight.

"The thing on your back is a GPS tracker. The camera on the front connects via Bluetooth to the cell phone, which is livestreaming to a private channel. That's also on your back, so I should be able to see the video. Battery life is shit, from what I was able to test, so the video lasts less than three hours. The GPS should last longer."

"Are we done here?" Arbuckle says, obviously getting impatient.

I check the signals and make sure everything is turned on. "Signal looks good," I reply, looking at my phone, which shows a split screen of map and video.

Arbuckle is at the sink, looking in, ready to jump.

"Oops, almost forgot," I reach up and undo a clasp on the top of the vest, and a little antenna pops up, briefly waving back and forth as it springs to.

"You've got to be shitting me," Arbuckle says as I watch him launch himself into the air, and land right in the sink face first, where he never hits bottom. The last thing I see is the nub of his tail disappearing.

Francis deflates, and Poly jumps down from the table onto his lap. He looks at her, his face a sad mash of uncertainty.

"Don't worry," Poly says, "I don't mind things that smell funky."

Francis laughs, reaches down, and scratches Poly behind the ears.

My phone is clamped onto the magnetic arm I attached to the van's dashboard, and we watch as the video goes from a grainy picture of nothing to the inside of a metal sink. Then up onto the counter looking at a wall, with the top half of the frame Arbuckle's lower jaw. He scans the kitchen for a second before jumping down. Walking along, he paws open the few cabinets at the floor level, peering inside for long enough to determine that Alexander isn't there.

Moving along the living room floor, he passes by the box portal on his way to the sofa, which he jumps up on. Alexander is gone, but he jumps onto the back of the sofa and peers into the void between it and the wall. The camera picks up mostly fabric on this, but we can tell what he's doing.

Off the sofa again and onto the floor. Then the bedroom, where he crawls under the bed, coming out the other side. Then he jumps up on the mattress, which is still freshly made. Scanning the room, then the floor again and into the bathroom. He opens the cabinet under the sink. Again nothing.

"Alexander must have made a mistake with where he wanted to go when he entered the portal," Francis says.

"Well, I guess we're about to find out," I say, as we watch Arbuckle approach the box. "Let's hope it takes him where Alexander went."

The camera jumps in the air, then black again as the box sides slide away.

There's a tense minute as we wait for the video to clear, so I tap the map to see if it has a GPS location. It appears to have found him. Moving and skipping well out of Oklahoma and repositioning in Tennessee, the map shows Arbuckle back in Knoxville. It lands in the Fourth and Gill neighborhood.

I tap over to the video. It's grainy, but we can make it out. He's in the front yard of an old Victorian house, obviously refurbished. Even in the dim light of the streetlamps, I can make out the bright, festive colors it's painted in. Then his head whip pans to the right, and we see Alexander's butt round the side of the house, disappearing. Arbuckle follows.

Francis lets out a small sigh of understanding. "He went back to where it all began."

"Where what began?" I ask, still not entirely understanding.

"That house, that's where he was born, Alexander. That's where we conjured them."

Poly has jumped up and is sitting on the seat near my shoulder, leaning forward and looking at the video feed, which clears as the phone finds fresh cell towers.

"How does he remember it so well? I have no memory of it at all," she says.

"I'm not sure," says Francis. "If it wasn't for some of those flourishes on the porch, I'm not sure I would have recognized it either."

"Whose house, is it?" I ask.

"I thought you would have recognized it," Francis says, surprised.

"Why would I have?"

"It's your Great-aunt Miriam's house."

∞

chapter six

Sly and Haut,
The Hero's Foil,
The Thaumaturge of Poison.
The Baleful Gaze,
The Quiet Step,
The Monarch Beast—Monvoisin.

—ALD
transcribed by AC

T en hours until twilight. Francis, Poly, and I push through
to Tennessee, rattling down I-40. We're all hoping that by
the time we get there, Arbuckle will have calmed Alexander,
allowing us to scoop them up and head home.

We gain two hours driving into the rising sun, so we should
reach a place where we can jump through the Gloam in about eight
hours, shaving off roughly four hours from the estimated twelve-hour
drive. That's assuming my math is right—though I doubt it's exact because this feels like a word problem. I hate word problems.

"*You leave Oklahoma City at 9:00 PM Central Time, driving east at a speed
of 58 miles per hour in your VW Type 2 van. You plan to arrive in Knoxville,
Tennessee, 12 hours later, assuming no delays. The twilight sunrise in Knoxville
is at 5:06 AM Eastern Time. At what point in the journey can you engage the
Gloam drive?*"

Don't forget to show your work and let me know if you figure it out. I plan to tap my address, hit 'GO' and pull the red knob as soon as I see the sun breaking across the horizon.

Francis still has no idea why the portal sent Alexander to my aunt's house. They'd both left town after the accident and had never returned. We talked it through for about an hour, after which we all agreed we'd run it well into the ground with no concrete answer. Portal spells work on a simple principle: if you don't assign a specific destination—and Francis hadn't—you go where you want to go, or as close to it as possible.

If you think, *I want to go to the Grand Canyon*, you'll appear somewhere in the Grand Canyon—but always on solid ground. Never above it or inside it. There are classic safeguards woven into even the simplest portal spell. Otherwise, you could step into a portal and end up in a wall, in a mountain, or over a canyon. So, for Arbuckle, he would have been able to think, *I want to go where Alexander went*. But Alexander would have had to be more specific.

On the off chance Arbuckle hasn't been successful, I plan to drop by my place first and pick up Em in case we need someone—that isn't me, a mystical one-eyed cat, or a stage one revenant to do a little recon. My great-aunt's house is less than a fifteen-minute drive from mine. It's probably now home to a perfectly nice family, and there's no reason to creep them out if we don't have to.

Francis and Poly monitor the video feed until the battery on the cell attached to Arbuckle runs out. Most of the video involves Arbuckle sniffing things and wandering around the yard and house chasing after Alexander, who is a surprisingly spry chonk. Unfortunately, Arbuckle spends most of the time staring down, so the image is mostly grass with the occasional blurry outline of a tree or house.

I grab some takeout before midnight hits. We won't find many 24-hour restaurants crossing into Arkansas. Everything along the interstate turns into a barren wasteland of abandoned warehouses. We hit a couple of rest stops for Poly and I. Since Francis doesn't eat, we leave him to guard the van. Secretly, I hope someone tries something.

While I focus on driving, Poly and Francis get reacquainted, and I eavesdrop a little to stay awake. After listening for a while, I ask a stupid question.

"Poly, are you named after the *Treasure Island* parrot? I mean, people called Jane 'Pirate Jane,' so I figure—"

"You're thinking of Captain Flint, Long John Silver's parrot," Johnathan says.

"I'm named for Polyphemus," she says.

"Oh," I say. "Who's that?"

"Didn't you go to school?" Johnathan chuckles.

"Not really," I say. "My uncle homeschooled me, so it was mostly magic, folklore, and slave labor."

"Polyphemus is a type of folklore," she says, jumping up behind me and sitting to my right. "Technically, it's from mythology—a sacred story. However, it could be argued that mythology and folklore often intersect."

"So, like Odin and Zeus," I say confidently.

"Yes, but Odin belongs to Norse mythology, and Zeus is from Greek mythology—like Polyphemus. Polyphemus was a famous Cyclops. One of the Argonauts."

"I get it—a little play on words. Named after a cyclops but abbreviated like the parrot."

"The parrot's name is spelled *P-o-l-l-y*, but I have only one 'l' in my name. It's an abbreviation that's also a homophone."

"I feel like I'm about to be homeschooled again," I say.

Poly gives me a quick nuzzle against the side of my head. "It's never too late to learn something new, Aubrey," she says, and I smile.

"Alright, I'll bite. What's a homophone?"

"Homophones are words that sound the same but have different meanings and spellings. *Poly* and *Polly* are pronounced the same but mean different things. I have one eye—therefore, I am a Cyclops. I am a cat and not a cat, here and yet not from here. I am a multitude. *Poly*, as a prefix, means 'many.' It was Jane's little inside joke, a clever play on words, just for us."

"How is your name a prefix, too?"

"I was Jane's prefix. She said I was the thing added, the introduction to her new life," Poly says, and I hear a shift in her tone—uncertainty, as if she's worried I might mock it. "Like I said, it was just a silly thing between us."

"I didn't mean for you to tell me if it was private," I say, feeling a little guilty.

"It's OK, It's our secret now."

Even though I want to take my eyes off the road to thank her for sharing it, I don't.

She rubs against me, letting me know everything is alright, before jumping down and continuing her conversation with Francis. I think about what I'll do when we arrive as they talk.

* * *

Eight hours into the drive, I see a small patch of sun barely break the horizon. "Hang on," I say as I mumble under my breath to add a cloak to the van just before we pop into the Gloam and come out again on the runway at DKX—as a plane lifts off the ground in front of us and almost scrapes the van's roof with its wheels. I try not to scream or pee myself and yank the wheel to the right a little too hard, and we almost tip over. Poly is behind me, cursing up a storm in her sweet, quiet voice while Francis claps his hands and laughs.

Part of me wishes this van had some classic safeguards like a portal spell does, but after that near-miss, I know it doesn't. I get us aiming straight again and move off the runway. I keep the cloak on until we're through the gates.

I park in my yard and run in to find Em. She's in the front, watching the rabbits eat their breakfast of dew-covered grass. It's like a fairy tale waiting on a bluebird that I destroy by rounding the corner fast, out of breath, causing the bunnies to scatter.

"This better be good, Aubrey," she says, giving me a disapproving look.

"Scooby level," I say, and her eyes grow big as saucers.

She hikes her dress up for reasons I still don't understand, other than muscle memory, and follows me at a quick clip to the van. She passes through the side door before I can even open it. I slap it and jog around front to climb in. Cranking it up, and we're gone.

Passing over the Henley Street Bridge, the sun pushes through the morning fog, creating an image to rival the best of the Hudson River School, as we roll over the Tennessee. A right, a left onto Summit Hill, and a right onto Gill. Thirteen minutes to get everybody on the same page, and I lay out what I want to happen once we reach our destination.

A block from the house, I park on the street. Double-checking Arbuckle's location one last time, I see he hasn't moved since the night before when the camera died. I put my phone in my pocket. Em is the first one through the door, and her job is to get in the house and do a full recon since no one will see her.

I give Francis a walkie from the glovebox in case we need him once we find Alexander. He doesn't argue with me about staying in the van. We both know it's for the best. For Poly, I put on a quick harness and leash, and we head toward the house on the opposite side of the road. Just a middle-aged man walking his one-eyed cat.

We keep an eye on the house until we're directly across from it. Polly stops and pretends to occupy herself with something in the grass. I take the time to give it a once-over. It's nice, a classic Victorian, painstakingly restored and painted in bright contrasting colors I'm unsure the Victorians could have achieved. But it fits into this street where care has been made to return everything to its former glory. I cross my fingers that we can resolve this amicably. I'd hate to be known as the wizard that destroyed Fourth and Gill.

Satisfied I've seen everything I need to, which is nothing I might add, we walk to the closest crosswalk and cross the street. We walk to the municipal access road behind the houses and turn onto it, reaching the back yard fence. I signal Poly with a pull on her leash, and she falls and rolls on her back like she's found something that smells funny but requires her to cover herself in it.

Then I see Em, resembling the rainbow on a soap bubble, pushing out of the back of the house, crossing the yard, and moving through the fence. She stops near me where she's hard to see in the bright sun, but I know she's there.

"There aren't any people in the house. Arbuckle and Alexander are downstairs in the basement arguing," she says, and I nod imperceptibly to let her know I've heard her.

I don't want to come off as crazy, should someone be watching.

"What was the argument about?"

"Alexander wants to go through the rift and return to the Gloam."

"How is there a rift in the basement?" I say, startled.

"I don't know. I've never been here before."

"How do you know it's a rift to the Gloam?"

"I can feel its pull. I kept back as soon as I felt it. It's small too, about a foot and a half tall."

"OK. This complicates things. We need Alexander until we figure out how to remove Francis's quintessence from his corpse."

"How are we going to do that?" she asks.

"I don't know yet. Get in the basement and tell Alexander we're coming and to wait for us. I'll get Francis, and we'll figure it out. If he's returning to the Gloam, I'd rather he takes Francis with him."

"See you in a minute, then," she says, flitting off into the house.

I look around before pulling out the walkie. I depress the talk button.

"Francis, over?"

"Go for Francis, over," he says, a little too loudly, and I crank the volume down.

"Meet us in the access alley behind the house, over," I say, trying to whisper loudly.

"10-4," Francis says, followed by "Out."

I stuff the walkie into my pocket, feeling an unmistakable childlike glee that I got to use it. This kerfuffle has already ticked off quite a few childhood nostalgia adventure boxes.

A few minutes later, I hear Francis shuffle up behind us.

It startles me more than I care to admit, and I wonder if he used to shuffle his feet like that before he became a revenant.

"Where's Alexander?"

"Lower your voice," I say. "We're still working on a plan. Em is inside. There's a rift. Alexander wants to go through, and Arbuckle is stopping him from now."

"How is there a rift?"

"That's the million-dollar question, but how did Alexander know it was here? More importantly, Alexander is very close to leaving you here to rot. So, let's go change his mind."

We're halfway across the well-kept back lawn before I notice the tree—an enormous, broad pedunculate oak with a small Parisian-style table and chairs, painted white, shaded beneath it. It's the tree from my uncle's memory, after we chased the phantom from the basement. But looking at it now, it feels like it's just waiting for a fun summer afternoon, ready to host some crusty bread, cheese, and wine. My stomach growls at the thought as we reach the back porch. I'd taken the leash off Poly so we could each go at our own pace, and she'd been watching us approach for the better part of a minute, having sprinted all the way.

The porch is small, and I have Francis crouch low. I mumble under my breath, popping the two locks on the back door. This is one instance where a spell trumps a hobby. We enter as quickly as we can. I'm hoping it's still too early for the neighbors to be awake enough to notice suspicious activity.

The back door leads into the kitchen, and I see Em pop out of the door to the basement, waving her arm for us to hurry. We head that way. Stepping onto the stairs, I last saw my young doppelgänger descend before my mother died— my entire body shivers in anticipation of what I might find.

There isn't much refurbishing that's been done down here, so the stairs end like my Craftsman, on the poured concrete foundation, with drainage, a furnace, and a laundry area off to the side. The dais is gone, but the rift in the middle of the room is giving me the heebie-jeebies. The light emanating from it is the same pallid green from the apothecary where I almost died before standing on the mesa staring at the Perpetuation.

Poly is already across the room, gently approaching Alexander, who's shrunk against the far wall, covered by the malformed shadow of Arbuckle, produced by the bright light flooding from the rift. Arbuckle's stalwart guard against Alexander's escape into the Gloam has taken its toll. He's sitting on his haunches, the harness still snug around him, slowly wobbling back and forth, close to falling over. *I mumble under my breath,* pushing a shield between Alexander and the rift, then watch Arbuckle relax to the point of almost falling over.

I'm across the room and to him, picking him up in my arms as Francis crosses to Alexander, stopping short of this side of the shield where he sits down gently, cross-legged on the floor feet from the scared cat. Alexander approaches him out of the shadow, slow and apprehensive, the shield tempering his fear of Francis until he's just on the other side.

"I'm sorry," Alexander says, lifting his head slightly to look at Francis's face. "I was planning to join you in the van, but when I stepped into the portal, the last thing I thought was, *I want to go home.* I ended up here because of the rift.

"Then I was uncertain. But then I was brave. But Arbuckle stopped me. He said I should wait for you."

Alexander's tail hangs low as he lets out a mournful yowl. "I don't know what to do. I don't know how to help you."

"I have waited a long time to hear you speak outside our meditations, my friend," Francis says smiling, "You have a lovely voice. I've always wanted more than what we had. A better understanding."

"I'm sorry," Alexander says, dropping his head.

"I am sorry too. This isn't how I thought our life together would end. I know this has been very scary for you, full of uncertainty." Francis removes his glasses and places them on the floor. "Now, we need to find a solution."

Poly, on the other side of the shield with Alexander, rubs against him to let him know he's not alone. Em steps forward, keeping as far from the rift as she can, her visage now the same pallid green, crystal clear in a way I've never witnessed. She moves across the room and kneels beside Francis.

"Hello, Alexander, you're very handsome," Em says, smiling, and I watch Alexander's ears slowly relax and stand up.

"Hello," he says, his voice trembling and boyish, delicate without any hint of malice or threat as he takes a step forward, releasing the tension in his shoulders. "Who are you?"

"My name is Em."

"Can you help us Em? Can you free Francis?"

"I don't know how I can," she replies.

"You've talked to Death," Alexander says. "I see it in your aura."

"What does that matter?" Em says, looking at me as if Alexander has revealed a secret.

"She's a Death Runner," I say to Alexander. I look at Em, shrug my shoulders lightly, and make a face that says, *He might be onto something.*

Alexander turns to Francis. "You're like a butterfly stuck in a chrysalis. The question is, why are you stuck? I think it's because you're scared."

"Scared of what?" Francis replies, curious now.

"Death," Alexander says.

I watch this statement wash over Francis. "I suppose I am," he says.

"What does that have to do with me being a Death Runner?" Em asks.

Alexander becomes more animated and excited, looking between Francis and Em. "Don't you see?"

"I'm not sure I do," Em says. She looks at me, and I give her that patent-pending shrug of noncommittal reassurance.

"I think I understand," Francis says, looking toward Em. "You're not afraid of death, are you?"

"No," says Em.

"Well, maybe you can show me why I shouldn't be either."

"I guess I can try," Em says. She lowers herself onto her knees in front of Francis.

I mumble under my breath and lower the shield. Still holding Arbuckle, who feels weak in my arms, I watch Em reach out her hand to Alexander. He moves to her, letting her touch his head, and gives him a comforting scratch—her practice interacting with this plane paying off. She holds her other hand out to Francis, who looks at me for a split second, mouths the words, *Thank you*, before taking Em's hand.

"Francis, I want you to close your eyes and listen to my voice," she says before closing her own. "What do you see?"

"Darkness," he says, sighing in resignation.

"No light at all?"

"I don't know. Maybe?"

Em rubs her thumb rhythmically against Alexander's head, keeping him calm, while doing the same for the back of Francis's hand. "Give it time."

Arbuckle is asleep in my arms, twitching lightly, kicking, dreaming. I wonder what his dream is and if it has a place for me. Leaning down, I kiss him gently on the head. It makes me feel better, but I don't know why.

"Wait," Francis says, breaking the silence. "I think I see something?"

"What do you see?" Em prompts, stopping her thumb and squeezing Francis's hand.

"It's dim. Very far away."

"Walk toward it, Francis. Imagine that with every step you take, you halve the distance between it and you."

"I'll try," he responds, his voice an uncertain whisper. "I'm getting closer."

"What do you see now?"

"A light, maybe," his head moves involuntarily as he cranes it to see what only he can see. "Orange, maybe yellow, on the horizon."

"That's good, a horizon is very good."

"Oh," Francis says, almost a sob. "All the colors now, the brightness, I can feel it, it's warm on my face. I've been so cold; I'd almost forgotten what warmth felt like." He's crying now, but no tears come from his desiccated ducts. "It's wondrous."

"Yes, Francis. Yes, it is."

"What is it?"

"It's you, your quintessence. All the things you ever did, learned, experienced. All your love, hate, fear, and bravado. A spark, become a sun," Em says, leaning in close now. It's hard to hear her as she whispers to Francis.

"It's below me now, the light is coming from a large hole in the ground. It's deep, but the light is so bright. I'm on the edge. I'm afraid I'll fall."

"What do you think happens when you fall?" Em asks. removing her hand from his arm and placing it on his chest.

"I don't know," Francis says, uncertain.

"Is that what scares you?" She asks.

"Yes?"

"Why?"

"Because if I fall, it's the end of me."

"It's the beginning," I hear Alexander say, and he pushes closer, nudging Francis's free hand.

Francis moves his hand to touch Alexander's head, and Em takes hers out of the way. A broad smile crosses his face, and he stares deeply into Alexander's eyes as they connect.

"How do I get down there, old friend?"

"Jump," Alexander says.

"Don't be afraid," Em's voice lowers, "Leap."

"I'll catch you," Alexander whispers.

Francis's body goes rigid, and he shakes uncontrollably. But then, just as suddenly, he goes limp and slumps. His body, his chrysalis, falls to the floor as the quintessence emerges, shimmering and mirroring Em in color and clarity.

"There you are," Em says, smiling.

Alexander climbs onto Francis's body, moving toward the fading ghost. Francis runs his hands down Alexander, from his head to his haunches, taking in the entirety of him. Then Francis is holding Alexander in his arms. Their foreheads touch, and Francis is gone.

Alexander jumps down from his corpse, tall now, proud, and whole, turning to Em, "Thank you."

"You're very welcome," she says and stands.

Poly comes over and rubs against Alexander, who returns the favor, their tails momentarily twirling about each other.

"Can we go now?" I ask, killing the moment.

"I think that would be a mistake," a voice behind me says.

I turn and see Aunt Miriam's Maine Coon, Monvoisin, sitting on her haunches, staring at all of us. I look at Em. "I thought you said no one was in here?"

"I said there were no people here."

I motion around to Alexander and Poly, then I hold up Arbuckle, who wakes from his short nap. "This is the one time where cats count very much."

As quickly as I can, I drop Arbuckle, turn, and *I mumble under my breath,* bringing up the shield again, but this time isolating us from Monvoisin.

"Not bad," she says walking around the shield, looking at us all as though examining animals in the zoo. "But I have no reason to harm you, Aubrey."

"You were with Miriam the night my parents died. The night Alistair tried turning everyone into shadow wizards. And who I think is also connected to the death of my uncle and Jane." I say, motioning to the rift. "And who happens to be the one cat I know who has a rift in her basement."

"I didn't put it there. They keep popping up ever since that night. We closed it, but it's been permeable ever since. It's why your great-aunt left the house to me in her will. I stand guard here and keep what happened that night from spreading into the greater world," Monvoisin says.

Walking up to the rift and staring at it, almost transfixed by it, until she turns and looks directly at me. "I'm part of the pact too, you know. Miriam is inside me. After Alexander and Arbuckle appeared, I left the rift open. We usually close them as soon as they appear, but I thought maybe it was starting again. Why else would they return? So, I waited to see what would happen, and you showed up. So, what say you drop the shield, and we figure out what to do with that corpse? Then we can discuss what happens next."

"Is this true?" I ask Arbuckle.

"Yes," he says. "The order enlisted her help after it was concluded that Alistair was controlling her."

"Then I only have one question," I say to Monvoisin.

"What's that?"

"Who was Miriam talking to that night? I've seen my uncle's memory. Someone else was there, but they were somehow erased. Alistair may have controlled Miriam, but someone else was pulling the strings."

"I don't know what you mean," she says.

"Alright," I say. "After we're done here, you can prove it."

"How?" she asks.

"Show me my great-aunt's memory of that night. But before we do that, I think I know what we can do with the body."

* * *

I wasn't sure if it was a good idea, but I convinced everyone that we should push Francis's corpse into the rift. We'd saved the part of him worth saving, and now that his quintessence had been removed, he was rapidly decomposing.

What I'd seen when I had been there was mostly wasteland, so what could it hurt? Only after I convinced everyone this was the best plan did I realize I was talking to four cats and an eidolon. So, it would be up to me to do it. First, though, I had to untangle Francis's crossed legs and get him supine.

After collecting his glasses, the walkie, and his wand from his sleeve, I mumble under my breath and use his wand to add a dash of precision as I gently lift his body off the ground. Turning him around so his feet aim toward the rift, I pause as the cats split up, two on each side.

"Any last words?" I ask.

"Goodbye, old friend," Arbuckle says, and I wonder if it's him or my uncle forcing the sentiment through him.

Poly is next. "Sleep well, Francis," she says, butting her head gently against his hand as it lies still against his body.

His head hung low, Alexander begins a yowl, distressing at first, that morphs into a rhythmic chant. It surprises me. There's beauty to it, and it isn't like anything I've heard before. Soon, Poly adds her voice, higher pitched and melodic, followed by Arbuckle, and eventually Monvoisin, as though the song Alexander is singing has entranced the others to join in.

I wait a beat, treat it like a dirge, before moving Francis's body forward, feet first into the rift. As it slides in, the dirge changes. The notes seep through my skin, vibrating my whole body. As the crown of Francis's head slips beyond our world, the song is brought to a low hum, stopping. We stand in silence for a time.

When it ends, I put a dome shield over the rift in case something decides to come through, and we all go upstairs. We're in the parlor before I finally remove the harness from Arbuckle. He flops onto the floor for a nap. Em seems at home in the room and busies herself flitting about, looking at every knickknack, bauble, trinket, and piece of bric-a-brac with a kind of childlike joy.

"Come with me," Monvoisin says, as she rubs against my leg to get my attention.

I follow her to the kitchen. She has me turn on the electric kettle and grab four saucers and a teacup from the cabinet. Liberating a pint of half-and-half from the fridge, I instinctively check the best-by date. Good for another few weeks, which means it's fresh. How is there fresh half-and-half in the fridge? Who's using it? Who's buying it? I keep that to myself for now, as I rummage through the loose tea bags until I find a sachet of English Breakfast. It should go well with the whiskey I saw in the parlor.

"How does someone leave a house to a cat?" I ask, waiting for the water to boil.

"Miriam put everything into a trust, which is administered by a law firm, who are paid very well not to go poking around. Every month, money is deposited into an account to which I have online access."

I hold up the half-and-half and give her an inquisitive look.

"Everything is bought online and delivered," she says, like it's normal and I'm an idiot.

"How do you work the keyboard?"

"Oh, I don't. I have a man for that," she says as the water boils.

I decide that makes as much sense as anything, "Can you, you know, communicate with my aunt? Her quintessence has been in you for a while," I ask, pouring the water over the tea bag. I set an alarm on my watch for five minutes.

Monvoisin jumps up onto the counter and sits near me. "In a way, yes, and in a way, no. Early on, she tried to force herself through, using me as a conduit, but it was too painful."

"My uncle did the same to Arbuckle. It didn't look fun."

"She'd be nowhere if she killed me trying, so she retreated. She's like a reference book more than a second consciousness. You are welcome to ask questions, but it won't be like you're talking to her," she says.

I motion to the parlor. "Everyone else is just getting the hang of it, so I was curious how it works long-term."

"It gets easier, less confusing if that makes sense. I've learned that I am more likely to connect with it when I am quiet, open to the experience."

I bob the teabag up and down a little with the string. "What would happen if we transferred her quintessence to a human?"

"I'm sure it would be more compatible, but also dangerous, trying to hold two life essences in a single vessel. A person might go mad."

I look for something to carry all this stuff into the parlor with.

"You said you wanted me to share one of her memories with you, but I don't know how," she says.

"Arbuckle does," I say. "He bonked me on the head, and I saw the memory. Well, more like I was in the memory."

"I'm happy to try. You have a few minutes before your tea is done steeping."

"Sure, what the Hell," I say and walk to her. I lean down.

Monvoisin head butts me, hard.

"Ow, that hurt," I say, rubbing my head.

"Anything?" she asks.

"Nothing but pain," I say.

"Maybe we can try again later," she says, jumping down and heading into the parlor.

"Maybe not," I say.

I find a tray in a lower cupboard, put everything on it, and walk to the parlor. I pour the half-and-half into the saucers, finishing just as my watch vibrates. While everyone but Em is lapping up their treat, I pour a little treat of my own into the tea from the liquor cart sitting to the left of the fireplace and wonder why it's even here if Monvoisin is the house's only permanent resident.

Sipping my tea, I survey the room from the surprisingly comfortable wingback chair near the fireplace. A bookshelf with a built-in writing desk sits behind me, and hanging over the fireplace is a portrait of a young woman in Victorian garb, sitting in what appears to be the same or very similar chair. Her dress is black and painted to resemble silk or satin, the brush strokes bright and vibrant. On her lap is a large grey, black, and white Maine Coon.

"Who's that?" Em asks, startling me and almost causing me to spill my tea.

"There's a brass plaque at the bottom," I point out.

Em moves closer, reading it. "Miss Miriam Cockcroft, and her Maine Coon 'Monvoisin,'"

"I've never seen her that young. In my uncle's memories, she's got to be in her seventies."

"She was quite the lady, Mr. Cockcroft," a voice says behind me, in a thick Southern accent.

Em and I turn toward the parlor door. Standing there is a slim man in overalls, muck boots, and a sweat-stained long john shirt, a toothy grin on his face.

"And you are?" I ask.

"Hollis. I'm here 'bout 'dat tear, Aubrey, the one you got yourself downstairs in the basement."

"How do you know me?"

Hollis grabs the suspenders on his overalls and makes an almost comical gesture of pulling them away from his chest while he rocks on his feet. It seems impossible, but his grin gets larger.

"Well, shucks, everybody 'round here knows about the Wizard of Island Home," he says, letting go of his suspenders that make a loud *snap* against his chest. Then, after a beat. "I'm messing with you," he says, dropping the southern accent entirely. "Monvoisin asked me to come take a look," he says, now in a British accent as he heads toward the basement. "Rifts to the Gloam are not an ideal thing to have in the house."

"Wait a second," I say, throwing back the rest of the tea and walking after him. By the time I get to the basement, Hollis is bent over my dome spell while Em watches, having dropped through the floor.

"Here, I can remove that," I say, as Hollis pulls a small branch flute from his back pocket.

Putting it in his mouth, he plays seven discordant notes, cracking the dome like a thin candy shell that collapses to the floor and dissipates.

Waving me away, "No worries, nothing I can't undo." Hollis walks around the rift, looking at it from all angles, then peers down at it from overhead. "Looks like it was opened from this side." He turns to look at me, a serious expression on his face. "You didn't stick anything in here, did you?" He stares at me, concerned.

"Uh, we—" is all I get out before his smile is back as wide as ever.

"Don't worry. Most people do. It's like they can't help themselves. Something shows up, spewing green light, like a nineties cover of a Stephen King novel, and next thing you know, they're sticking something in it. A broom, a shovel, a hoe. Whatever's lying around," he says, turning to the rift.

He puts a short brown stick from his back pocket into his mouth—chewing on it like a cow chewing cud and giving the rift a final once-over. Satisfied, he stops, returning the stick to his pocket. Opening his hands, palms up, he spits on them, rubbing them together before kneeling in front of the rift and folding it over itself, crimping it like a pie crust.

As he does, he makes small exhalation utterances that sound like *whew, whew, whew,* like he's pulling hot, freshly baked bread out of the oven with his hands. He even blows on them as though cooling them down. He does this until he's at the bottom. Then the whole crimped distortion fades away.

"That'll do it," he says, standing up. "It'll be a little weak here for a few days, but it should firm up."

"How did you do that?" I ask him, truly intrigued.

"Oh, that? My nan taught me how to do that," he says, and there's that smile again.

"But how did you do it?" I respond.

"Oh, I couldn't tell you that. It's a family secret," he says, turning toward Em, lifting an imaginary hat, "Ma'am." Pretending to return it to his head, he walks past me and up the stairs.

Em stands there as though his action has frozen her in place. "He can see me," she says.

I head up the stairs after Hollis, catching him in the foyer. I reach out, grabbing him by the arm. "Who are you?"

He turns around quickly, shaking off my grip. "It's impolite to manhandle another person without permission," he says, his face stern and menacing.

"Look, I'm sorry, but you waltz in here, unannounced, close a rift to the Gloam like you're making a pie on a Sunday, and we don't even know who you are. But, you seem to know me," I point to Em behind me, "And you can see her," I say.

Hollis takes another opportunity to look at Em and lift his invisible hat again. "Ma'am," he says, smiling, before returning it to his head and turning to me.

"Which is also not something everyone can do," I get out, which causes a contemplation to cross his face, and Hollis shakes his head up and down a little like he might be seeing my point, and he eases back, no longer menacing.

"I guess that'd be fair," he says. "If I was in your house, instead of in this one," Hollis turns again and walks toward the front door, which he opens, pauses, then loudly, over his shoulder yells, "See you later, Monvoisin."

From the parlor, I hear Monvoisin reply, "Hollis."

Then Hollis closes the front door behind himself.

I head into the parlor, where Monvoisin is now lounging on the fainting couch. "Who was that?" I demand.

"That was Hollis," she says, again like I'm an idiot.

"I know his name; I meant, who is he?"

"He's a tree sprite. He lives in the oak out back. It's not as big a thing as you're making it. He's served your aunt loyally for almost the entirety of her life," she says, before laying her head on her paws. "I told you I had a man."

"He's a little big for a spite, isn't he?" I say, knowing Monvoisin isn't going to answer me.

Looking around the room, the cats are all asleep, with Poly and Arbuckle huddled close to Alexander on the ornate throw rug in front of the fireplace.

I turn to Em, who shrugs. "I guess it's nap time," she says.

∞

chapter seven

Style and grace,
The Coat of Floof,
The Inverse of Inertia.
The Belle of Zoom,
The Cunning Look,
The Sovereign—Mistress Sorchea.

—ALD
transcribed by AC

Standing outside in the early afternoon sun, walking around the base of the oak, I feel a little silly. A much more beautiful and majestic tree than I had noticed when we first approached the house, but then my attention was on getting to Alexander and Arbuckle. Now that everyone is safe and asleep, I'm indulging my wonder. The base is easily four feet in diameter, and its height is over sixty feet. It's been here a long time.

Running my hand along its bark, I'm curious if Monvoisin was telling the truth and whether I could see any signs of Hollis being a sprite and occupying it. My knowledge of the Fae is slim, and my uncle had talked about them like they were a long-lost species. He painted them as tricksters and fraudsters, mostly unsavory but occasionally useful. The Americas have little folklore regarding them. They're mostly a British and European phenomenon. America, however, was, as they say, built by immigrants. So, I have no doubt Fae made the journey with those same immigrants. I also imagine them being forgotten as science overcame folklore.

As I make my way around, I find a knot about the size of a softball, roughly at my eye level. The one thing I remember from reading a treatise—no pun intended—on certain types of Fae, *Hamadryad Confabulations: Reaching Détente Through Discourse,* is that they are more intrigued by questions than statements. They love to espouse endlessly on subjects and consider themselves the most knowledgeable of all species. So, you're better off getting information by asking a single, well-worded question. The best way to ask this question is to direct it to the tree in which they live.

So, I lean in close and whisper my question into the knot, laughing at the childishness of believing it will do anything. Continuing my circuit, I find Hollis waiting for me on the other side.

"Well, that's an interesting question, I must admit," he says, motioning for me to sit.

"What's the answer?" I ask, trying to get comfortable in the tiny chair.

"Let's sit a while and talk about other things. If I find you interesting enough, I'll think on your question and let you know."

"Monvoisin tells me you're a sprite," I say, sounding stupid, like someone who's about to say they have many sprites as friends.

"It's bold of her to mention it," he says, and I wonder what makes it bold.

"We've just met, so I couldn't say. Have you known her long?"

"I've known Monvoisin since she was conjured. I knew your aunt when she was a little girl. You could say she's the reason I'm here."

"She conjured you?"

Hollis looks at me like I spit on his shoes. "We are not conjured, Mr. Cockcroft. We were here long before your kind and will be here long after."

"Now that is a bold statement."

"It's the truth of the matter."

"I wasn't aware there were tree sprites in Tennessee," changing the subject, or at least bringing it back to my question.

"Not many, but a few. I came over with your great-aunt from England in an acorn she carried in her pocket. I'd gone into the acorn in search of a wise worm to help me solve a riddle posed to me by a Badger. I was still relatively young and not as facile as I am today. While I was journeying through the plumule, having been told the worm had taken up residence near the radicle, a storm swept through. The winds were strong and unrelenting. They dethatched the acorn from the tree, which would have been fine if the wise worm had been there since I could have escaped through the hole he burrowed. But he wasn't, so there I was, trapped in a perfectly viable acorn.

"That doesn't sound good," I say.

"What must have only been a few days later, your great-aunt, on a walk in the park with her mother, while her father gave a lecture on the use of clitics in spell writing to the Hounslow Collective, found the acorn and put it in her pocket. Once they returned to America, she discovered it again and buried it here, which was fortunate. I was able to escape once it sprouted, splitting the shell."

"That's good, I guess." Hoping the story is almost over.

"So, here I was, a young sprite without a tree, surrounded by foreign species. I spent some time wandering the neighborhood, trying on different varieties, but none of them felt like home. Every day for five years, I checked on this little sapling, waiting for it to be mature enough for me to inhabit. Then one day it was, and I did, and here I am, no luckier a sprite you will find. And her—" he says, leaning back and rubbing his hand along the bark. "She's a roomy ol' girl,"

I nod, trying not to think too deeply about what that means. "I wanted to ask about the rift. Why didn't seeing it cause you any alarm?"

"That? I've been closing those for forty years, ever since your—" Hollis stops a second and appears to be thinking about what he said, unsure if he should go on. "Ever since Alistair did what he did," he says.

"Were you there that night?"

"Ask what you mean, Mr. Cockcroft."

"Was he controlling you like he was my aunt?"

"No," Hollis says, looking away, a touch of regret in his voice. "What do you know about allegiance bonds?"

"Nothing," I say, which was the truth. The term sounded familiar, but I was getting nothing back from my memory.

"When the wind knocked the acorn from the tree, I became trapped. The only way I was getting out was if the acorn took root. Lying on the ground rotting, I would have rotted with it. Putting it on a shelf to dry would have desiccated me, too. Because your aunt chose to bury it, and it sprouted naturally, I lived and was able to escape owing her my allegiance. Bound to do as she asked. When Alistair took control of her, he had her banish me to my tree. It was only after his defeat and her subsequent return to normalcy that she let me free."

"So, you never saw what happened."

"I only know what I was told."

"What do you know about Alastair?"

Hollis looks stunned. "It's not my place," he says and gets up. "That's a family matter."

"Well, they're all dead, so being the last member living, I give you permission."

"I don't know," he says, motioning to the house. "Ask a cat."

"What about my other question? You never answered it."

"Some questions you have to answer for yourself," is all he says, and then he's up and around the tree, and I follow, but when I get to the other side, he's gone.

Inside, I find everyone still napping in the parlor, with Em watching. She smiles when she sees me enter. "Aren't they the best when sleeping?" she says.

Each of the cats, their sides rising and falling gently in rhythm, is still and calm. Arbuckle's head is turned upside down, in an awkward position to the rest of his body. Alexander has fully turned onto his back, his arms and legs limp and suspended above him, his plush orange belly exposed with confidence. Poly is curled tight into a ball without a head or tail, and Monvoisin is lying belly down against the cushion of the fainting couch, one arm draped over the side hanging in the air.

"Yes," I say, walking into the room, where I lie on the floor and close my eyes.

As I drift off, I hear Em whisper it again, "Just the best when they're sleeping."

I know I'm safe here, that we are safe here, at least for now.

* * *

Arbuckle wakes me about thirty minutes before twilight by standing on my chest and screaming in my face. "Wake up, Aubrey, we need to get to Mia and Saoirse."

I reflexively bring my right hand up and lay it on his back, where the fur is soft and warm, and I pet him from neck to tail a few times, trying to coax myself from sleep. He's a little itchy because as I open my eyes, he's gnawing involuntarily on his front paw while I scratch him near his tail.

"Alright," is all I get out before he jumps off, and I roll over and push myself up, my shoulder and thigh both screaming with a deep throbbing discomfort.

Making the requisite noises of age as I coax my body up, grunting and cursing under my breath, standing—still a little groggy from sleep. Hollis is there with a tray and a fresh cup of coffee.

"Thanks," I say, grabbing it.

"I normally don't perform domestic duties," he says, letting the tray drop to his side, clanging against his leg.

"Well, I appreciate it," I say, sipping it.

I know it's not coffee quickly, but I don't spit it out. It's comforting, with a hint of licorice and a slight but not unpleasing bitterness—which runs smoothly down my throat. I take another sip, and I feel it warming my entire body. The throbbing in my leg and shoulder gets pushed out as the warmth radiates down my limbs. I finish it on the third sip and feel rejuvenated and almost young.

"What is this?" I ask Hollis.

"An old family secret," is all he says.

"That's a hell of a secret."

Hollis smiles and holds out his hand. It's a green acorn, about two and a half centimeters long. "Here, this might come in handy."

I take the acorn and hold it up to look at it more closely, then I look at him for an explanation.

"It's a calling card. If other Fae are in the area, they will come to your aid. Simply remove the cap, place the acorn in your mouth, and crack its shell with your teeth."

"That's it, crack the shell."

"Yes."

"OK, thanks," I say, slipping it into my shirt pocket and buttoning the flap. Then, I turn to Arbuckle. "You ready to go?"

"Yes, and we should take Monvoisin."

I look at Monvoisin and feel like everyone must have been talking while I slept. "Why?" I ask.

"Because I think it's important that you two get to know each other, outside of here."

"OK, but she's your responsibility."

"Naturally," Arbuckle says, in a tone that makes me think of someone rolling their eyes.

"Em, are you coming?"

"I think I've had enough excitement for today," she says.

"We'll drop you off at the house."

"I think I'll walk," she replies without hesitation.

"Up to you." I know I never had a say in it anyway.

"Yes, it is," she says, and I'm already worried.

"Just keep an eye out for reapers."

Em smiles sarcastically. "I always do." She disappears through the parlor wall.

Sometimes with Em, I'm not sure what to say. We've known each other for a long time now, and I know she doesn't feel the same about me as I do about her, so I'm careful. I don't want her to leave, and I often wonder why she even stays, other than she knows my house is the safest place she can be if the reapers come. It's a bit reckless traveling without protection, but then I think about all the years she was a recluse and can't begrudge her the freedom she has now.

As she once told me, 'Death was the only thing I ever found that cured me of my fear.'

"Hollis, do you care to look after Poly and Alexander for me?" I ask before we head out to the van.

"We're not children," Poly says.

"I didn't mean to imply you were, but we still don't know who's doing all of this, and I need you safe."

"Miriam Cockcroft was a powerful witch. There are more whispers in these walls than any threat could account for. My tree is also rooted deep, wrapping the foundation. They are safe here," Hollis replies with confidence.

"OK, we'll be back as quickly as we can."

I open the front door, and Arbuckle and Monvoisin pad across the threshold.

I turn to Hollis, "I've been meaning to ask. Why the muck boots?"

Hollis smiles, "Because it's always deeper than you think it is before you step in it," he says, looking from me to Monvoisin.

I think about this for a second, smile, and close the door behind me.

A few minutes later, we're in the van. I pull out onto Gill, then head south onto Fourth, a part of me not caring if anyone sees us. What are they going to do—call the police and report a hippie van disappearing right in front of their eyes?

As the sun dips below the concrete retaining wall lining the highway to my left, I bring up the GPS, push the gas pedal to the floor, tap Mia's address, hit 'GO,' and reach out with my right hand for the red knob. As we hit fifty-eight, I pull it—catching a glimpse of the gas gauge, the needle trembling below the white 'R' on the left side.

Shit. I'm out of gas.

* * *

We come up short as usual, heading north on Five West behind the Rio Grande train station in downtown Salt Lake City. Slowing down, I wait for the GPS to correct then make a U-turn at the end of the median heading down South Five West—hoping no cops have their eyes on us. Our destination is Pioneer Park, so I'm unsure what to look for.

Taking a left on University, we find the park a block up, and I turn onto Four West, parking in the lot on its north side. It's a nice night out, and there's still a bit of light left in the sky. When the sun goes down, I'll need all the eyes I can get. We should have done this in the morning. I grab a couple of harnesses from the glove box and outfit Arbuckle and Monvoisin, who's jumped up front to join us.

"Since we can't communicate outside, here's the plan. If anything—and I mean anything—happens and we get split up, meet back here as soon as you can. You two are small enough to take shelter under the van if it comes to that, right?"

I give them the classic *Dad face*, raising my eyebrows to emphasize the last word.

"OK," is all I get out of Arbuckle.

"I'm just glad to be out of the house," Monvoisin says.

I make a mental note to ask her why she said that. For now, I open the door and step down, waiting for them to jump. Attaching a leash to the harnesses, I mumble under my breath rubbing my hand down the length of the van securing it. My hand is dark with dirt when I pull it away.

"Remind me to wash this when we get home," I say, as we walk toward the park.

The park is scattered with people carrying their lives on their backs, in a grocery cart, or with handbags slung over bicycle handlebars—lashed so thick that there's no way the bikes can be ridden. They're hanging bars with wheels, making relocation easier. There are lots of trees, and anywhere there's a tree, there's at least one person.

The trees are well-established. Littleleaf Lindens line the perimeter, joined by American Elms along West Four and White Ash along South Four. Walking through, I imagine the area gets cleared out frequently for events. Nothing spoils family fun faster than having to explain the realities of life to little kids.

This makes me wonder if Mia is homeless, and all my uncle had for her was the location of the last place he'd known she had camped. So, I scan for cats. If she's here, there's no way Saoirse isn't with her. Pulling the photo out of my pocket, I try to figure out what kind of cat she is and look at Mia's face. Of course, it's too small for me to make it out well enough to attempt to match it to its owner sixty years later.

Saoirse is long-haired, with a dark face and a light-colored body. I put the photo in my pocket and pull out my cell. I search for "dark face light-colored body longhair cat," then scroll through a list on dembeans. com, settling on Ragamuffin, Himalayan, or Ragdoll. I'm talking out loud to myself while I do this, so we're getting stares as both cats pull on their leashes, trying to separate themselves from me in embarrassment.

Occasionally, we stop because people want to pet them, and I let them. It's cruel, I know, but there's something about watching these cats get annoyed by strangers that I enjoy. There aren't as many light poles as I'd like—maybe one every hundred feet—and those who've chosen to camp here for the night mostly keep the sidewalk clear, opting to put their backs against the tree trunks, which makes sense to me.

Having gone down all of West Four, we turn left and walk along South Four, keeping our eyes open. Worst-case scenario, we'll spend the night in the van and try again when the sun comes up.

Suddenly, Monvoisin pulls her leash taut, and I turn to see where she's heading. We cross the sidewalk and angle across the central lawn, where a few tents are erected, finally stopping at the Dog Park. Monvoisin pushes through the fence, scratches at the mulch, and drops a deuce.

"Monvoisin," I say in a low, menacing whisper. "Now we have to walk around so I can pick that up."

Monvoisin walks back through the fence just as a dog comes charging over. It's barking at the cats, but they hold their ground. The owner heads our way as Monvoisin bends over backward to clean herself. I look at the dog, who's eating her turd.

I hear the owner shout, "What are you eating? Put that down!"

Monvoisin finishes cleaning herself, makes eye contact with me as though to say, *Problem solved*, then stands up and walks away. Arbuckle and I follow quickly.

Once we're a good bit away, I pop Monvoisin's leash. "What was that all about?"

She refuses to go further, flopping on the ground like a fluffy rock and staring at me.

"Fine, if that's how you want to play it," I say before I pick her up and carry her like a football across my arm while Arbuckle continues to behave. Lifting Monvoisin so she can hear me, I whisper, "You're a jerk," into her ear, and she gives me the side-eye.

Arbuckle tugs his leash, and I follow his gaze to a small cluster of trees ahead in the northeastern quadrant of the park. There, a flash of white jets across the dark lawn. I put Monvoisin down, walking toward it.

Zoom!

There it goes, running between the trees and attacking their base. I unleash Monvoisin and Arbuckle and let them go first. They both hunker down and move forward like they're stalking a giant moth or something.

Heading right, onto the sidewalk along Three West, I push north, keeping Arbuckle and Monvoisin in my periphery. If they have the cat, I'll look for the woman. She's close to her mid-eighties like everyone else in the order, so I'm looking for light hair or the frail movement of someone in the light shining down through the leaves of the trees.

Most of those camped here are young and easily dismissed, but there are a few I scrutinize a bit more, and when they see me looking at them, I either get awkward smiles or the middle finger before they slink back into the shadows, trying to disappear.

Movement in my periphery brings me back to the grove, where Arbuckle and Monvoisin have gotten close enough that the white blur is still, crouched in the grass, like they are, all staring at each other. I'm about to step off the sidewalk to head toward them when I hear someone mumble under their breath and feel my heart clench in my chest like I'm having a heart attack. It hurts like hell, and I go down fast, but on the way down, *I mumble under my breath* and perform a blocking maneuver before I almost pass out.

I'm halfway up when I get hit by another spell, this one intent on keeping me from speaking. It stitches my lips shut. Weaving a casting anyone who susurrates the Gloam is familiar with, I unstitch the threads that bind my lips and pull them free with my left hand as I conjure the fireball in my right.

As soon as my lips are free, *I mumble under my breath* and give the fireball a target, and it's off and flying like a fastball thrown in the last second of the last inning of a game that's impossible to win. It finds its target, but they catch it.

They're about my height, thinner, and wearing a hoodie to disguise their face. I'm not a combat wizard, so I have no idea what comes next, but I start running. They caught my fireball in their hand, and the thing about fireballs is that they're unique to each person who summons them. Technically, no one can wield your fireball but you. So now, I have no idea how powerful they are or what they intend to do with it, but I'm pretty sure it's Alistair.

Running, for me, is a last resort. It hurts, and after a few minutes, I have trouble breathing and start tasting copper in my mouth. But I'm doing it now—right as my own fireball hits me in the back of the head—and I'm thankful I don't have much hair left. I drop, roll, and come up with it back in my hand, suppressing it as I watch the figure crossing the field, heading straight for me, obviously undeterred by my crude attempts to stop them. I glance over and see Arbuckle, Monvoisin, and Saoirse huddled together, watching me get clobbered.

I mumble under my breath and raise a shield seconds before a small sapling with a root ball explodes upon impact, pushing me back. If this is Alistair, as I suspect, he's powerful, and the next thing that comes flying at me is a metal bench torn from the concrete it was bolted to. It hits the shield and almost knocks me over. I need to think a little faster because I'm outgunned here. I mumble under my breath and turn the grass at his feet into a swamp, and he sinks fast as he steps in it.

It doesn't last long. Halving the distance between us, running again, this time straight at him, I try to get there in time to end this. He puts his hands on either side of the pit and pushes up, levitating up and out of the small quagmire. I should have made it deeper, but I didn't want to do any permanent damage to the park. Now, because I was being considerate, I'm about to have my fat ass handed to me.

Still running, but away this time, I change course—the copper taste fills my mouth as my legs go numb. Afraid I won't make it, I head for the trees on the perimeter. Even though I'm getting short of breath, I yell for everyone to get out of the way. A whole audience is now staring at me, running from sudden death. They're jeering me, calling me names, and I'm in grade school again, being bullied by a bunch of itinerant mundane.

"What is wrong with you people?" I scream as I make it into the tree line just before small rocks, traveling at the speed of bullets, slam into the trunk of one of the Littleleaf Linden, and the bark goes flying.

That turns the jeers into screams, as everyone runs away. Hunkering at the base, I peer out from behind it. He's floating there, waiting for me to stick my head out.

Thunk, right next to my head. Splinters pepper my face even as I pull back instinctively.

"It's about time we met," he yells.

"Is it?" I call out. "Maybe we can put it off a little longer. You seem upset."

"Come out and face me, brother," he yells, spitting the last word. Though lower and gravellier, I recognize the voice. It's mine.

Suddenly, my train of thought is broken by yelling across the lawn.

"I know who you are! It's me you want."

In the distance, Mia is standing on the great lawn, lit by the blue light coming off the top of a smooth-hewn walking stick. It's a solid wizard move. The brightness is a sign of your power, and she's shining bright.

"You don't scare me, old woman," Alistair yells.

As Alistair heads toward Mia, I make a break for it. Heading north, up the sidewalk parallel to Four West, I try to beat him to back up Mia. To my right, a light show has already started as they send strike after strike against each other in a well-matched duel. I make it to the sidewalk that cuts between the playgrounds, and my sides are killing me, I can feel the blood stretching the veins against my head as I breathe hard.

Alistair sees me and sends a strike my way. It's a short bright bolt of lightning, yellow and orange. But he shoots it off too quickly, and I dodge it. It leaves a molten puddle of sidewalk where it hits in front of me, causing me to trip and jump to miss the puddle of hot liquid rock. I *Yelp!* as I do. Like I said, not a combat wizard.

The next one hits me in the side of the arm, grazing across it, burning, and I go spinning with the force of it and land face down. As I hit the ground, something presses into my left tit, like I landed on a rock. It's the acorn in my pocket. It feels too early to use it. Hollis just gave it to me. But as I lift my head from the dirt, I see Mia drop to one knee, her staff supporting her, its blue light flickering.

Reaching into my pocket, I grab the acorn. Ripping the crown off and putting it in my mouth, I bite down hard, and an imperceptible *squeak* comes from my teeth, scraping against the acorn's shell as it cracks. The bitterness is strong on my tongue as the tannins release from the acorn's flesh. I try to remember if Hollis said I needed to chew it or if cracking it would do. All the saliva leaves my mouth as I stand up, spitting the acorn onto the ground. Like an adrenaline shot to the heart, I'm flush with energy.

Alistair is almost to Mia, bombarding her with shots, which she's deflecting like she's still twenty years old. It's something to witness as I run toward her, feeling strong. Alistair moves his focus from Mia, sensing my approach, and flings strike after strike at me. I see them coming and deflect them like they're nothing—gnats on a windy day.

A bright light flashes from behind me, illuminating the great lawn. Even Mia turns. I stop running and stroll confidently toward Alistair, because I know what's happening. They heard the calling card, and in my periphery, I see them—a hundred Tree Nymphs—stepping forth from their trees like neighbors turning on their porch lights, opening their doors, and stepping outside in their robes to see what all the commotion is about.

Alistair takes a step back, then another. One for every step forward I take, and then he holds up his finger, and on it, a silver needle like the one the shade from the apothecary had on the end of its finger. He slices into the air and opens a rift. But before he steps in, he pulls back his hoodie, and I'm looking at myself, a mirror image, except he's younger and thinner.

"Next time, brother," he says before stepping through and closing the rift behind himself.

Ahead of me, the Nymphs have gathered around Mia, helping her up. As I approach, one of their number steps forward. They're glowing faintly, vibrating in and out of focus, producing a sound like a hundred hummingbirds, hovering near the same flower.

"Thanks," I say,

It nods and then they're off, fast, like lightning bugs on crystal meth, each shrinking from almost human size to a mere pinprick of light—making tiny popping sounds as they enter their trees.

"It's good to see you, Aubrey Cockcroft."

"You too," I say to Mia, extending my hand.

She takes it and holds my gaze with her bright hazel eyes before we walk toward the cats, who greet us as we arrive.

"Where's your stuff?" I ask her, waving my hand around the area. "I'll get it for you. Then you can come with us."

"I have everything I need right here," she says as she squeezes my arm and smiles.

We walk the short distance to the van, and Mia laughs when she sees it.

"This old thing?"

"This old thing," I say.

I mumble under my breath and remove the security, unlocking the door. I help Mia in. All three cats jump up, Saoirse onto the seat with her. Shutting the door, I walk to the driver's side. Arbuckle meets me as I open the door and climb in.

"Good job," he says, and it feels good, that little bit of validation, even if it is from a cat.

Closing the door, I put the key in the ignition, and it putters and doesn't turn over.

"Oh yeah," I say. "We're out of gas." If this were a sitcom, we'd have all laughed at that, but instead, I turn to Mia, "Is there a gas station around here?"

"You're in luck," she says. "South end of the east side of the park."

"Great," I say. "The best news I've heard all night. Hope they sell cans."

It's a nice night as I walk the quarter mile to the gas station and back. Fortunately, they do sell cans. Unfortunately, it's one of the new ones, so I spill half a cup of gasoline on the ground trying to get the stupid self-closing spout to work. I leave the empty can in the parking spot next to the van and climb in, smelling like a pump attendant.

Mia gets a kick out of us passing through the Gloam. We exit at the airport again. So, we drive the fifteen minutes to Monvoisin's house.

Inside, Hollis shows Mia to a bedroom. I tell her to get some rest before I head into the parlor where Saoirse is holding court with the rest of the stupid poofs. All their tails are up, and they're nose-bopping and butt-sniffing, seeming to be genuinely happy to see each other.

I leave them to it and head outside, settling into the chair beneath the oak. I look down at my hands, then sniff them to see if the gasoline smell is still strong. It is. When I look up, Hollis is there.

"So," Hollis says, "I hear you met your brother."

"Can confirm. Definitely not locked in a binding stone anymore. He also tried to kill Mia, so I'm going to go out on a limb and say he's the killer."

"Well, that goes a long way to getting this sorted."

"You want to tell me about him now?"

Hollis takes a second to think it over, then says, "He was powerful from the start. I guess it was the shadow energy, but I'm not sure. When your aunt brought him home, I could already feel it radiating off him."

"You knew what she had done?"

Hollis takes a deep breath. "She had told me what she had done, but not before she brought him home. There wasn't anything I could do; like I said, I was bonded to her. What I never figured out was why she did it. Why did she call forth your shadow energy into your mother in the first place? But I can tell you, from the first moment I saw Alistair in her arms, I knew she wasn't in control."

"Who let him out? That's what I want to know, and why? It's been a very long time. Why now?"

Hollis shakes his head. "It doesn't make any sense. He reaped nothing but chaos in his short life."

"So, who do we know who thrives on chaos?" I ask.

∞

chapter eight

Young and Fit,
The Stolen Child,
The Doppelgänger with Flair.
The Ornament,
The Sad Boy Lost,
The Shadow Twin—Alistair.

— Em

After four days with little sleep and nearly twice-daily trips through the Gloam in the magic bus, I'm tired. We still have one pair left to find—Johnathan Priest and Augustus—but there's no address in the GPS for him. Under his name, it just says *Everywhere and Nowhere*, which isn't helpful. So, I gather everyone into the parlor to help figure out where he might be. Hollis has set out a nice spread: pâtés and chopped meats for the cats, along with bowls of cream, clam juice, and water. I'm having a cup of Hollis's magic elixir, and so is Mia, who's regaining her strength after her little skirmish with Alastair.

"Has anyone had contact with Johnathan recently?" I ask, getting the ball rolling.

"We ran into him in 1983 at an Occult Expo in Virginia," Poly says.

"Anyone more recently than forty years ago?" Side-glancing at Poly, I can see I've hurt her feelings, her tail is drooping. "Thank you, Poly.

That's a helpful start," I add, hoping not to lose the room.

"He was reclusive even in the beginning," Arbuckle says. "He and Augustus would disappear for weeks and never talk about where they had been."

I nod at Arbuckle's addition. "Anyone else? Think hard. Maybe poke around in the quintessence you're carrying. Maybe you weren't there when your human met with him."

"Is that a thing? Can you interact with the quintessence once you've acquired it? That would be lovely, if Saoirse and I could still communicate after," Mia says, stroking Saoirse, who is curled in her lap, listening, eyes half-closed.

"Your first instinct will be to try and dominate your vessel. Resist this—it's excruciatingly painful for us."

Mia looks at Saoirse with concern. "Oh. I'll try and keep that in mind." Reaching out, she gently strokes Saoirse's head.

"Otherwise, unfortunately, it's not as grand as one might hope. It does become part of us, but it's more like intuiting your opinion on a subject," Monvoisin says, then looks directly at me. "For instance, I know Miriam regrets what happened all those years ago, and is saddened by the secrets that were kept from you, Aubrey," she says, walking toward me slowly but confidently, as though listening to a voice no one else can hear. "She'd be proud of you, doing what you're doing—putting an end to all of this."

Monvoisin rubs against my legs.

"Thank you," I say, reaching down to rub my hand against her side.

"I'm sure Monvoisin is right," adds Arbuckle. "Once William settled down and stopped trying to come to the surface, we became more—" he pauses, searching for the right word, "—fluid in our understanding. I've known exactly what William would have thought and done in several situations I've faced this week."

"That's very comforting," Mia says. "And I may know a way to find Johnathan."

"How?" I say, jazzed, there might already be a solution.

"Well," she says, "he spent a great deal of time in the woods. We all know this. Hollis might be able to find him through the Sprite Network."

I turn and look at Hollis, and he's looking at all of us as though he thought he was invisible until that moment.

"It's not impossible, but it could take some time. Like I said, there aren't that many in North America."

"What are you talking about? There were over a hundred in that park in Salt Lake City."

"America is a big place. It's unlike Britain, where almost every tree has a sprite, nymph, or dryad. Copses here are small and spread out."

"What's a copse?" asks Poly, sitting up on her haunches.

"For sprites, a copse is the group they live in—like a prickle of porcupines, a fluffle of rabbits, or a dray of squirrels," Hollis says.

"Like a pack of dogs," I say, trying to clarify it in terms they might understand—and end up sending negative energy across the room. The cats slink back a bit.

Alexander's eyes grow large as he drops low to the floor.

"Nothing good comes from packs," he says in his low, frightened voice, backing under a chair.

"Well, it's nothing this clowder can't handle," I say, trying hard to recover. The statement dies a slow death in the room. "It's what they call a group of cats."

"That's a stupid name for a group of cats," Saoirse says from Mia's lap, still half asleep but paying attention.

"It sure is," Alexander says, in an oddly confident voice, standing a little taller now, having tentatively poked his head out from under the chair. "What sort of idiot came up with that?" he says, creeping across the floor to a bowl of cream. "A *clowder* of cats," he reiterates with contempt, then punctuates this final opinion with lapping noises.

"Back to the point. Hollis?" I say.

"I can put the word out; I'm not guaranteeing a response."

"If we got a response, how long would it take?"

"Not long. Word travels fast through the copses—well, technically under them. Ten hours at the most."

"Ten hours?" I say, honestly impressed. "How does it travel that fast?"

"The mycorrhizal network," Hollis says, sounding disappointed in my ignorance.

"What?" I say, reinforcing his opinion.

"Mushrooms," Monvoisin interjects, with a fair modicum of pride. "The mycelium connects to plant roots, allowing the forests to talk to each other."

"Very good," says Hollis. "Most of the land in the world is connected by mycelium. It's a real wonder—the planet's brain," he adds. "All I need is a description. My oak outside is a mother tree."

"Great," I say, turning to everyone. "Who can describe Johnathan and Augustus?" I realize I don't speak cricket.

I quickly get the feeling we'll have to try and extrapolate from the only thing we have. I pull the picture out of my pocket and pass it to Hollis.

"He's that one," I say, pointing to Johnathan in the photo.

"I wouldn't call this helpful," is all Hollis says.

"Let me see it," Mia says, reaching for it. "I haven't seen Johnathan for a long time, but if what you say is true about the quintessence of William, Francis, and Jane, I might be able to do something."

Saoirse jumps down from Mia's lap, and Hollis helps her stand. Handing the photo to Hollis, she steadies herself against her staff with both hands.

"Everyone gather 'round." She waves the cats toward her with a free hand. "Hollis, I need a pad of paper and a pencil or pen—as fine a tip as you can find."

Hollis nods and walks off as I move out of the way, making room for the cats, who begrudgingly get up from whatever position they've been sitting or lying in. As they take their first steps—almost in unison—they stretch their hind legs out one at a time, then come closer to Mia until they are gathered at her feet.

"Now, I'm going to attempt drawing from each of you your last visual memories of Johnathan and Augustus. This spell should also be able to access the quintessence you hold. I'll then combine them all, and hopefully we'll have a good enough likeness for Hollis to use. So everyone, remain still, calm your minds, and think of Johnathan and Augustus."

Mia sings softly, and the top of her staff glows with blue light, soon forming six wispy snakes that reach out toward the cats, the sixth turning to her. It slithers into her ear. As the others reach the cats, they do the same, worming their way into their brains—or at least that's what it looks like. Surprisingly, the cats don't flinch or show signs of pain or discomfort. If anything, they stand taller, becoming rigid. I hold my breath to keep from making any sudden movements and feel Hollis return behind me.

The song Mia is singing crescendos, and the tendrils disconnect from her and the cats, braiding themselves into a single strand emanating from the top of her staff. At its end, a six-fingered protrusion. Reaching out to Hollis, Mia motions for the pad. He moves quickly to the table and lays it down. He hands her the fine-tipped Sharpie, and she removes the cap with her teeth, spitting it onto the floor. Positioning the pen over the paper, the tendril grasps it and begins drawing.

We all stand watching, the cats jumping up—either on the table or the chair where Mia had sat—as it draws a near-photorealistic image of Johnathan and Augustus.

Finished, the pen drops, and the tendrils retreat into the staff. Mia sighs, sitting abruptly, almost on Alexander, who jumps from the chair just in time.

Saoirse returns to Mia's side in the chair.

"She can rest now," I say, picking up the drawing.

Johnathan is older here, a man in his sixties—not the young man in the photo. His face is worn and learned, a vagabond raconteur. Layers of clothing cover him, ready to be removed or added as the weather requires. He, like Mia, carries a staff, and riding on his shoulder is a surprisingly large and well-muscled American Bobtail, with the wizened face of an owl.

"Now, that's much better," Hollis says, picking up the pad and admiring the image. "I'll get it on the network and see what comes up."

"That's a nice trick," I say, kneeling in front of Mia, who looks haggard. "Anything I can get you?"

Smiling, Mia reaches out, touching my face. "Finish what we started. Send that little shit where he belongs."

"That's the plan," I say.

"She needs to rest," Saoirse says—and she's right.

I stand up. "I'll have Hollis mix her up some more elixir."

Saoirse sniffs Mia's face. "She used too much of her strength performing that spell."

* * *

"What's your plan if I hear something?" Hollis asks, shutting the door to Mia's room.

We've just moved her upstairs to rest. Saoirse is curled next to her head.

"Well, if they find him, we go get him. If not, we start working on how to lure Alistair somewhere I can deal with him."

"Aren't you worried that'll affect you too?"

"Why would it?"

"He's your monoamniotic twin. The egg only split because two energies showed up instead of one. That's a rare kind of bonding."

"So what you're saying is—killing him could kill me?"

"Not all of you, but a part of you."

"I'll keep that in mind. While I do, can you hold down the fort? I need to run to the house and grab some things if we're making this home base."

"Certainly."

"Thanks," I say, hitting the stairs. "You're starting to grow on me, Hollis."

"That's unfortunate," he says, which makes me laugh as I head to find Arbuckle.

He and the others are enjoying the grass and sun in the backyard. I tell him I'm heading to the house, and he runs across the lawn to join me—but so does Alexander. Figuring it couldn't hurt anything, I let him tag along. We head through the kitchen. I'm feeling pretty good, like I might finally have a handle on this thing.

But when I open the front door, Alistair is standing on the porch—hoodie down, and a rift shimmering behind him.

"Hey, old man," he says, before hitting me full force with a push spell that throws me across the foyer, knocking the wind out of me as I hit the wall.

I hear Hollis running down the stairs, but he's too late. Alistair grabs Arbuckle, steps through the rift, and shuts it behind him.

Filling both lungs, I scream—yelling obscenities, some of which I'm pretty sure I make up on the spot. Hollis is at the rift, stepping around and looking intently at where it used to be.

"It's fresh. I think I can open it back up."

"What happens if I enter it? It's not like I have the van to protect me."

"You shared a water bag, and that's strong magic. If he can do it, so can you."

Hollis is already chewing on his stick as I cross the doorjamb. He spits in his hands, then pushes his fingers between the molecules, splitting the rift open right along the previous seam.

"I'll have to close it once you go through," he says.

"Count to three before you do. I'll find another way out—be ready for it," I say, stepping through, raising my hands, ready to kill.

"Nobody takes my fucking cat."

* * *

It's not what I expect, coming out the other side like I'd passed through a curtain between rooms. I mumble under my breath, so my shield is up as my feet hit the ground. Nothing comes my way, so I orient myself before what little I can see is gone as Hollis closes the rift behind me. I barely get a good look at my surroundings before he does.

Reaching down, I feel the ground. It's full of gravel. I grab six pieces about the same size, tossing them in the air as I mumble under my breath and transmute them into werelights. I bring them close and orient them along a small circumference, as I bring the shield down, pushing them ten feet away, increasing the diameter until they illuminate the area in front of me. It's a risk, but I don't know what else I can do except trip on something in the dark without them.

It's some kind of an abandoned train tunnel, with tracks under my feet and all that gravel as ballast. Walking on the gravel will make it obvious I'm here, which sucks, so I get up onto one of the beams of the track and walk along it, slowly, listening. I'm trying to keep my balance. The rails are less than two and a half inches wide, making it more difficult than expected. Note to self: Learn how to levitate.

A *yowl* reverberates through the tunnel, and I almost slip off the rail. It's low and echoes out from somewhere ahead of me. Arbuckle's alive and pissed, which is good. The only bad thing is I don't hear another one, so either he's subdued now, or they've gone somewhere else. Into a room, or up a stairway, there's no way for me to know until I get there. But hearing it makes me think Alistair had no idea I'd be able to get through, otherwise, he would have been waiting for me. So, maybe when I find him, I'll have the upper hand.

I'm not sure what I'll do when I find him. I'm no killer; I never have been. Regardless of what twisted plans float through my head or feelings swirl in my brain, I know I'll fight against those urges. He didn't ask to be brought here. He had no hand in being born, but he's my brother, and I need to stop him one way or another.

Staying on this rail is wearing me out. I'm racking my brain for another solution when I look up from watching my feet and see a bright spot thirty yards away, so I suck it up and put my arms out and try and think about something other than that my feet are killing me and starting to go numb. I still haven't heard any more signs of Arbuckle, which worries me.

The closer I get, the more I can tell that the light is coming from a doorway up a small flight of stairs with a metal railing, all tucked inside an alcove off the main tunnel. Taking it slow, as I step off the rail head, and my shoes settle awkwardly on the gravel, I wait for the numbness to subside and for the pins and needles in my feet to run their course.

Snuffing out the werelights, I pull the shield close and make it small, attaching it to my left arm like I'm a centurion out of time. Making my way up the stairs, I pause, listening at the door. I don't hear anything.

I take a breath and count to three. Grabbing the handle and pulling, I give myself away. The door is locked, making a loud *clang* as the bolt hits the strike plate. The sound reverberates down the tunnel. I mumble under my breath and pop the lock to the sound of scuttling inside. Pushing the handle down, I conjure my fireball as I open the door. The adrenaline pumping through me makes me yell out a war cry. I sound stupid and feel even dumber, but it came out like the darkness had pulled my inner neanderthal to the surface. I stop screaming once I see what's behind the door.

Four people, illuminated by the green glow of the flame in my hand, huddle together in what must have been a storage closet at one time. A large flashlight sits between them, pointed at the ceiling. They stare at me like I'm about to kill them, and it makes me wonder what my face looks like at this moment. Maybe there is a killer inside of me, and I've never let him out. I hope not, but these faces tell another story.

"Wrong apartment," I say, closing the door. Walking down the stairs, I think about what a monumental mistake it was to follow Alistair through the rift in the first place. If I don't find him, I'm stuck here, wherever this is.

Back on the gravel, I pick up another handful. I mumble under my breath, throwing them into the air, making another ring of werelights.

This time, I don't worry about whether anyone can hear me coming. My primal scream killed any advantage I may have had. I continue deeper into the tunnel, surrounded by the echoes of people slipping on gravel as they try and get traction to run away.

Ten minutes later, I hit a wall, literally. I mumble under my breath almost as a joke so I can feel good about turning around and walking the other way. Pushing the reveal spell onto it, the whole thing lights up with runes like it's Christmas. The runes are like the ones written on the wall behind my uncle and the basement ceiling in my uncle's memories. This is magic in a foreign tongue, from a place different than here. This is Alistair's shadow magic, and I have no idea where he learned it or what it means.

I take a few steps away to see if I can discern a pattern. I pull out my cell phone and take some pictures. Then I get a silly idea. I hadn't switched the microSD since I had flipped through them with Arbuckle. Pulling up the ones I took at my uncle's place, I stop on the wide shot of his living room, his death diorama, and I hold it up to compare it to the wall.

Stepping forward and placing my hand on one of the runes, it flashes and goes active, and I move it to the location in the photo. I do the same with the next one and the next one. I'm hoping the runes are the solution to this puzzle, left for someone to find, and I am now pretty sure that someone is me.

Blood rushes to my head. He did expect me to follow. Maybe not this time, but eventually. He brought me to his home court and gave me the combination to unlock his door. Continuing to move each rune into its place, I wonder what kind of idiot would do this other than me.

The last one moves into place, and they flare—moving across the wall, forming a circle. The circle spins, and the stone inside disappears, creating a way through. I hesitate for a second, before bringing up the shield again as I step over the threshold. As soon as I do, I turn to look—and the wall is solid again. I mumble under my breath, but no runes appear. I'm trapped here, whether I like it or not.

Extending the shield out in front of me, I step into a cavernous space lit by bare bulbs strung on wires looping across the ceiling and adorning the rough-hewn rock walls. It's full of books and mismatched furniture that looks stolen from apartment complex dumpsters. I hear him before I see him.

"You came through. I had a wager with your cat that you'd be too scared."

"Where is he?" I say.

"He's fine. Scratched the shit out of my face, though," he says, stepping out from behind a bookcase, holding Arbuckle by the scruff of his neck. "You can lower the shield. If I'd wanted you dead, you'd be dead already."

I make it look like I'm dropping the shield by shrinking it to the size of a watch face and leaving it on my left wrist, ready to go at a moment's notice.

"Put him down. You can hurt him that way."

"A normal cat, yes. But he's not a cat."

I see what he means about his face—there's a good, long gash on his right cheek, beaded with blood.

"Put him down, or whatever you have planned for me isn't going to happen."

He takes a step forward and tosses Arbuckle toward me. Arbuckle spins and rights himself before hitting the floor on all fours and skidding to a stop. He turns toward Alistair and hisses, arching his back.

"Arbuckle. Over here," I say, and he slinks toward me. When he's close, I reach down—keeping my eyes on Alistair—and scoop him up in my right arm.

"You alright, bud?" I ask. Sure, he can't respond.

"As good as can be expected," he says, and it's enough of a distraction for me to take my eyes off Alistair for a split second to look at Arbuckle.

"I'm glad you're OK. I guess we can add this evil lair to our list of places I can understand you."

Turning to Alistair—who is now pouring himself a cup of something hot from a small service on a side cart—I feel the anger rising in me.

"Why are you doing this?"

"Tea?" he says, holding up a glass to me.

I don't respond.

"Suit yourself," he says, picking up his cup, walking over to a wing-back chair, and taking a seat. He takes a sip and motions to the chair across from him.

I remain standing.

He shrugs. "Why am I doing what? Getting even? Having my revenge?"

"You're killing people."

"They tried to kill me."

"You shouldn't be here."

"Says who?"

"It's not how things work."

"Oh, you know how things work?" he says, letting out a laugh—part scoff, part incredulity. "Are you sure about that?" He pauses and takes another sip before turning to me and pointing his finger. "Because when I rode your spark out of the Gloam, what did the universe do?"

He waits for me to answer him, but I don't have an answer.

"It gave me a body. It said this spark, too, is worthy."

"But look what you did with it. I'm no philosopher or theologian. I don't know enough to say whether you being born was right or wrong, but what I can tell you is that you had no right to do what you did once you were here."

"Didn't I? Are you any less true to your nature?"

"So, your nature is being a killer and a manipulator?"

"My nature is being superior."

"Superior? Is that what you call enslaving Miriam—whom you used against the order to subdue them—then chaining them to a bunch of posts so you could extract their quintessence, leaving you with seven vessels that you planned to fill with their shadow energy in hopes of creating an enclave of wizards who answered only to you? Correct me if I'm wrong."

"When you put it like that, it does have a negative overtone. But when you consider the fact that they all came to murder me first, it does flip the narrative."

"No, it doesn't. You should've never been born—but you were. And I'll admit, I'm still a little hazy on this, but somehow, even as an infant, you beguiled her, and she took you in, erasing your existence to raise you as her own. But she left fragments in my mother's head, and she dreamed of you. The order figured it out, and you had no choice—even though you were still young—but to enact your plan then or risk losing everything."

"I'm a scorpion. But that doesn't mean my right to exist is any less than yours."

"I'm saying it does, at least in this world."

"That's sad to hear, brother," he says, standing and putting down his cup. "You and I together would be unstoppable," he adds, steepling his fingers like a Bond villain.

Both of his index fingers are skin all the way. The silver adornment isn't on his hand. I scan the room to see if I can find it.

"I'll find a way. I'll send you back."

"No, you won't."

"Why not?"

"Because you're not like me. You don't have it in you."

Then I see it—the adornment—on the lampstand next to the chair he was sitting in. I twist Arbuckle's head so he's looking at it.

"I see it," he says quietly.

Bending down, I place Arbuckle on the floor and step toward my brother.

"Hollis says we're connected more deeply than I understood. Something to do with a water sac."

"The bag of waters," he corrects me, and I let him. "A much more poetic term, don't you think?"

"I guess," I respond, stepping deeper into his lair.

"We were the same egg, you and I," he says. "It was my spark. I split us into two," he adds, eyeing me, sizing me up. "So, in many ways, I made you who you are."

"Don't expect me to thank you for it."

"I'm not looking for your thanks. I'm looking for your—acceptance."

"More like my obedience."

"Obedience is a form of acceptance."

"You got me on that one," I say, feeling more emboldened now that I have a plan in motion. Moving more freely, looking around, I'm warming to his little dungeon.

"You got a lot of stuff here. How long have you been out?"

"A couple years now."

I make eye contact.

"A couple of years? What took you so long to start... revenging?"

"I didn't know where I was. It took me a bit to get orientated. I'd been locked in a crystal for forty-seven years. You don't shake that off. It took time to reorient to this plane."

From the corner of my eye, I can see Arbuckle slinking imperceptibly forward—his prey the adornment. I'm doing everything possible to get my brother as far away from it as I can.

"That dream I had—it was you?"

"Dream?"

"I dreamt killing Jane and my uncle. Our uncle. Saw the whole thing through the killer's eyes. Through your eyes."

"Huh," he says. "That's odd." He turns toward the chair where he'd been sitting.

I don't want him to see Arbuckle, so I clap my hands together, and he turns toward me, dropping into a fighting stance.

"So it wasn't you? Some sick spell to make me watch?"

"I can do many things, but giving people dreams isn't one of them."

"Then who was it?"

"I guess someone else wanted your attention as much as I did. I left you the runes on the wall in the trailer, but I expected it to take days, if not weeks, to come to your attention—if it ever did."

"What was your plan then, after you got my attention?"

"I figured I'd be done with my little task at that point, and we could, I don't know, get to know each other."

"Get to know each other? You do understand how crazy that sounds. You thought after you'd murdered everyone, I'd track you down and what, forgive you over a couple of beers?"

"We're brothers. That must count for something?"

"Not as much as you might think," I say.

"Don't you want it?"

"Want what?"

"The power?"

"Why would I want that?"

"Why wouldn't you?"

"Because most days—" I say, unsure if what I'm about to say even matters. "Most days, my brother, I can barely muster enough energy to eat, let alone sit down. I don't need the world to cower before me. I don't need to pound it into submission to feel good about myself. What I need is for the world to slow down and be quiet. I need to feel like I'm not constantly struggling against a never-ending tide of other people's agendas and desires. I don't have it in me to bully the world."

"It bullied you, didn't it?"

"The world didn't bully me, Alistair. Small-minded people did."

"Don't you want revenge? Don't you want them to suffer?"

"No."

"If that's the case, I should put you out of your misery. No one will miss you," he says.

He's right, of course—or at least that's what goes through my head. It almost sticks there, too, but then I hear Em.

"Well, that's not entirely true," she says, coming through the wall.

Alistair claps his hands with delight and laughs.

"A ghost? That's your saving grace?"

"Brother, she's all the grace I need," I say, looking at Em and already feeling better. "Also, she's a great distraction," I add, watching Arbuckle sprint toward me.

Alistair sees him, too, firing off a hex that barely misses. Arbuckle's moving so fast even I can't keep up.

"You really shouldn't have left the adornment unguarded," I say, trying to sound confident as Arbuckle takes position behind me.

"Give that back!" Alistair screams, dropping into a striking stance.

Pulling the shield from my wrist, I expand it as he fires off a couple more nasty hexes that hit so hard they barely deflect. Dropping to retrieve the adornment from Arbuckle's mouth, I extend the shield to cover Em as she moves close to me. I slice a rift in front of us.

"How do you know where this leads?" Em asks.

"I don't," I say, as we all push through.

We land on grass, and Arbuckle tears ass across it, while Em moves straight up into the air above the rift, and I roll to the side.

The last thing I hear is my brother screaming,

"You can't leave me here!" as Hollis spits in his hands and crimps the rift shut.

"That worked better than I expected," I say, sitting up, looking at the silver adornment in my hand.

"He sounded pissed," Hollis says.

"That's OK," I say. "I'll get over it."

* * *

"When did you plan that?" Arbuckle asks, walking into the parlor.

"I kind of didn't," I say, enjoying a cup of Hollis' elixir. "All I did was ask Em to keep an eye on me, so she pretended to walk home. I told Hollis to be ready if something weird happened, which was why he was hanging around the house more. I was sure Alistair would make a move at some point after what happened in Salt Lake City, but I had no way of knowing what or when. I didn't think it would happen that quickly or he'd show up, sucker punch me, and kidnap you."

I shake my head and take a sip of the tea, enjoying its calming, warming effect, and think for a second that it might be addictive.

"In all honesty, I got a little worried once I got through, because even if Em had been able to scoot through with me on such short notice, I had no way of returning other than figuring out where I was and making a call to Hollis, and hoping he knew how to drive the van to come pick me us up. I need to see how far he can travel from his tree. I forgot to think about that, too."

"Focus," Arbuckle says.

I snap out of my tangent. "When I saw the adornment on the table, I waited for the opportunity to grab it, or for you to grab it. All in all, I think it worked out well."

"Yeah," says Arbuckle, before jumping onto the counter and looking me in the eyes. "Assuming it's not exactly what he wanted you to do."

"What do you mean?"

"It was pretty easy."

"It wasn't that easy."

"It was pretty easy."

"Why would he want me to have the adornment?"

"I don't know yet, but there must be a catch. You got it, but he learned how far you're willing to go, what makes you angry, what you think about him, and who's working with you. All of those are weaknesses he can exploit."

"Maybe so, but he's only one man."

"So are you, Aubrey, so are you," Arbuckle says.

* * *

I'm examining the adornment and seeing which of my fingers it might fit on, hoping it's the right index finger because that might look cool. I try and slide it on, but I'm heavier, so I keep trying each finger until it slips comfortably onto my pinkie, which isn't as flattering as it sounds. I look up as Hollis walks into the room, smiling.

"I think we found your man," he says.

"So where do the mushrooms say he is?" I ask.

"Close. Maybe ten miles. Headed straight for us."

"He's been that close all this time?"

"No, he appeared in the Smokey Mountain National Forest six days ago."

"From where?"

He shakes his head. "They don't know."

"How do you show up somewhere suddenly, out of nowhere?" I ask.

Hollis claps me on the shoulder with his right hand, looks me in the eyes, laughs, and says, "You step through a rift between planes," then he walks out of the room.

So, Johnathan and Augustus are coming to us. I'm not going to lie—that's the best news I've heard all week. It means I can take another nap. I'm getting better at them. Standing up, I put the adornment into my pocket and stretch, feeling a few places pop and a few others throb.

Sometimes, I wonder how people make it to eighty when everything is so worn out at fifty. I walk from the kitchen into the dining room and down the hall to the parlor, where all the cats have beat me to that nap. I count them all to ensure they're all there and then climb the stairs.

I gently open the door to Mia's room and peek in. Saoirse is still curled up on the pillow next to her head, and I wait until I see the slightest rise and fall of the sheets covering Mia before I quietly shut the door again. I need to know she's still breathing before I lie down, or I'll never get to sleep.

I probably should have asked to use one of the bedrooms, but I figured Hollis would have said something if it wasn't alright. Opening a few doors, I find a small one with a small bed, and I take my shoes off, lie down on my back, and close my eyes. I don't even bother getting under the covers. It's cool and soft, and I'm sinking the right amount into the mattress.

I'm almost asleep when something jumps onto the bed—then another and another. Cracking my eyes, I see Arbuckle land. He walks along the mattress's edge until he's close enough to curl up next to my head. Surrounded now on all sides by cats. I feel safe and warm as I drift off.

As I sink beneath awareness I wonder if I'm strong enough to face what's coming as my mind pieces things together, realizing I still haven't found the anomaly—the missing person in my uncle's memories— which makes me feel like that little kid who was told he was 'lucky to be alive' but was never asked how he felt about it.

∞

chapter nine

Proud and True,
The Loyal Friend,
The Minister of Justice.
The Best of Us,
The Tailless One,
The One They Call—Augustus.

—ALD
transcribed by AC

We gather on the front porch to greet Johnathan and Augustus. The mushrooms let Hollis know when they are less than a mile away. It's a little surreal, and I hope the scene makes him feel welcome. Em, Hollis, and I stand on the porch, with the five cats presented like ornaments on the steps.

Figuring he'd want to get here under his own steam, I chose not to drive out and pick him up, even though I wasn't sure how he'd fare. People around here drive like the world has ended and all the blinkers have broken. Knoxville's traffic is legendary in its stupidity, and a man and his cat must take care if traveling by foot.

Augustus rounds the corner first, and he seems different than the other cats. More confident. There's a sense of purpose in his stride, and without a tail to tell me, I must assume he's in a good mood. His coloring is unique—noticeably light, almost white, with complex, subtle hues of beige where he needs it to define his features.

When Johnathan appears, it's like watching a mystic enter a village. His hair and linen clothes are almost entirely white. Even his staff is made of light-colored wood, possibly holly. He's wearing sandals, and the hood of his bohemian-cut shirt covers his head. Augustus stops at the foot of the walkway and stares up at us but doesn't move. Johnathan soon joins him, removing his hood. He stares, smiling.

"The gang's all here," he says, then walks toward us, Augustus trailing behind.

The cats lose their composure and rush to greet Augustus, who seems uncertain of all the attention. Johnathan strides forward, looking very strong for his age, and I walk down the steps to greet him.

"Aubrey, you've grown up," he says as we shake hands.

"Doesn't feel like it," I say.

Johnathan turns to Hollis. "Do I know you, Sprite?"

"I've never had the pleasure," Hollis replies.

"Are you sure? There's something about you," he says, scrunching his face, trying to remember before being distracted and heading up the stairs.

He approaches Em. "And who is this young Eidolon?"

"You can call me Em."

"Nice to meet you, Em," he says before turning to me. "I take it everyone is dead."

"Mia is upstairs, but other than that, yes."

"It was inevitable," is all he says.

"Let's go inside," I say, walking up and opening the door. Johnathan enters, and so does Hollis.

"Arbuckle," I call down, and he looks up at me, then tears up the stairs and into the house. The rest of the cats follow at a more leisurely pace. Once everyone is inside, I close the door.

These little moments that happen between all the insanity seem odd. Little pockets of normalcy where you can catch your breath, eat, chat, and sleep. It's like the universe knows that if everything happened at once without a break, we'd all keel over from exhaustion. The quiet moments before the storm. It's something I'm beginning to understand.

These are the moments to cherish. You'd think it obvious, but it's not until you have something to compare them to.

Hollis has become quite the host, and I'm not sure exactly where the food keeps coming from since I haven't seen a single delivery, despite what Monvoisin said. He fixes a complete lunch spread fit for both man and beast. We're all seated at the dining room table like we're civilized— and we've always been this way.

Mia has roused herself to join us, so she, Johnathan, and I are sitting at one end of the table while the cats occupy the other. I haven't formulated an opinion of whether cats should be on the table, and I'm thinking that if they didn't talk, it would be no. But since they all come across as intelligent and thoughtful, I have a hard time putting my foot down over it.

Once everyone has finished eating, the humans stay at the table, and Hollis brings out some coffee, like we're European or something.

"So, Johnathan, we understand you suddenly showed up six days ago in the mountains. Want to tell me about that?" I ask.

"You want to know why it coincided with your uncle's death and the appearance of Alistair," he says, wasting no time cutting through my indelicate dance.

"Pretty much."

"Augustus and I were consulting the Akashic record when we were summoned to return."

"Where's the Akashic record?"

"Are you familiar with Theosophy or Anthroposophy?"

"No."

"Then it doesn't matter. We were somewhere, and then we were here."

"Who summoned you?"

"Your uncle. He sensed Jane's death and anticipated his own. Machinations were put in place long ago for such an occurrence." Johnathan looks at me like he's trying to see through me to the wall. "I'm curious— how did you discover what was happening?"

"It was a dream—" I say.

"It did work," Johnathan says, cutting me off and jovially turning to Mia, looking for affirmation.

"I saw through his eyes. Through Alistair's eyes."

Johnathan looks slightly aghast. "Oh, goodness. It was only supposed to warn you with a sense of foreboding. Temporarily fill you with hypervigilance so you would be on guard until we resolved the issue."

"Well, after I watched Alistair kill Jane and my uncle, I was hypervigilant." I take a sip of coffee, letting it sink in. "I guess I did feel a sense of foreboding." I put my cup down harder than I intended, startling Mia and Johnathan. "It was pretty traumatic," I say.

Johnathan is quiet. He's staring intently into his cup, trying to divine a response.

Mia reaches across the table and gently grabs my wrist to get my attention.

"Aubrey, I understand you're upset and confused after everything that's happened, but you must understand that what we did was to protect you. It may not have been the best way to go about it, but we were young, and it was the best we could do. Our intent was pure."

"Maybe so, but no one seems to know how Alistair got free and how he hid for two years without anyone knowing."

Johnathan and Mia have a short conversation with their eyes.

"He couldn't have gotten out on his own. I'm certain of that," Johnathan says, turning to me.

"How can you be so sure?"

"We didn't just shove him through and hope for the best. Miriam contacted the Caretakers after we had bound him in the holding stone."

"My father mentioned them in his notebook, and I've met a shade."

"Oh, how was that?" Johnathan asks, excitedly.

"It tried to kill me."

"Well, that sounds like a shade. They aren't supposed to attack us. They're like the enforcement arm of the Caretakers," he says, sipping his coffee, happy to be on a subject other than his complicity in my nightmare. "Anyway, we contacted them, and they were waiting on the other side of the rift to take custody of him. They said he'd be kept there, in the Gloam. A warning, should anyone else try something similar."

"I've been there too—the Gloam."

Johnathan looks at me, aghast. "How?"

"The shade sucked my quintessence right out of me. The next thing I know, I'm on a mesa, looking at a throbbing city in the distance."

"The Perpetuation. You saw it? What was it like?" Johnathan asks, mesmerized by what I haven't even told him yet.

"Like looking at the world through emerald glasses. I saw a woman too."

"A woman?"

"Yeah, but her face was covered."

Johnathan looks to Mia. "Do you think?"

"I don't know," she says, obviously getting irritated with him.

"How can you be sure that just because they took possession of him, he couldn't escape? He's been passing through the Gloam like he owns the place. He was using this to hop around," I say, pulling the adornment from my pocket.

"Where did you get that?" Johnathan tries to reach for it, but I pull it back.

"Off Alistair. It's what opens the rifts."

"Only the Shades have those. They're the only ones allowed to pass through in that way."

"Tell that to my brother."

Johnathan looks confused, which quickly changes to flustered. "Well, I guess there's only one thing to do now."

"What's that?"

"Augustus!" Johnathan yells over his shoulder, and Augustus appears almost instantly. "Gather the cats in the basement. We'll need protection."

"Yes, sir," Augustus replies before sprinting off.

"Mia, feel free to sit this one out. You look tired," Johnathan says, standing and grabbing his staff. Turning to me, "You, on the other hand, are required to attend—and leave that here," he says, pointing to the adornment.

"Attend what?" I say, putting it on the table in front of Mia. She nods, letting me know she'll look after it.

"A meeting with the Caretakers."

"And where are we going to do that?"

"In the basement, of course," he says, like it's something everyone should know.

"Why the basement?" I ask, finally hoping to understand why it's always the basement.

Johnathan shrugs. "Good a place as any," he says, walking out of the kitchen.

Mia shakes her head. "He's always been like this, acting in charge. He's never been afraid of anything."

"Must be nice," I say.

Mia skips the tête-à-tête with the slugs, and I can't blame her. I didn't enjoy my last encounter, but if Johnathan is confident the cats can keep us safe, then it's the least I can do to join him. I'm not confident they'll be helpful or informative, but I guess it can't hurt.

When I get downstairs, Johnathan is holding court with the cats, who all seem intent on listening to his story. They're sitting on their haunches, staring at him and following the tip of his staff as it bobs up and down and side to side as he talks. I've missed most of it, so I wait at the bottom of the stairs until he says, "And that's how I knew the Gorwrath was pregnant."

He laughs, and I can't tell if what he's told them is true or just a story to impress them.

I clear my throat, and Johnathan looks up, the cats still talking like it's the most interesting thing they've ever heard.

"What's a Gorwrath?" I ask, sincerely curious if he has an answer.

"There you are. Are you ready to meet the Caretakers, Aubrey?"

"Sure," is all I can muster, and I make a mental note to ask him about the Gorwrath again later.

"OK, I need all of you to spread out and look menacing, so it doesn't get any ideas," he says, gesturing with his staff to direct where each cat should position itself, then waves me over. "And Aubrey, you'd better stand next to me."

Walking over, I stand slightly behind him—just in case I decide to run. I've never been ashamed of it. Running has saved my life more than once, and if there's a plus side to social anxiety, it's this: if people are going to judge you anyway, let them judge you while you're running. You stay alive, and they get an opinion on how you do it.

Johnathan takes another minute to prepare, then does something I wasn't expecting. He taps the air three times with the end of his staff like he's knocking on a door: *gong, gong, gong,* reverberating the air as if striking an invisible church bell.

"And now we wait," he says, bringing his staff to his side and grasping it with both hands.

I've never been much for staves or wands, but I have to say the staff is growing on me.

"Where did you learn how to do this?" I ask him to kill time.

"I learned it from the monks of the Astral Plane. It's a kind of universal knock. If you can find the door, that is."

"Wow," I reply, curious if he learned the knock before or after he figured out how to find the door. I'm about to ask him when I see a small point of pallid green light appear in front of us, followed by the silver fingernail of an adornment. It cuts straight down, splitting space right in front of us. At first, I feel a strong flight response, but I'm also curious about what it'd be like to meet one without it attacking me.

Before anything comes through, Johnathan puts his arm out and nudges me to step back with him, and I do. We take maybe three steps, and the cats move forward, positioning themselves in an arc around the opening.

The lamprey mouth pokes through first, probing the air, reading the room. It senses Johnathan and then me, where it lingers, its mouth opening and closing, tasting the air. Then it spits out a warning hiss, and I reflexively step back. Then it notices the cats, screeches, and immediately retracts.

"I guess it doesn't want to talk."

"Shades seldom linger; think of them like a tongue, sensing what's in the room. Although it can act independently, as I believe the one you encountered did, they rarely leave their Caretaker."

"Great," I say, hoping that's the last time I see one. "What are the cats?" I ask. "In my uncle's memories and the apothecary, I saw their shadows created from the light of the Gloam."

"Wonderful, aren't they?"

"Yes, very nice, but what are they?"

"Life energy comes from the Perpetuation, the potential city, whose very act of living produces both potential and shadow energy, filling the world around it and giving rise to possibilities, of which the Caretakers and Shades are but a few."

"I get that, but what are the cats?"

"They're micro-possibilities. They feed off the energy that bleeds from the Perpetuation, like the radiation-eating bacterium used to clean up nuclear waste. Hardy as a tardigrade."

"Why are Shades scared of them?"

"Oh, they aren't scared, they're disgusted. Caretakers and Shades react to them like we might to bedbugs."

"Rude," Arbuckle says.

I look at the cats; they're all giving Johnathan the stink eye.

"It's an honest analogy," Johnathan says, defending himself.

The cats' indignation is interrupted by a rumbling that shakes the whole house. Dust dislodges, falling and swirling through the room.

"Here it comes," Johnathan says over the loud din of a low groaning chant so deep that I can feel it as much as I can hear it.

We turn our attention to the rift, where the shape of a man comes through, but it's awkward and unsteady. I notice once it settles that it's hardly a man but a construct of a man. A puppet standing before us, manipulated by the monstrosity remaining on the other side.

"We call that an Emissary," Johnathan whispers to me from the side of his mouth.

The Emissary is crudely rendered in something akin to clay, formed and dried, stitched together with interconnecting pieces. These ill-fitted pieces are bound together with the same silverish wire used to weave the adornment. All wired up, the puppet's movements are orchestrated by the thing that oozes from the gaping rift—a black-clad puppeteer.

"Lovely," Johnathan says. "They're getting much better at it," he remarks to me before slapping me on the arm and stepping forward to greet the crudely rendered facsimile of a man.

As Johnathan steps forward, the cats move to the sides but remain close to the opening. The Emissary feigns lips with a protrusion like the fisted thumb of a hand puppet, bobbing up and down as it talks.

"Speak," it says, shaking the house with a single word.

"Yes, Great Caretaker of the Perpetuation. We humbly seek your counsel on a matter of some urgency. It concerns the shadow-born Alistair—"

"Fugitive!" it screams, cutting off Johnathan.

"Yes, we know. But how?"

"The Stone—cracked!"

"Cracked?" I hear myself say before I even realize I've said it.

The puppet turns to me, tilting its head slowly to the side in a weird, stilted gait—its body twisting as it steps forward, dragging more of its blackness from the rift.

The cats scatter, their disgusting nature forgotten. Johnathan moves too, stepping behind me as the thing approaches, racking its head side to side with each step.

Holding my ground as best I can, uncertain what I can do if it wants to take me—my heart races as my blood pressure pushes a headache into my face. Compared to me, it's a god with a puppet on its finger, scaring a mouse in its hole. Stopping in front of me, leaning in close, I feel its breath on my face even though I know it's not breathing.

"Other half," it says, lower in tone but more physical in vibration. I feel nauseous almost immediately.

"Other half," I respond, shaking my head up and down. "Good half," I add, pointing to myself.

"Guilty half," it says, and I feel my bowels shift.

"If I may, Oh Great One," Johnathan says, holding up his finger and stepping forward.

The Emissary jerks toward him, the charade broken.

"Silence!"

Johnathan lowers his head and arm, stepping back even further this time.

"Guilty half? Guilty of what?" I ask.

The Emissary jerks so hard toward me this time that one of its fingers rips free of the wire and clinks to the ground.

"Life!" it rumbles.

"You're putting it on me, aren't you?" I say, stepping forward. It's a bad idea, and I know it. Bending down, I pick up the Emissary's finger and tap on the chest plate with it to punctuate what I'm saying. "You think all of this is my fault, don't you? You think if I hadn't ever been born, we wouldn't be in this mess. You think Alistair is my responsibility. Like I had any say in the matter. Well, let me tell you something—"

The force of the Emissary puppet headbutting me brings me to my knees so fast I almost pass out. I throw up for the second time in a week, my head swirling and my insides loosening. Then, the puppet's mouth is staring me down, and I feel the word inside my head rather than hear it in my ears.

"Worthless," it says.

The Emissary rips away, flying across the room like a stuntman in a cable pull, arms and legs out straight, trying to catch up to the body as it disappears into the rift, which stitches up almost instantly.

I turn around and look at Johnathan, who's smiling. "Let's never do that again," I say, picking myself up off the floor and walking past him and the cats—heading upstairs.

"What did it say?" I hear Johnathan ask from behind me. "What was the last thing it said to you?"

"None of your fucking business," I yell down the stairs, before heading to the kitchen, where I find Mia still sitting at the table.

"Did it do that creepy puppet thing?" she asks.

"Yes," I say, still feeling sick to my stomach.

"You should have been there, Mia," Johnathan says gleefully.

"I was fine, feeling nauseous up here, thanks," she says.

"They're getting good at making The Emissary," Johnathan adds, ignoring her complaint, acting like a minute ago, he hadn't been reduced to a sniveling sycophant.

"It was not good," I say, angry and still shaken from what it said to me. "It was a nightmare. It could have killed us both."

"Well, at least we know they did have him, and they want him back," Johnathan says, pouring himself a cup of cold coffee from the coffee maker, ignoring me and talking to Mia.

"How do we get him to them?" I ask.

"We trick him into knocking on the door?" Mia says.

"The Caretaker said the stone had cracked," I add.

"How can a binding stone crack?" Mia says.

"I'm not sure," Johnathan says, sitting at the table.

"Maybe they cracked it after they took him?" I add.

"I didn't think of that. Maybe they're just covering up for their mistake," Mia says, shaking her head. "Not that that makes any sense."

"Who would have the ability and the power to do it?" I ask.

"Let's make a list," Mia says.

"A list of what?" Johnathan asks.

"Suspects," she replies.

"We made it. We should be the only ones who could break it," Johnathan says.

"Yes, true," Mia says, looking down. "I've forgotten so many things." She takes a sip of coffee and looks at us both. "How are we going to do this? How are we going to stop Alistair?"

"We'll figure something out," Johnathan says, looking at me.

"I don't know," I say, feeling drained and unsure. Maybe it was just being in the presence of the Caretaker. Maybe it sucked some energy out of me like the Shade had done. I felt tired again, like I had so often since this whole thing began.

"Do you remember the poems we wrote about the cats?" Johnathan says, trying to cheer Mia up.

Mia furrows her brow. "Monvoisin was the first," she says, her eyes lighting up.

"Yes," Johnathan says, a big grin crossing his face. He looks at me and winks, then turns to Mia. "Sly and Crafty—The Hero's Foil," he says.

"The Thaumaturge of Poison," Mia says and laughs.

"The Eyes of Night." Johnathan points his finger at Mia, pleased he remembered.

Mia takes a second, and I see her lips move as she repeats it to herself. Then she claps her hands. "The Quiet Step,"

"The Monarch Beast – Monvoisin," they both say together.

"Ha," Mia brings her hands together without a clap this time and puts them against her lips, gone off somewhere in her memory for a quick moment.

"We made up a poem for each of the cats," Mia says, looking up at me. "Nothing much, just a little rhyming thing." Mia pushes out her chair and stands, steadying herself with her staff. "Let's go see if we remember them," she says, walking out of the kitchen, Johnathan following.

I remain seated, glad for the momentary silence. But in this silence, as it does, the doubt creeps in. The doubt telling me I'm not a part of this. The doubt that I'm not up to this. The doubt that I don't belong, an interloper. Worthless.

* * *

I find them in the parlor working through the rhymes. None of the cats appear amused, but Em is enjoying herself, laughing and clapping as they finish each one. I envy her smile.

"Pascal and Silas, poor things. Let us not forget them," Mia says, silence falling across the room.

"We should write them down, Aubrey," Em says as she sees me standing in the doorway.

"Why?" I ask.

"Because they're fun."

"I don't like fun," I say.

"I know you don't," she says, making a funny frowning face. "But you are carrying a pen and pad."

I look down at my hands, and she's right—I am. I don't remember getting it or why I thought I needed it, but I do as she asks. Mia and Johnathan go through them while Em looks over my shoulder, whispering punctuation corrections to me as I write them down.

"We should make up one for Aubrey," Em announces.

"No thanks," I say, putting the pen and pad on the lamp table. I leave them to their fun.

"Oh, come on, Aubrey. Don't be like that," I hear Em call behind me.

"Let him go, dear. He's..."

Worthless. I finish the sentence for them.

Heading out back looking for Arbuckle, I find him and the other cats lying in the sun on the warm concrete walkway. I lay down in the grass next to him. He gives me a gentle headbutt and then rolls onto his back, and I drift off, the warmth of the sun making me feel calm. And Arbuckle, my transmuted tardigrade from the Gloam, makes me feel safe and as snug as a bug in a—

* * *

I wake up alone. The sun is low, blocked by the house. My watch shows it's just past four in the afternoon. Rolling off my back, I make my proprietary mixture of groans and grunts as bones and tendons pop and my muscles complain. I'm groggy and have no idea what to do. Where I had felt hopeful and even energized by the thought of having Mia, Johnathan, and Hollis on my side—finally having a group of skilled companions to help me figure out who had freed Alistair and ultimately who was behind all of this—I now feel empty.

'Worthless,' the Caretaker had called me. And that's how I suddenly feel. Why had it all become my problem anyway? Why was it all on me to fix this mess? Last week, the worst thing that could happen to me was that I would spend another week without a paying gig. This week, I had been attacked by the Skittering, forced to cram myself into a refrigerator, bitten by a spider the size of a bulldog, almost had my life essence drained by a slug from another dimension, had a tree thrown at me, not to mention a bench and a couple of nasty hexes from my estranged brother, and I had a slug god puppeteer passive-aggressively blame me for the whole thing.

Maybe it is me. Maybe if I weren't here, none of this would be happening. Alistair wouldn't exist if I hadn't been born. It's not a great thought to have at any age. But I'm having it now. Just another thing I did wrong. Living. So right now, standing here in the warm afternoon, all I want to do is go home, back to my life. The life I was perfectly content with last week before I learned all the shit I'd learned. Me, Em, and Arbuckle, because now I want Arbuckle to want to go too and be a part of that—be a part of my life, the one I used to have. The simple, quiet, boring life I used to have.

I find Em in the library, reading a book of poetry that someone left on a bookstand. Alexander has perched himself on a chair next to the stand, and I see why. Em is practicing interacting with objects again. I stay quiet and watch as Alexander reaches out to paw the page but stops as Em holds up her hand.

"Let me try. I think I've got it this time."

She puts two fingers at the top of the left-hand page, and slowly, it moves as she successfully pushes it across so that it flips over. It takes her a bit longer to flip it back, but she finally gets it turned. She beams at Alexander, who holds out his head for her to pet like he's the one who accomplished something. She obliges, scratching his head while reading the poem. When she's finished, she tries turning the page again but doesn't have the same level of success. Frustrated, she nods to Alexander, who turns it for her by dragging his paw across it. I take a step and make it loud. She looks up and smiles like she always does.

"Have you read T.S. Eliot? He's very good," Em says.

"He wrote a poem about naming cats," I say, having intended to read The Waste Land at least once in my life but having failed to do so thus far. I had read the one about the cats, though.

"Augustus's name is in it," says Alexander proudly.

"Isn't that nice," I say to Alexander, then to Em. "I'm going home, Em. Are you coming?"

"What's happened, Aubrey?"

"Nothing. I'm tired. It's all too much, and I want to go home."

"OK, I'll come with you," she says, maintaining a worried look as I walk out of the room. I hear Alexander jump down and pad heavily behind me, so I know Em is either there too or already dropped through the floor.

I find Johnathan downstairs in the parlor with Mia and the cats. Hollis is passing out refreshments, and he holds the tray out to me, where a nice hot cup of his elixir beckons.

"No thanks," I say, holding up my hand to wave him off. "I came to tell everyone I'm going home."

"When do you want to meet back?" Johnathan asks. "We still need to work out exactly how we're going to deal with Alistair."

"Yeah," I say, pausing for a second to think about it. "I'm not sure I'm returning. But it was nice to meet everyone. Sorry I couldn't save Jane or my uncle. But there are two of you and Hollis left. He's a powerful sprite. Plus, you have Augustus, Alexander, Monvoisin, Saoirse," I say, pointing at each cat. My finger moves to point at Arbuckle. I take a deep breath, sigh, and catch myself before I get upset. "And this guy."

"Aubrey, we need you," says Mia, concerned.

"Do you? I mean, I've been in the dark about all of this for a very long time—most of my life. And I don't think I'm prepared for it. I'm not the kind of person you need. I investigate liars, not killers. I take pictures of people doing things they shouldn't do with people they aren't married to. I find people who don't want to be found. Rarely do they try to kill me or anyone I care about. When not doing that, I like the world to be quiet so I can pretend it's still and peaceful and enjoys having me around. I like to think I'm worth something without constantly having to prove it.

"You waited too long to let me in. I grew old thinking I had abandoned the only family I ever knew because he wouldn't stop keeping secrets from me. An order sworn to make sure my brother, as evil as he might be, remained imprisoned in another realm, dimension, plane, whatever, so he wouldn't destroy the world," I say a little too loud. I'm angry, but I'm also frustrated, not with them, but with myself. I've got imposter syndrome leaking out my pores.

I point to Mia, "You fought like a boss in that park. That was some solid combat magic."

I point to Johnathan, "You knocked on the door to another dimension in the basement of a house in Tennessee, and a slug god answered."

Hollis is last. "You're a tree sprite who can summon an army with an acorn and find a man with a network of mushrooms."

"I've got a fireball, shield, reveal spell, and I can pop a lock and lay a little security down. What's that against a dark wizard like Alistair when it comes down to it?"

"You got away from him," Johnathan chimes in.

"Only because he thought he had the advantage. If Em hadn't followed me, I probably wouldn't have. This is out of my league. My life may be simple, and I may be a little out of shape and neurotic, but I don't have a death wish, and I sure as hell don't know what I'm doing."

No one has anything to say to that but Arbuckle, who's made his way across the room to rub against my leg. I look down at him, overwhelmed by his loyalty.

"Let's go home, Aubrey," is all he says.

"I'm sorry," I say, walking toward the front door before anyone can say anything.

Arbuckle pads behind me. Em has already passed through, and I only hesitate a second before I open it. I glance toward the parlor, but no one watches me go.

* * *

We ride home in silence, which is probably best. I'm feeling guilty for what I did. It wouldn't be going away anytime soon, either. Entering my back door calms me down as I smell the comforting aroma of home. It's not a great smell, especially after not smelling it for a few days, but it's mine.

I exhale, feeling the weight of the week slide off me. I walk across the kitchen and up the stairs, heading straight for the bathroom, where I strip off my grungy clothes and take a very long shower. It's been a few days since I've had one, and the water feels good. After I've soaped up and rinsed off, I stand there, letting the water run over me. My muscles loosen, and my brain clears. I stand that way for a minute or two longer than I should. I can feel my wrinkled fingertips as I run my thumb across them.

Since I had forgotten to get a change of clothes before I showered, I wrap the towel around my waist. Picking my dirty clothes off the floor, I cross into my room, throwing them into a hamper. All the clothes in my closet are the same, so it doesn't matter which pants or shirt I grab. The colors might shift, but the brand, size, and cut are always the same. I grab a black t-shirt off the hanger and a pair of socks and underwear from the dresser. I put everything on standing next to the bed in case I lose my balance pulling on a sock or trying to get my foot into the pants leg.

I sit in the chair next to the dresser and put on my shoes one at a time. When I look in the mirror over the dresser, I realize it's been a bit since I cut my hair, and there's a scrubland up there now. The last time I looked in the mirror was at the motel in Florida, and that was to body shame myself. This time, here, I feel OK. I recognize this guy. I like this guy.

Downstairs, I raid the fridge. I pull out some extra sharp white cheddar and a piece of salami and find a jar of olives. Grabbing some saltines out of the cabinet, I make myself a poor man's charcuterie platter. I find a clean wide-mouth mason jar in the dishwasher. Shaking the box of Buttery Pinot Noir, praying it has some weight, I pour a good six ounces and head out onto my deck.

The sun's almost down, and I realize this is one of the few twilights I've been able to enjoy in a while. A northeasterly breeze, strong enough to notice, takes the edge off the temperature, as the lightning bugs tell the universe a story in Morse code. I take a sip of wine and eat a cracker, stacked just right with salami and cheese. I have an olive and take another sip of wine—exactly what I needed.

I'm working on building another cracker stack when something catches my eye. It slinks across my lawn under the cover of shadow. Cayote, maybe. They aren't uncommon around here. Then I see it, leave the grass, and cling to the side of my house. About the size of a dog but with the speed and agility of a monkey, it clambers upward— heading for Em's room. As I slowly put the glass down, another one runs onto the deck and looks at me for a quick second, trying to decide if I'm a target. It decides not, snorts, hisses, and shoots up my siding.

Pushing the chair back slowly from the table, I keep an eye on my yard—where impossible shadows writhe—and move toward the side door. I bump into it, then I mumble under my breath, slap my right hand against the wall next to the door, and activate the reaper protocols. Then I take a breath and scramble to open the door as fast as I can and get it shut behind me before one of them breaches it.

No one knows where the reapers came from. The only thing they eat are eidola. We're pretty sure we know which came first. Some have speculated they found a way in from another plane. Sensed a food source once the eidola population increased to the point of being sensed. But that's hard to swallow since they aren't very bright. I think one smelled a single num num in the space between atoms, and the rest followed.

Reapers are like lizard dogs with armored plates down their backs and claws that can attach to anything. They communicate by making bird-like chirping sounds. They move fast and cooperatively, too. But it's less graceful and more like watching alligators run on land.

Em is where she's supposed to be, in the basement. Even though ghosts are non-corporeal and can move through objects like walls and floors, reapers are not. They're solid enough in this world that they can't go through stuff. Maybe it's the universe's way of leveling the playing field between predator and prey. Who knows. Either way, it helps, and that's why Em is down here. It's the hardest place to get to and the most defensible. Even down here, I can hear them tearing at the roof tiles. It's going to look like a tornado hit it before it's over.

Em has moved against the solid concrete wall that isn't exposed to the coal chute or the small ground-level window that I'm hoping they take a bit longer to find. Arbuckle is standing in front of her, his tail puffed, popping back and forth in staccato movements like a wind noodle, outside a used car lot—in a hurricane. I bolted the basement door from this side when I closed it. I bet there aren't many houses with dual surface bolts on the backside of their cellar door. I also doubt many cellar doors are made from solid wood.

The protocols I'd put into place would keep us safe for a little bit as the reapers worked their way through them. They'll have to sacrifice a quarter of the pack before they get in. Not that they'll mind doing that.

"How do you think they found me?" Em asks, her voice shaking—scared.

"I'm not sure, but the timing seems coincidental," I say. "Reapers attack just after we break off from the group. Not to mention they haven't found you once since you moved in here, and that was a decade ago. This was coordinated. It has to be Alistair."

"Aubrey," Em says as we hear a loud *pop*—like a giant bug zapper

frying something big—followed by a *thump*, which I hope is a dead reaper hitting the ground outside the small window.

"Yeah," I reply, scanning the ceiling, listening for any signs that
they've breached the outer defenses.

"I told you it was too easy," Arbuckle says.

"What do you mean?"

"He's tracking us somehow, feigned being trapped when you stole the
adornment. He's out there somewhere coordinating this."

Reaching into my pocket, I pull out the adornment. "What if he's
using this to track us? Why not send reapers to my aunt's house?"

"He was waiting until we were separated from the others," Arbuckle
says.

I let that sink in, making me mad and afraid. "And I gave him the
opening."

"What opening?" Em says.

"He's going after everyone else while he has us trapped here," I say,
trying to figure out what to do next.

"Can't we use the adornment to open a portal back to your aunt's
house to help them?" Arbuckle asks.

"Maybe, but he knows I still have it, and if he's using it to track us, I'd
rather not risk it. My biggest concern right now is the reapers. With the
quintessence inside you, you're as vulnerable as Em is."

"I know how to fight," Arbuckle says.

"So can they, and there's more of them. There's a solution here—I
know there is," I say, pacing. My mind filled with a hundred variables,
but no pattern to connect them.

"Revenants," Arbuckle says.

"What?" I say, stopping and staring at Arbuckle.

"Reapers eat eidola. The quintessence in me reads as eidola—"

"Your point?"

"Wouldn't reapers be attracted to revenants as well?" Arbuckle says.

"Yes, but most revenants these days end up in hospice, and those
buildings are deeply warded."

"Warded against reapers?" Em asks.

"Warded the way I wish this house could be," I say.

"If only we knew where a revenant hospice was," Arbuckle says, a wink in his voice.

∞

chapter ten

Dense and dull,
The Newts from Hell,
The Slimy Little Creepers.
The Clawing Jerks,
The Gnashing Teeth,
The Hellhounds known as—Reapers.

— Em

"The plan is simple. Don't die," I say out loud, as if it'll make a difference. Underpinning that overall goal is a series of other things that require some well-timed maneuvering.

Since the reapers haven't made it inside, Arbuckle and I head upstairs, where I pop the two bolts holding the door closed and crack it open a bit. My wards tell me the reapers aren't in yet. If they were, the inside of the house would be going off like the bridge of the *Enterprise* on Red Alert. There's an old saying in magic: 'Cocky gets you dead.' So, I'm getting a second opinion from my eyes and ears.

Since nothing appears to be moving in the kitchen, I open the door enough for Arbuckle and me to slip through. Closing it gently, I mumble under my breath, sliding the bolts into place on the other side. Em is going to stay in the basement, where it's safe. She'll join us once I get to the van and back it against the house's exterior. It's the best way to keep her exposure to a minimum.

Technically, there isn't much the reapers can do to me since I'm alive, and the universe doesn't allow them to go around killing living people. Otherwise, they'd be out there like Gila monsters in a bird's nest, sucking our quintessence out like yolk from an egg. Unfortunately, my uncle's quintessence inside Arbuckle is fair game. And even though I've seen Arbuckle's true form, I have yet to see it do him any physical good on this plane. So, he and I need to get to the van, and right now, I'm looking out on the deck where two reapers are prowling back and forth, waiting for their quarry to spook.

"Hey, man," I whisper to Arbuckle. "Can you see them?"

"Yes," he says in a shallow voice before he slinks low to the ground and moves so slowly I can barely tell he is.

"That's good in a way," I whisper. "Head for the back door and wait there."

He doesn't respond, but I see his body turn in that direction. I move out of the kitchen and edge down the hall into my office. It's admittedly a bad time to do some research, but I'd become complacent since meeting Em and warding the house a decade ago. Sure, I do regular maintenance to keep them primed, but I've never really made a contingency plan for trying to leave the house while it was surrounded. It's like buying a bear-proof cage to put your trash in but never really thinking about what you would do if one came into the house. Well, it's more like the opposite of that, but you get the point.

The book I'm looking for is relatively easy to find. It's sitting in the hamper from my uncle's. The book is a small tome called *Among the Eidola* by Lady Penelope Stanton. Considered to be a definitive work because Lady Penelope claimed to have lived with a small haunting in an abandoned abbey in Lancashire. She not only studied them but also the many encounters they had with reapers. There isn't much work on reapers for obvious reasons. Most eidola can't write things down, and most people can't see eidola. The book is a confluence of the right person, in the right place, at the right time.

Flipping through it, I look for anything to distract or divert the reapers outside. While I do, I hear a guttural growl from the kitchen.

Arbuckle. I stay low and move swiftly down the hall. My movements are careful so I don't attract any attention. When I get to the kitchen, Arbuckle's at the back door like I told him, but a reaper has gotten through the small back porch door, and the two of them are having a staring contest through the glass panel at its base. Arbuckle's back is arched, and he's making the distress call while the reaper growls like a hungry coyote.

The fact that it got onto the porch already tells me there are workarounds to my wards, which I suspected, but now I know for sure. Since it already sees Arbuckle, I dispense with caution and walk toward the door. It looks at me for a second but then returns its hungry gaze to the only thing it can eat.

"I guess we're going out this way," I say to Arbuckle, who backs away slowly from the door until he's behind me, continuing to growl between my legs at the reaper.

"Here it is," I say, finally finding what I'd been looking for. I look down at Arbuckle. "You know what reapers can't stand?"

"No, what?" Arbuckle says through his growl.

"Bells."

Arbuckle stops growling and stares up at me. "Really? Bells?"

"Yeah, bells."

"Do we have any bells?"

"Kind of," I say, throwing the book over my head while I retreat slowly down the hallway. Arbuckle keeps pace with me as we watch the reaper, bumping the glass panel with its snout, testing—each bump getting firmer and more forceful.

"Keep an eye on it," I say, stopping on the other side of a small storage closet. Opening it, I grab a bag of treats, shoving them into my pocket, then grab what I came for. "I got these when I got the harnesses and leashes. I was going to surprise you with it, but now is as good a time as any," I say, pulling a small, clear cellophane package from the closet.

"What is it?" says Arbuckle, his eyes now off the reaper and on the bag.

"They're little plastic balls you can chase around."

"Oh," Arbuckle says, his eyes getting wider.

"Guess what's inside the balls."

"Bells? Like the one Poly had?"

"That's the one," I say, ripping the package open, pulling out the three balls, and dropping the wrapper to the floor. Looking toward the reaper, I shake one, rattling the bell inside. At first, the reaper is more interested than worried, its head turned sideways until I start shaking all three and walking toward the door. Then I roll one down the floor where it bounces off, sending the bell sound through the glass pane. The reaper is gone, and I mean fast.

Picking up the one I tossed, I look out the door, scanning left and right for the reaper. It's five feet away, looking at me. It retreated, but it did not go far.

"Alright, bud," I say. "This will hopefully keep them at bay but not scare them that far off. But I have an idea that might keep you safe. Do you trust me?"

"Yes," says Arbuckle.

I lean down and hold one of the balls out. "See if you can grip this with your teeth. If you run with it like that, the tintinnabulation should be enough to keep them away."

Arbuckle takes a few tentative bites until he finally has a good grip on it with his teeth.

"Fanks," he says.

"I'm going to open the door on the count of three, and you run for the van, try get under it, and I'll open the driver's side door, and you can jump in, OK?"

Arbuckle nods, the little bell inside the ball letting out a *tinkle*.

"One," I mumble under my breath and unlock the door. "Two," I grab the knob with my right hand, the balls in my left. "Three," I throw open the door, and Arbuckle takes off across the small porch and down the steps— ringing all the way. I'm behind him, a ball in each hand, shaking them like churning butter in a mason jar.

The reaper that had been eyeing Arbuckle through the door has followed him to the van, actively trying to get at him. In all fairness, the bells are small, and the deterrent is minimal. However, I can still hear Arbuckle's little bell ringing out. It sounds like he's shaking his head furiously, and the reaper is still jumping like it's getting shocked with every *tinkle*.

I'm moving slower because part of the plan is to get the attention of all the reapers. So, that's what I'm working on. I'm turning as I go, counting them while the bells keep them at a distance. The sound also draws the attention of the ones further afield. I even see the one that made it onto the roof jump down and join the two on the deck. Another one comes around the side of the house shaking its head, so I assume it's the one the ward blew off the roof earlier.

To say that my hands and wrists are getting tired from shaking these balls would be an understatement. But it's working, and I now count nine reapers keeping their distance. They're all focused on me now, except for the one keeping Arbuckle trapped under the van. Before I walk around to the driver's side, I chuck one of the balls at it, and it reacts to getting hit in the head and then to the sound of the bell. It snaps up, slamming right into another one, who takes it as aggression, and they start fighting, rolling on the ground.

I get the key in the door and jerk it open. Arbuckle shoots from under the van and is up and in, followed by me as fast as I can. I slam the door as a reaper hits it head-on.

Cranking up the van, I don't even worry about looking in the rearview mirror as I hit the gas, dropping into reverse. I feel one of the reapers roll under the tires, but I keep going. Tearing up the grass, the van skids, its tire unable to get a grip. The grass is so high, it's turning slick, ground beneath the weight. Eventually, the tires grab ahold, and we lurch back as I turn the wheel, slamming into the house with the rear of the van. Arbuckle is up on the seat, keeping his eyes peeled.

"Go," he yells.

I glance in the rearview to see Em pushing through the fold-down seat. Cranking the van into first, I hit the gas, and we tear out of my yard, heading for the airport.

"Where are they?" I yell, trying to keep my eye on the road.

"Right behind us," says Em. "Gaining fast."

"How many?"

"I count nine," she says, which is what I was hoping for.

Reaching the gates, the airport is still open. *I mumble under my breath,* camouflaging the van, and mentally cross my fingers that it's a slow night on the tarmac. As we round the corner of the main hanger, a little Piper Cub takes off in the distance. I don't see anything else.

"Still on us?" I ask Em.

"Yes," she says, a little worried. I hear one hit the back door, sinking its claws in and climbing onto the van's roof.

The brakes squeal as I do a U-turn, giving me the most runway possible. I'm hoping the force of the turn won't knock the one on the roof off, and it doesn't. It somehow clings on, and the short period we spend slowing and turning allows a few more to catch up. I hold the van here, waiting for all of them. They're going to have to be close for this to work.

The van rocks as two more climb on. Arbuckle picks the bell up in his mouth, and I can see little drops of saliva fall from his lips as he holds it there. The ball keeps him from being able to swallow. I check the rearview. Em is tense, looking around at the sound of them latching on, climbing up, and securing themselves to the van—hoping to pry it open like a can of sardines.

Satisfied we've got them all, I hit the gas, and we rock forward. The weight of the reapers is affecting our speed. I've got the pedal to the floor, watching the needle on the speedometer climb.

"Come on, baby, hold together," I say, then, "Hold on," and *I mumble under my breath.* The van lurches ahead, given a short burst of additional speed by a focused gust of wind at our tail. The speedometer pushes forward, and I'm hoping to force this poor thing up to sixty-one. I've figured we always come up short on the destination because we're under speed. If I push it over slightly, I'm hoping we'll land beyond the point I'm aiming for.

Reaching out my right hand, I select the address on the GPS, while the speedometer keeps climbing. For a second, I wonder what it looks like outside as the camouflaged van with nine reapers clinging to it zips down the runway. The theme to the *Benny Hill Show* comes into my head as we reach sixty-one, I hit 'GO' and pull the red knob. I count to two and hit the brakes. *I mumble under my breath,* surrounding Em, Arbuckle, and me in a shield.

We come out of the Gloam, squealing across the lobby of The Township, slamming the driver's side of the van into the wall at the far end. This throws Arbuckle across the seat, but luckily, the shield takes the lion's share of the impact. *I mumble under my breath,* removing it from around us, and focusing it on Em. Climbing over the seat, I accidentally smack it with my foot, sending a shot of pain up my leg. I've never hit my shield before. It hurts.

I push open the door, shaking my bell, as Arbuckle jumps out with the bell in his mouth. We're looking around for reapers, but I don't see any. However, there is a fine mist of particulate in the air I don't remember from the last time I was here. At the end of the lobby, Bernice gives me that look again as she gets up from behind the reception desk.

"I know you didn't drive that van into my lobby from out of nowhere," she says, walking toward us.

"It wasn't nowhere," I say. "It was Knoxville." Being smart right now isn't exactly polite.

"If you're looking for those reapers, they're all gone. Incinerated the instant they appeared. We're a hospice, not a buffet. No reapers allowed."

I mumble under my breath and lower the shield around Em. Arbuckle drops his ball onto the floor, and so do I.

"Aubrey?" I hear Em say timidly from behind me.

"Yeah?" I say as I turn and see Em fading away.

"What's happening?" Her voice is panicked. She's looking at her hands as they disappear. She looks at me for a second and is gone.

"Em! Em!" I scream.

"What happened to Em?" I yell, turning to Bernice. "What happened to her?"

"Oh, she's gone," she says, still walking and flipping her right hand at us in a scooting motion. "Did you think you could pop into a warded revenant hospice with a ghost?"

"She's an eidolon," I protest for some reason, like it'll make a difference.

"You can call her a popsicle, but it won't make no difference," Bernice says, almost to the van now.

"What harm could she have done?" I plead, not understanding why Em is gone.

"You think they warded this place with exceptions? You think your ghost was going to be safe?"

"I don't even understand why it's warded against eidola in the first place."

Bernice stops and looks at me like she's met an alien for the first time. "Where'd you think poltergeists come from, genius? A stork flies them through a window so they can possess a house?"

In the haste to save Em, I'd forgotten.

"They come from revenants. About five percent of the time, what's left of their quintessence finally splits away from their decomposed corpse. But now it's deteriorated, angry, mean, and plain ugly." Bernice makes a smug snort.

"But Em isn't a poltergeist," I say, the energy draining from me with each passing minute. I sit heavily on the edge of the open van door. Arbuckle jumps up next to me. I look up at Bernice, pleading, "She's a nineteenth-century poet."

"That's the most irrelevant thing you've said so far. Eidolon, ghost, poltergeist, wraith, phantom, specter. Those are words. They might seem different to you, but not to the state." She pauses, looking me over, shaking her head. "I should have known you were a little screwy when you tried to sneak out of here with that stage one revenant. You looked silly as hell, carrying him around thinking he was glamoured. You can't glamour nothing I can't see for real."

With this, she looks over at Arbuckle, then looks at me, holds her hand up perpendicular to her face, and hides her other hand as she points in his direction. "That ain't no cat, neither," she whispers, laughing. She drops her hands and looks at him like he might change when she does. "He's cute, though."

"If you knew I was leaving with a revenant, why didn't you stop me?"

"That's security. I'm reception."

"Why didn't you call security?"

"He retired. They haven't replaced him yet," Bernice shrugs. "Cutbacks." She pauses, then walks off. "Anyway, all ghosts who apparate in this building get a one-way ticket to subbasement six."

"What?" I say, my spirits suddenly lifting. "So, she's not dead?"

"She was dead when you brought her in here," she yells over her shoulder.

"You know what I mean."

"If you mean, has she evaporated? No, of course not," Bernice turns and gives me that side-eye again. "Do you even know the definition of hospice?"

"How do I get to subbasement six?" I ask, standing up, ready to get Em.

"Why would you want to go there? There ain't nothing but poltergeists down there, packed in like fart spray in a can," she says dismissively, having given up on dealing with me. She turns and walks away.

"I need to get Em," I yell, and it echoes a bit in the empty lobby.

"Then you better sign your ass in," she says, heading to the desk. "And you better figure out how you're getting that van out of my lobby."

I look at Arbuckle, who is cleaning his face, and step into the van. He catches me out of the corner of his eye, makes a few more passes on his nose with his paw, and jumps up to join me.

"I want you to—" I start to say, but he doesn't let me finish.

"Stay here. Sounds good," he says.

"You aren't going to argue with me?"

"Why would I? We wouldn't be able to communicate, and I hate poltergeists."

"That's fair," I say. "Try and think how we'll get the van out."

"I already have an idea."

"Good," I say, climbing out.

"I'll be back as soon as I get Em."

"Try and hurry, Aubrey. There's no telling what Alistair is doing, and this little detour could cost lives."

"I know," I say, heading to the reception desk, racked with guilt for all the stupid things I've done this week. Hell, all the stupid things I've ever done. Losing Em won't be one of them, at least not losing her permanently. I'm the reason she's in the subbasement in the first place. I should have left her at the house, where she'd probably still be safe.

I sign my name and date it. Bernice swivels the book around and hands me a maintenance pass.

"I could get fired for this."

"I'll tell you what. If they fire you, I'll hire you."

"I ain't cheap."

"Never said you were."

"The pass accesses the elevator. I've limited it to subbasement six, so don't try and go anywhere else."

"Cross my heart," I say, making the gesture.

"Mm-hmm," she replies, and I'm pretty sure it's sarcastic.

Across the lobby, I tap the pass on the elevator's keypad and listen as the motor kicks in.

"If I don't survive, enjoy Oklahoma City," I say to Arbuckle.

He doesn't say anything because he can't, and as the door opens and I step in, I hear Bernice yell to me across the lobby.

"You got a flashlight?"

"Why do I need a flashlight?" I yell.

"There's no lights down there," she yells, and I hear her laugh as the doors close.

I mumble under my breath and conjure the fireball as the elevator counts off the floors with dings, illuminating the floor indicators. The ride music is Herb Alpert and the Tijuana Brass performing *Spanish Flea*, a surprisingly upbeat tune for a descent into a dark subbasement full of malevolent spirits.

As the elevator comes to a halt, it jostles me for a second before the door opens, illuminating a space about twenty feet square just beyond. I pause and listen but don't hear or see anything, so I step out. As the door closes behind me and the light from the elevator slowly fades, I'm left alone.

"Em?" I yell. The cavernous echoes return to me.

The subbasement must encompass the entire footprint of the building.

"Em?" I yell louder this time, and so does the echo.

Growing the fireball, I hold it in front of me as I walk deeper into the space.

"Aubrey!" I hear her voice call to me, her distance immeasurable.

"Hang on, Em, I'm coming," I yell, stepping forward. Suddenly, something screams past me, snuffing out the light of my fireball and pitching me into blackness.

"Aubrey!" Em yells again, but now her voice is to my left.

"Don't move, Em. Stay where you are, and let me come to you."

"That wasn't me," I hear from my right.

"I'm here," this voice rings out from behind me. Even though I know the elevator is less than ten paces away, her voice sounds as though it's a football field away.

I conjure the fireball again, revealing a hideous face—its flesh fallen from most of its skull, ravaged by decomposition. I step back as my flame is once again extinguished.

This time, *I mumble under my breath,* calling up the shield before I conjure the flame. Let's see them get through that. Something brushes against my back leg. How is that possible? Unless I've somehow trapped one inside the shield with me. I turn and hold out the flame. At my feet, Arbuckle stares up at me.

"I told you to stay with Van," I say, unsure how he got here.

"I did," he answers.

"Then how are you here?"

"I died," he says. "And you weren't there to save me. You were down here, saving your girlfriend."

"She's not my girlfriend," I respond, knowing there's truth in his statement, but wishing she wasn't a ghost, and that we had a life together. That isn't something to think about now.

"Isn't she? The way you think about her all the time, the things you do when no one is looking," it says. The irises of its little eyes open full and round. "You think we can't see what you do in the dark?"

"Shut up. You're not Arbuckle. Cats don't have quintessence."

"Yours does," it says, now my uncle. The rune on his forehead oozes blood. He smiles and blows out my fireball. Something touches my face.

"Do you want me to be your girlfriend?" it asks, in Em's voice.

When I try to knock the hand away, I end up slapping myself. I hear it laugh and feel it touch the inside of my leg. It slides upward. *I mumble under my breath,* gulping air as I make a small opening in the shield, hoping to force it out with the air rushing through. I bring the outer edges so close I can feel the shield hug me, waiting even after it constricts around me like a second skin. I know I can't stay this way for long, because the only air in here to breathe is what I have in my lungs.

As I exhale, I mumble under my breath, conjure a tiny fireball, and push it through the small opening as it closes. I expand the shield until it has a twenty-foot diameter, with me at the center, and I call the fireball back to me, wrapping my shield in flame.

"Em?" I yell as I push through an onslaught of poltergeists trying to get to me—laughing, moaning, and screaming as they slam into the shield like insects into a light bulb.

I'm attracting them all now; their presence has weight, making movement an effort, like wading a beach ball through Jell-O. Bernice wasn't kidding—this place is packed. The sound of their torment is almost deafening as I yell out Em's name again. It's too much.

I don't know how I'll find her in this quagmire of noncorporeal quintessence. All the forward momentum—the drive to save her—drains away from me. I'm not half as good at this as my uncle was. He would've had a solution before the elevator even touched the ground. I try to think of what he would've done, but so much time has passed, he's become a feeling more than a memory. And I realize that's on me too. I chose to leave, he chose not to find me, and I let him—another of his sacrifices to keep me safe.

Once again, I'm proving that I am not worthy. Once again, I'm failing to achieve anything. I keep pressing forward, no longer sure why, feeling more alone with each step. Trapped in my bubble, I push through the darkness, my light diminishing.

Around me, they swirl—mocking, belittling, disparaging me. A cacophony of ridicule muddles my brain. They all use her voice. But still, I press on, one step at a time, my prison moving with me. Each hit they land shrinks my shield as they drain energy from it.

"Em!" I call out one last time and hear it echo into the cavernous space.

Nothing.

Then, from the darkness, I hear her voice. There's something different about it now. The words are not mocking, lascivious, belittling, or cruel. They are her words—her verse, her magic—and they call to me.

"I can wade grief,"

I close my eyes.

"Whole pools of it,—"
And let her words guide me.
"I'm used to that."
Strength returns to me.
"But the least push of joy"
The phantasmagoria gives.
"Breaks up my feet,"
I push forward.
"And I tip—drunken."
My steps grow surer.
"Let no pebble smile,"
Every word a lifeline.
"'Twas the new liquor,—"
I laugh.
"That was all!"
Warm tears roll down my face.
"Power is only pain,"
I continue pushing.
"Stranded, through discipline,"
Forward.
"Till weights will hang."
I open my eyes.
"Give balm to giants,"
The path before me illuminates.
"And they'll wilt, like men."
She stands before me, glowing, keeping the demons away.
"Give Himmaleh,—" her hands outstretched.
I mumble under my breath, extending the shield of fire around her.
"They'll carry him!"
She walks toward me, smiling.
"I thought I had lost you," is all I say.

Em reaches toward me, and I close my eyes. I feel her thumb wipe a tear from my face.

I snuffle, take a deep breath, and open my eyes. "I liked that poem a lot."

Em smiles. "You ready to get out of here?"

"Yes, ma'am. Stay close."

Em places her hand on my shoulder as we turn toward the elevator—this time, I feel it.

I mumble under my breath, bring my hands up, extend the shield, and we walk together across the divide. The calls and jeers, quiet now—they know they have no power here in the bubble that envelops us. I shrink the shield as the elevator opens, and we walk in.

"I'm sorry Em," I say, unable to meet her eyes.

"For what?"

I sigh, releasing the tension I've been carrying. "For almost getting you killed." I refuse to wipe the sadness from my face.

Em's fingers touch my chin as she motions for me to look up, so I do.

"I'm already dead, silly," she says, smiling. "But I appreciate you not leaving me there."

I laugh a cry, punch the button for the lobby, and I mumble under my breath, making sure the building's wards no longer see her. We ride in silence until the elevator dings, indicating the lobby.

Stepping out, I deploy a wardstealer to crib the ward that vaporized the reapers.

"I'll never let anything else happen to you," I say.

"Don't be stupid, Aubrey," she says, stepping off the elevator. "That'll get you killed."

Arbuckle is at the receptionist's desk, getting scratched by Bernice. I give her the keycard and sign us out.

"You must be one powerful wizard to get out of subbasement six alive," Bernice says.

"You thought I was going to die?"

"Why else do you think I gave you access?"

"Thanks for believing in me."

"Why should I have believed in you? You didn't even believe in yourself. Now go on, take your cat and your girlfriend, and get out of my lobby."

"Thanks, Bernice."

"I'm not his girlfriend," Em says.

"Tell him that," I hear Bernice say, but I ignore it as I'm halfway across the lobby, Arbuckle plodding beside me.

Closing the side door, I climb into the front passenger side, brushing the window glass off the driver's seat before scooching onto it. Em slides into the back, and Arbuckle jumps into the passenger seat.

"Stay away from the closing doors," I say, as *I mumble under my breath* and pull it shut.

I put the key in the ignition and cross my fingers. The van turns over, but it sounds awful—like a dying mammal. I push gently on the gas, and the whole thing squeals as I turn it perpendicular to the wall, where there's now a van-sized depression.

"Well, I guess we're about to find out how far we can get at five miles an hour."

I input my aunt's address, hit the gas, press 'GO,' and pull the red lever—right before we hit the opposite wall.

We get disgorged a few miles east onto a baseball field as the van gasps and spits black smoke out the back.

"I'm pretty sure it died," I announce, and no one responds. "We're going to have to use the adornment to get home, and I'm not sure how safe it is traveling that distance."

"We'll never know until we try," Arbuckle says.

The first thing I do is detach the license plate. Then I open the engine compartment and remove the VIN plate, followed by the one on the left front part of the dash. I had to Google how to find it, which allowed me to know there were two. I stuff the leashes and harnesses from the glove box into my side pockets.

I no longer care if anyone sees us. They'd only see Arbuckle and me anyway—and who'd believe it? But before we go, I have one more thing I want to check. It's been bugging me since we first took the van into the Gloam.

Climbing up into the driver's seat, I reach across and grab the red knob and pull it. Since we're not moving forward, I assume the van won't pass through—and I'm right—but the curtain's there, sitting about two feet from the front. Jumping down, I walk around to see what's creating it.

Arbuckle and Em are staring at the front of the van, not the curtain.

Where the VW logo should be is a hole, and sticking out of the hole is a rod with a three-pronged grip on it. Grasped in the grip's metal fingers is a sphere, about the size of a bowling ball.

I walk up to it and touch it with my fingers to test the temperature. It's cold as ice, and the longer it sits exposed, the more it frosts over in the humid Oklahoma air. The sphere is translucent, and something is moving inside it. Whatever's in there is getting agitated.

I mumble under my breath the reveal spell, and what I see makes me angry and sad.

Em gasps audibly, and Arbuckle backs up, slouching low to the ground and moving slowly backward. There's an eidolon in there, encased in the orb. That's what's opening the curtain—like Em had when she slipped through, escaping the reapers in Amherst. My uncle had imprisoned someone here so he could drive his van through the Gloam.

What price is this toll road? I'd been using it. I should have asked the question first. I should have investigated. Instead, I'm complicit in this exploitation.

The fact that it could open a curtain at any time to anywhere meant that my uncle had also found a way to untether it from its place. I hesitate to wonder how he had done that. I'm also having a hard time understanding why he had done it. Whoever was trapped in here must have pissed him off—but even so, I still have a hard time imagining my uncle being this cruel.

"You have to free them, Aubrey," Em pleads.

"Don't worry," I say. "That's what I'm going to do. But not here. Whoever this is, they've been trapped in this thing for a long time. They've probably gone mad. They can wait until I figure out the best way to do it."

"Why weren't they taken with me to the subbasement at The Township?"

"If I had to guess, it's because this orb is a vessel. It makes them appear corporeal to the wards."

I pull the leashes out of my pocket, making a cradle knot around the orb. Pulling it taut, I reach behind it and pull the pin, keeping the claw grip locked around it. I can feel the cold coming off it as I carry it away from the van.

"Let's all think about my aunt's backyard, in case it helps," I say—even though my intent should be enough to get us close. And I have intent in spades. Intent to get Arbuckle and Em home safe. Intent to put an end to Alistair. And most importantly, the intent to get back to my boring life.

I pull the adornment out of my pocket, cut a slash in the air, and we all step through.

∞

chapter eleven

Taut and Stern,
The Teacher's Pet,
The Acumen of Guileless.
The Muscle Tone,
The Midnight Coat,
The Senior Statesman—Silas.

—ALD
transcribed by AC

We exit the rift quietly, and I seal it behind us. We're not passing through the Gloam as I had thought. Shades do because they're cutting through from the other side— that's an actual rift between the planes. When I use the adornment, like Alistair, it's like accessing the membrane surrounding the Gloam. Stepping through, we skip off it like a stone across a pond. Where we stop has everything to do with intent.

Being my first time, we ended up farther from my aunt's house than I'd hoped, but it's not bad for a first try. Not to mention that being a half mile away could be an advantage if Alistair is tracking us. Either way, I drop the adornment, the license plate, and the VIN plates into a drain grate near a cross street and memorize the street name—Gratz. I have no idea what that is. Maybe it's a person, a last name? I don't have time to puzzle it out, but it's memorable enough.

If I survive this, I'll retrieve the adornment. Otherwise, it can sit in the city's stormwater system for eternity. There's no way it's staying in my pocket and giving Alistair the upper hand.

"You need to go home, Em. There aren't any reapers left."

"How do you know? Besides, I'm not leaving," she says.

"The wards—they'd be going off in my head instead of this headache if they were still around. You'll be safer there."

"What do you expect me to do? Sit at home and wait for you to return from the war? I won't do that again," she says.

"Alistair will leverage you against me," I say, looking away from her. "I won't be able to resist that. I care about you, Em."

"I know you do, Aubrey, and I appreciate that. The world isn't so lonely with you in it. But I'm not sitting it out this time."

"OK," I say, then look at her—just in case it's the last time. "Maybe we can work on a poem together when it's over," I say. "I don't know much about it, but I'd like to learn."

"I'd be happy to teach you," she says.

I watch her grab the sides of her dress, hiking the hem—marching down the street toward the house.

"Who's coming?" she yells over her shoulder.

"She doesn't even have to do that," I say to Arbuckle, who runs after her.

Following behind, I switch the orb to my other hand so my fingers don't freeze off.

The closer we get, the darker it becomes—before I realize the street her house is on has lost power. Turning down the side street, I crane my neck toward the front of the house, where I see a quick bright blue flash of lightning inside. Mia.

Running, I turn down the maintenance road, stopping at the back gate to the smell of burning wood. The oak is smoldering. It hasn't burned down, but it's taken some damage. Unlatching the gate, I step through, Arbuckle skirting by me, low to the ground—going wide on the grass toward the back door. I take the opposite side and hedge closer to the oak. Em heads straight, like nothing can hurt her—even though plenty of things can.

"Em, slow down, wait for us," I whisper-yell, but she's ignoring me, making rash decisions because I asked her to go home.

Hollis is leaning against the base of the tree. He looks injured but not dead, I think, because he appears to be breathing and emitting a faint glow. I have no idea what it takes to kill a tree sprite, but I bet it's a lot. Kneeling beside him, the smell is earthy and sweet, like a smoke pit. I shake his shoulder lightly, trying to rouse him. The more I know about what's inside, the better off I'll be.

It takes a second before he comes to—his eyelids open, and he smiles.

"Aubrey, glad you could make it."

"Sorry I'm late." I try to smile. "He ambushed us with reapers at my place. We had to take a detour to shake them."

"Better late than never." He winces in pain.

"You OK?" I ask, looking to see if I can find anything that resembles a wound.

"I'll survive if the tree does." His smile is weak, and he starts coughing. He spits a thick amber wad of something onto the ground.

"How long ago did Alistair attack?"

His eyes go wide as he grabs my arm—looking half-dead—but his grip is still like a gorilla trying to give me an Indian burn.

"Not Alistair—Mia."

"Mia?" I stand up, looking toward the house. Em has gone inside, but Arbuckle is waiting for me, crouched at the far-right side of the back porch.

"Hang tight," I say, clapping him on the shoulder, and he nods.

Moving as quietly as I can around the tree and staring at Arbuckle to get his attention, I indicate he needs to stay low as I run for the far-left edge of the porch. My calves burn almost immediately as I squat, but I give up and stand—unused muscles screaming. Waving Arbuckle over, I'm mad at myself for being so out of shape. He jumps onto the porch and walks to my side.

"Hollis says it's Mia," I tell him. "I have no idea why or how, but that may mean Saoirse is compromised too, or under some spell. I'd rather they not die before we figure it out, but looking at Hollis and seeing what she did in the park in Utah, I'm sure I'm outgunned. The closest thing I have to useful is my stupid fireball, so if we go in, we may not come out, is all I'm saying."

Arbuckle, listening intently, walks over and bonks me on the head in answer.

"In we go, then," I say, standing and switching the orb from my right hand to my left. I brush myself off with my right hand and pull Francis's wand from inside my jacket. I swish it around a few times like I know what I'm doing and head up the stairs to the back door.

"Stay close to me," I say to Arbuckle, who's at my feet. I mumble under my breath, running a shield around us. Using the wand, I break off the piece close to Arbuckle so he's autonomous. I reach for the knob, but the door is ajar, so I push it with my foot and peek inside. The kitchen is quiet, so I make my way across, with Arbuckle staying close.

I'm holding the wand like I'm about to conduct a symphony. It gives me a level of confidence I haven't felt before. I feel strong, powerful, and prepared. It's a stick—like a stylus on a phone—adding accuracy you wouldn't have without it. Maybe that's what I've been lacking: a level of accuracy.

The parlor has been turned upside down, and I see Alexander lying still under an overturned chair. We go to him, and I use the wand to break off another piece of the shield and place it around him. I can see his side rise and fall gently, giving me some sense of relief. Pulling the treats from my pocket, I shake a few out, pushing them through the shield with the wand, leaving them on the floor near Alexander's nose. At first, there's no reaction, but then his nose twitches. Then it twitches again, and his eyes pop open. I'm pretty sure he's eating the treats before he's even conscious.

"Hey," Arbuckle says, "What about me?"

I shake a few more out and shove them through Arbuckle's shield too.

Standing up, I notice Monvoisin standing at the door to the parlor, appearing from nowhere. She's staring at the treat bag. Shaking my head, I give her some too, popping off a small shield for her as well.

"Where are Jonathan and Mia?" I ask, as something—or someone—hits the floor above us with a *thud*.

"You all stay here," I say, putting the orb down and running up the stairs.

I point the wand in front of me as I wind my way up, unsure what kind of spell I'll use if I get into trouble. I feel better, though, holding it like it might go off unannounced. Reaching the top of the stairs, I see Augustus. He looks like he's been slung across the room and hit the wall hard. His breathing is shallow, and I don't have time to do much more than surround him with a shield before Jonathan is blown out of the master suite and across the hall.

He lands hard, and I hear his hip break as the wind is knocked out of him. Bringing the wand up, I move to his side, keeping my eyes on the door to the bedroom. I extend my shield around him.

"Johnathan, can you hear me?"

His eyes barely open as he takes a hitched breath.

"You came back," he says. "Augustus said you would. I don't know how it happened," he says, before he goes into a fit of coughing, and I see blood trickle from his mouth as he tries to get up. He screams in pain and lies back down. Augustus is trying to crawl to him, so I grab him, bring him into my shield, and move him to Jonathan so they can be together.

"What happened to Mia?" I ask.

"One minute she was fine, and the next she was attacking everyone." Jonathan grabs me by the arm, straining to say something else. His eyes go wide, and he stares me in the face.

"Hollis," he says, before his grip loosens. I watch him let go, closing his eyes as his chest drops, and he goes still.

I put my hand on Jonathan's neck—no pulse.

"What about Hollis?" I say.

"We came for you," Augustus says. "Don't let it be for nothing."

"I didn't ask you to," I say, standing up and watching as Jonathan's gossamer quintessence lifts from his body and enters Augustus.

The rest of the cats have arrived and are crouched on the step below the landing. Augustus joins them, and they huddle close.

"It's almost time, Aubrey," Arbuckle says from behind me.

I turn to look at him. "Time for what?" I ask.

"When Mia falls, the pact will be fulfilled."

"I don't know what that means."

"It means we will all be together at last."

"I'm not going to kill her."

"She'd want you to."

"Not happening. I'm not a killer."

"But you are the one we swore to protect, and Alistair is still out there. He's the one controlling Mia."

Turning toward the master suite, gripping the wand like my life depends on it, I walk through the shield wall—taking a piece of it with me. As I reach the door, the room is flooded with green light. I see Mia, her staff out full, blocking another rift. I assume it must be Alistair, who's found a way through, but I can't tell—Mia's spell is too dense to see through.

"Mia," I say, bringing the wand up.

Mia looks at me over her shoulder and yells, "You came back."

"I surprised even myself," I say, before she stops casting and turns her staff on me.

It was all an illusion. There wasn't anyone trying to come through a rift. She was making an illusion—for my sake.

"You need to run, Aubrey," she says, stepping toward me. "I'm not myself."

I can see her fighting it—whatever it is.

"How is Alistair doing this to you?" I say, keeping my wand pointed at her and remembering how my great-aunt looked—still and composed—under Alistair's spell in my uncle's memories.

"Going to hit me with a fireball?" she says mockingly. "Or maybe unlock something with a knocking spell?"

It's not Mia anymore.

"You're the worst wizard I've ever encountered," she says, trying to goad me into doing something stupid. "What do you know—like five whole susurrations? What a disappointment."

"You know, I wasn't disappointing anyone but myself until about a week ago," I say. "Then suddenly, for reasons I'm still not sure of, my brother reappeared, killed my uncle and Jane, and started a chain of events with no useful purpose to them."

"It got you here, didn't it?"

"But I'm a disappointment, aren't I? And what could you possibly want with the cats?"

"It's not the cats, you ignorant rube," she says, before putting her staff under her chin. Her eyes go sad, and she looks at me one last time. She's herself again. I can tell.

"It's the quintessence, Aubrey—the collected power of the order. You have to stop him."

"How's he doing this?"

She never answers me. A bolt of blue energy cuts through her head, leaving a scar of ash on the ceiling. Mia's body hits the floor as I run to her, screaming. I watch her gossamer quintessence leave her body.

Suddenly, all the cats are in the room, ricocheting off the bed, the side table, even the walls. It's like someone knocked a jar of superballs off a table—their shields intensifying the bounce. Something spooked them.

I turn and level the wand at the door, where Hollis strides in, holding Saoirse by the scruff of her neck. He holds her out like a catcher's mitt, claiming his final prize as Mia's quintessence flows into her.

"Whew," Hollis says. "That was a hoot."

The adrenaline washes away my aches and pains, filling me with focus, and I'm on my feet like I'm twenty again, bringing the wand to bear on Hollis. I start to mumble under my breath as he plays a note on his branch flute—which I hadn't noticed in his other hand—and I feel my throat catch.

I try again, and now I can't even move my tongue. Then all my muscles go rigid, and I freeze.

"Shouldn't have had so much of that acorn tea," he says, smiling. "It heals, for sure, but it also leaves enough tannins in your system for me to play you like a monkey plays a peanut."

Hollis drops Saoirse onto the floor. She lands on her feet, but she doesn't run. She stays where she is as he walks toward me.

"I put some in the half-and-half too," he says, reaching out and taking the wand from my hand before picking up Mia's staff. "So many wizard sticks lying all over the place."

He turns and heads for the door.

"Come on," he says, and we follow him.

* * *

If you guessed we're all in the basement, you're right. Like I said before, weird things happen in basements, and this is no exception. And when I say "all," I'm not including Em, who I haven't seen since we entered the house. I'm glad for that, in many ways—having no desire for her to see whatever Hollis is planning.

Arbuckle, Augustus, Alexander, Monvoisin, Poly, Saoirse, and I are all standing together, shields down, while a tree sprite controls us with his magic acorn tannins. It is, to be honest, embarrassing. It's also the first time I've realized that three cats' names begin with an "A," and I have no idea why. Funny, what we think about when we should be contemplating something else—like how to get out of this situation.

Hollis has us all collected at the base of the stairs. Crossing the room, holding his hand up like he's performing a ritual, he plays another little tune on his flute. The ground vibrates, and a tree root breaks through the foundation like a hot knife through butter. That one is followed by many more, and I watch as they thread through the room, weaving a dark brown, regal throne together.

While all this is happening, I watch Hollis remove his clothes as his skin hardens, taking on a bark-like texture. I'm relieved to see he has a doll's crotch, so I don't have to endure some twisted Pinocchio-style display in case he lies. Once all his clothes are off, and he's turned into something like a humanoid tree, he can't help but sit on the newly finished throne.

"I told you the roots run deep," he says, as water sprouts break from him to form a woven crown, which is placed gently on his head.

"That's better," he says.

I'm trying hard to break whatever hold he has over me so I can toss a few good zingers his way, but I'm not having any luck. I can barely move my eyes back and forth.

"Admittedly, for a while there, I wasn't sure you'd pull it off. All those people scattered all over, and their cats." Hollis stands and walks across the room toward me. "I couldn't do it myself, you see, because I'm attached to my tree—rooted to this place, if you will. But you, timid adventurer, tepid explorer, mediocre wizard." He says these things while gesticulating like he's performing a long-practiced speech. "You bungled your way right through it, marvelously. I must admit, you gave me a bit of a scare with Francis. Poor, living-dead Francis. But then your little girlfriend—whew! Quite a last-minute Hail Mary to a touchdown."

She's not my girlfriend, I try to say, but nothing comes out except spittle that drips down my chin.

"Oh, and good thing I gave you that acorn, so Alistair didn't kill you before you'd finished. He's more unpredictable than I thought he'd be. He got the ball rolling but then failed to bring me anything useful. Took him too long to figure out it was the cats. By that time, he didn't seem to care about fulfilling our bargain. He wanted to kill everyone. Thanks again for trapping him in that little hideout of his. Maybe I'll go see him when we're done here."

Hollis cups his hand over his ear, acting like he's trying to hear me.

"What's that? How can I leave this place? Aren't I attached to my tree?"

He drops his arms, miming sadness.

"It's true—poor old Hollis, stuck to his tree. If only there were a way to, I don't know, absorb enough quintessence to give him autonomy in the human world, like a real boy."

He spreads his arms, approaching us, then bends and counts the cats.

"One... two... three... four... five... six." He stops, looking at me.

"Looks like one's missing. Your daddy's cat. The one that slinked away in shame. He did, however, plant the seed that will turn my little defeat into a victory again. The pact they made that night—the one to keep little Aubrey safe. The one that brings us all together today. Admittedly, this all took longer than I had hoped, but what's a little time between friends?"

He puts the branch flute to his lips and plays a little tune. It sounds like sap boiling after lightning strikes a tree, and I wish I could cover my ears as the foundation before us cracks open and a large tuber, wrapped in roots, pushes through. The roots place the tuber on the floor and retreat into the earth.

What looked solid at first begins to writhe, as whatever's inside fights against the inner membrane like a snake hatching. Hollis reaches out and uses the sharp tip of his finger to pierce the rubbery shell. It splits, spilling amber sap across the floor as it disgorges Silas, his fur caked to his skin. He retches and vomits more sap—thinner, like amniotic fluid.

"Ta-da!" Hollis makes a grand gesture. "Look what I found. Poor thing must have gotten lost."

To say this is the moment I finally understand how long this plan has been in the making is an understatement. Hollis had Silas imprisoned since the night my father died. He was the phantom in the memories, having erased himself somehow from everyone's mind—like he did Alistair all those years ago when he kidnapped him and forced my aunt to raise him.

He controlled Alistair—and her—the night he tried to replace everyone's quintessence with shadow energy. Alistair would have gotten a group of shadow wizards to lead, and Hollis would have gotten their quintessence so he could break free from his tree. I had to guess he'd also called the shadow energy into my mother in the first place. Maybe as an experiment. Or maybe he'd known exactly what he was doing.

Picking up Silas, still hacking up sap, Hollis puts him on the floor closer to the other cats.

"A bit sticky, but he seems okay," he says.

Silas slumps against the concrete like all his bones are missing.

"All together again. Shouldn't take long now," Hollis says, backing up to take in this little clowder of interdimensional water bears.

I'm a bit confused about exactly what the pact is about. I mean, I understood that they were trying to preserve themselves in case Alistair or Hollis returned, but now, here we are—all trapped, with Hollis in control. Maybe a part was missing. Maybe it was never going to work. Maybe I came by my incompetence naturally. Wouldn't that be grand? We get to the end, and I find out we were all a bunch of failures.

That's when it happens—while I'm still arguing with the voices in my head, the ones always quick to let me know what I've done wrong and how stupid I am. The voices that make sure I rarely feel good about anything. The voices that keep me in place. That's when the air around me fires off little sparks of green light, and I can feel the stubble on the top of my head stand up straight.

"Here it comes," Hollis says, clapping his hands.

He turns on me, and before I even know what's happening, one of his vines runs me through, pinning me to the wall—still controlled—the scream of pain caught in my throat as I feel the blood seeping from my chest.

"Hold still, Aubrey. You're just the catalyst. I'm the vessel," I hear him say, distantly.

My bladder releases, and I don't care—my heart racing now, cold sweat dripping down my forehead, warm piss filling my shoes. I want to throw up, but I can't.

Through my tears, I see Hollis pull out his flute again.

"Here kitty, kitty, kitty," he says, before putting it in his mouth and blowing a high-pitched note that rises from within my range of hearing to beyond it.

For a second, I can move my head a little—his attention off me and on whatever is about to happen. Looking down, I see the cats getting up, walking in little circles like iron filings controlled by a magnet. Coming to a stop, they face each other—a kind of seven-point asterisk. Their quintessence rises from them, trailing upward and braiding together.

Hollis drops his hands from the flute—still blowing the note—and reaches into his chest, splitting the bark aside and exposing a dark black knot in the pale pulp, positioned like a human heart. His eyes go wide in anticipation. The combined quintessence rises, weaving back and forth like it's being charmed.

Behind me, I hear the cat flap first—then something heavy hits the first stair and rolls toward the next. Each thunk is louder than the last, and each one quicker as it picks up speed: *thunk, thunk, thunk, thunk, thunk,* coming down the stairs.

It takes a great deal of effort to turn my head enough to see the orb from the van hit the concrete floor at the bottom. It rolls a few inches and comes to a stop. The eidolon inside is swirling, beating itself against the glass. Blinking to clear my vision, I finally see it—right on the side of the orb—a crack spiraling out like a spider's web.

I look at Hollis to see if he noticed, but he's still blowing that note and holding his chest open. Beside me, the combined quintessence rises, weaving like smoke, like magic, like something divine. Without thinking about it, I lick my lips and realize—

Hollis can't control the quintessence and me at the same time.

I still can't move my arms or legs, but I can move my tongue and lips.

I mumble under my breath and do the only thing I can think to do. Behind me, the crack in the orb grows, and I see the eidolon inside whirling faster, aware of what's about to happen. It's about to be set free. I don't know how long it's been trapped in there, but if I had to guess, I'd say close to thirty years. Thirty years imprisoned. Plenty of time to go rotten.

The orb doesn't crack open like an egg—it explodes, shattering into a fine dust that peppers the room. I barely have time to shut my eyes before I'm hit. The eidolon, born again, broken and bitter, now a poltergeist of decayed quintessence, screams in rage and flies toward the source of the sound—the flute. It calls to it, too.

Hollis doesn't have time to react. The eidolon dives straight into his chest, right into the knot. Hollis screams, his hands releasing his bark-like skin as it seals shut again, locking the fetid thing inside.

Control returns to my body, and I try to take a step, but I fall to my knees instead, sliding down the vine that still pierces me. My scream joins Hollis's as I thrust a fireball from my hand. *I mumble under my breath* and cast a flaming shield around myself and the cats.

At that moment, the combined quintessence enters me—and the shield isn't the only thing on fire. I take a breath, my eyes dilating as the scene before me—Hollis screaming, the malevolent quintessence spreading through him like tar, rotting him and his tree from the inside—flares to white.

* * *

I'm surrounded by blinding light, a whiteness so pure it makes my head hurt. From this light, step seven forms. The Defenders of the Autumn Light, minus my mother, and joined now by my great-aunt. Standing directly in front of me is my father, like he was when he died. I feel overwhelmed. I have so much I want to tell him and ask him. I try and speak, but the words catch in my mouth.

Reaching out my father places his hand on my shoulder, and I feel it. "I'd hoped we'd have more time," he says.

"Me too," I say.

"The house is collapsing, Aubrey. You need to wake up."

"I'm pretty sure I'm dead already," I say. "Maybe I'll just stay here."

"There is no 'here,'" Aubrey. We're in you, and if you die, that's the end of us."

"Figures," I say.

* * *

The whole place is shaking when I come to. The cats are dazed. I'm on my knees, and when I look down, the vine running through me is limp and soft like boiled asparagus. Grabbing it with both hands, I break it off in front and reach behind me, slowly pulling it through, screaming with each tug until it's out. Close to passing out, I pick up each cat, one at a time, putting them on the bottom step, which spurs a subconscious memory of flight. One by one, they run up and out of the basement, except for Silas, who's too weak to walk.

Hollis sits slumped on his throne, looking soft like a bruise, mushrooms growing out of him as the mycelium network reclaims his nutrients. Walking across the floor, stepping on roots that squish like cooked fruit under my feet, I almost lose my balance stepping on something solid. I reach down and pluck Hollis's flute from the muck. Slipping it into my back pocket, I step toward him.

It's raining dust as the house squeals, shifting on what's left of the foundation. I'm not sure what I'm doing. Maybe I want to make sure he's dead, but I keep stepping closer and closer to him until I'm leaning down and looking him square in his eyes. They're matte, like unwaxed apples. He's dead. I feel the tension in my shoulders melt.

At the stairs, I pick up Silas. Each step is more difficult as I climb, leaving bloody footprints behind. The whole house shakes above me as the roots beneath it turn to slush.

Along the way, I grunt in pain, picking up the staves and the wand, where Hollis had dropped them on his way into the basement. Outside, the cats gather close to each other, Em too. As I step off the final step, the foundation gives. A sinkhole swallows the house deep into the Tennessee clay. It drags the oak with it, its leaves already brown. It deflates like a banana peel, whose innards are liquid and dank.

I place Silas near Arbuckle and drop everything but Johnathan's staff. Turning to the hole where the house once stood, my father speaks to me. A new spell ushers forth from my lips as I mumble under my breath, and the ground forms again, filling the hole. When that is done, Johnathan speaks, and we make the lot a liminal space. Here, but barely perceptible.

Finished, I drop the staff and fall again to my knees, too weak to stand anymore.

"Aubrey!" I hear Em yell. "Aubrey, what's happening?"

"I'm dying."

"You can't."

"Watch me." I try and smile, but I'm pretty sure it's just a wince.

"We need you."

"You'll be fine without me," I say, knowing it's true.

"I don't want to be fine," she says.

The cats have all gathered around me, and as my breathing becomes labored, Arbuckle rubs against me.

"You need to get them out of me, buddy," I say.

"Wait," Em says, panicked. "Aren't they going to help you? Can't they heal you with a spell or something?"

"It doesn't work that way," I say as the cats begin to yowl.

They're calling the quintessence from me. Each one feels like a shiver being pulled from my spine, but it doesn't hurt. Watching them flow back into the cats, I'm glad they made the pact, glad they'll live on.

Trying to stand, I fall over, landing on my face and rolling onto my back. I don't want to die, but the endorphins my body is releasing make it not so bad.

I look up at Em, hovering and worrying over me.

There's a kind of poetry to her being here. What were the odds we'd meet? She'd fled The Homestead, pushing through, skipping off the

Gloam's membrane to escape the reapers, and landed here in Knoxville.

Her intent was to go far away from the reapers while remaining close to family—to home. So it sent her here.

To her cousin Perez's house, perched on the hill overlooking his former land, now the home of the Tennessee School for the Deaf, and his island—Dickinson Island—where DKX airport now sits. Inside that house, a portrait of Perez Dickinson hangs in the foyer. On its cardboard backing, someone wrote: 'Emily Dickinson wrote some of her poetry in this house.'

It's unlikely to be true, but the intent of the writer—and of those who continue to tell the story—was strong enough to call her here. A haven in her time of need.

Em leans down, and I imagine her breath on my face as she whispers in my ear.

The words roll from her tongue, a conjuring. Words full of power, nuance, and intent flow through me, filling me up, and before I realize I'm doing it, I mumble under my breath, repeating them, connecting them to the Gloam, susurrating a new kind of magic.

Warmth spreads across me as my strength returns and flesh stitches itself together. Tears roll down my face as her power and grace flow through me, and I am made to feel whole and worthy.

* * *

Walking out the gate one last time, I feel a hand on my shoulder. It's Em, smiling.

"You know you saved us all by rolling that orb down the stairs. Not sure what I would have done if it hadn't been there."

"I was trying to distract him."

"You also saved my life just now, and I don't know how to repay that," I say.

Em stops, and I do too. She gives me the look she sometimes does when she feels bad for me.

"It isn't a thing that comes with a price, Aubrey," she says.

I nod to let her know I understand, even though I'll never agree.

When we get to Gratz Street, I mumble under my breath, the lifting spell I used on Francis's body when I pushed it through the rift, but the adornment doesn't even wiggle. It makes sense my magic doesn't work on it. I rack my brain on how I'm going to retrieve it.

The way the last week has gone, I'll be lucky to get up after I get down on my hands and knees to peer down into the storm drain. I see it, but it's out of reach when I stick my arm in to grab it. I'm straining against the concrete, feeling like I'm reopening the vine wound.

"I've got it," Em says.

So, I pull my arm out and watch her drop below the sidewalk. Then I see her head poke through the wall of the ditch. She looks around for a second before she sees the adornment. I reach in. Em concentrates as she picks the adornment up with her hand and gently passes it to me.

"You really are something," I say.

"Practice makes perfect," she says, disappearing into the concrete.

I stand up as she rises out.

We set off down the sidewalk toward home. The cats, trailing behind me, Em skipping a little ahead. And me, just an old man and his clowder taking an afternoon stroll.

∞

epilogue

Death is not stillness –
It's Journey –
Eternity's collected lands
Are roamed –
The Owner of our Mind
Is now the collective Soul –
Our Gloam.

—D & C

 not planning to kill my brother, and I would just as soon avoid a fight, but I'm prepared if we do. I've brought Johnathan's staff, and it feels good in my hand as I step out of the rift into Alistair's cave. Silas follows me, and once he's through, I seal the rift with the adornment.

The bulbs that once hung overhead now lie flickering on the ground. The furniture has all been tossed, and I imagine my brother, in a rage, destroying everything after I trapped him here. The runes I had initially used to enter were one-way. A large portion of that wall lies in rubble to one side, and I imagine Alistair, in his fury, trying to blast his way out.

When I find him, he's curled on the ground like a frightened child, which, in many ways, he still is. Strewn around him are empty bottles of acorn liquor. Hollis hadn't been the one who freed him. He'd found him when Alistair finally returned to my great-aunt's house a few weeks ago, having escaped the Gloam years before. Living like a rat in this cave, trying to remember where the house was.

Hollis saw an opportunity to go after the order and get their quintessence once and for all—finally obtaining what he had tried to get all those years ago. He hadn't counted on the fact that Alistair had entered the holding stone as a seven-year-old, arguably a mature seven-year-old, but still a child. Though his body had aged while imprisoned, his mind had not matured. When Jane's quintessence defied him, refusing to enter the vessel Alistair had brought, he did what any seven-year-old would have done: he threw a tantrum, going off-book and undermining Hollis's plan.

Luckily for Hollis, I appeared and nearly finished the job for him. I know this because Silas knows it. If there's an upside—and I'm certainly not saying there is—to being trapped, suspended in the sap of Hollis's tree, it's that for all those years, Silas and my father's quintessence became part of the tree, and therefore part of Hollis.

When I consulted with the clowder about how to approach Alistair, Silas told us what he knew—what the sap had known.

Alistair had escaped the Gloam because when they bound him in the stone, it had been done in anger. Anger weakens the intent of any spell. In this case, the stone had been formed with a tiny imperfection. The order itself had been responsible for Alistair's escape.

Over the decades, as it hung against the Perpetuation—where the Caretakers had placed it as a reminder to be more vigilant concerning shadow energy—the vibrations of the Perpetuation had turned that imperfection into a crack, and that crack had grown.

One day, the stone shattered, and Alistair was free. Because his quintessence was born of shadow energy, he had more power in the Gloam. When a shade tried to stop him, he killed it, taking its adornment and opening a rift. His intent was to hide where no one could find him, so it brought him here: a cave inside an abandoned train tunnel far from where he had been raised.

Years later, Alistair finally opened a rift into our great-aunt's basement. His roots sensing Alistair's return, Hollis approached him.

He reacquainted himself with Alistair, who remembered him fondly. Over acorn tea, Alistair confided in Hollis, as he was compelled to do, and they hatched the plan for Alistair to get his revenge. The members, too old to be of use as shadow wizards, were to be killed.

Hollis used the mycelium network to locate them, and Alistair was to repay him with their quintessence. But then the pact got in the way— and then I did.

Holding onto the staff for support, I crouch close to Alistair and shake his shoulder to wake him. He groans and looks at me.

"Come to kill me, brother?" All the fight gone out of him, the effects of the tea and liquor having faded with Hollis.

"No," I say. "But I've got to send you back."

"Better that you kill me, then."

"I've made a deal with the Caretakers. If you return to the Gloam and stay there, you can live the rest of your life in peace."

"Alone."

"No, not alone," I say, helping him to stand.

"And who will keep me company, you?"

"No, too many mouths to feed," I say, smiling.

Silas rubs against Alistair's leg.

"Your cat?" he asks.

"Dad's."

Alistair reaches down and picks up Silas, who is content to be held.

Holding up Johnathan's staff, I find the door and knock three times. We wait.

The Shade comes through first, chittering and angry. It shrieks in disgust when it sees Silas in Alistair's arms, and Silas hisses. I calm it down by returning the adornment, which it takes before passing back through.

Alistair hands Silas to me, and I place him on the ground.

"I thought you said I wouldn't be alone."

"You won't," the woman from the mesa says, stepping from the rift. Pulling her hood down and unwinding the scarf from her face, I immediately recognize her. It's our mother. She still looks younger than me, the same age as I saw her in my uncle's memories.

Pascal pokes his head out, looking around, then at me. I close my eyes and blink slowly. He returns the blink and then looks at Silas, who hurries over. They touch noses, and Pascal retreats into the rift.

"You're all grown up," my mother says.

"Why didn't you say anything when we first met?" I ask her.

"I was afraid if I did, you would stay. You belong here. You deserve to be here."

I look at her and know she's right. I would have. The little boy who lost his mother would have chosen to stay. I would have given up and walked away from this world.

I think of Em and Arbuckle. "I guess part of me is glad you didn't."

"I wish I could stay longer," she says, smiling.

"Me too," I say.

"I'm proud of who you've become," she says.

"And who's that?" I ask.

"The man I always hoped you would be," she says.

Turning away, she reaches out to Alistair, who takes her hand. They both step back through the rift.

Before he goes, Silas looks at me, and I kneel and give him a good scratch.

"Take care of Mom and Alistair," I say.

He gives me a good, strong bonk on the head before turning and walking into the rift.

Standing, I hear my tendons pop and feel my muscles burn. A moment passes before a silver adornment closes the rift. I wait until it's closed to tell my mother I love her.

What had come through the rift just now wasn't her but a glamour, projected by Pascal. He now contains her quintessence in the Gloam, the way the others here protect the order.

My father and Silas had decided to return with Alistair once we found out my mother still existed there. As much as we wanted time together, he needed time to heal. I hadn't been able to spend nearly as much time with him as I'd hoped, but we had talked. Being held captive for as long as he had, and in the way he had, was traumatizing. The Gloam would be a better environment for that healing to take place.

Alistair needed some time to heal too. It was far from perfect, but it meant he wouldn't be alone this time. He'd have family.

Looking around the hovel my brother called home, I think about how strong he had to be. He had survived a lot and had done it on his own. I had to give him credit for that. He'd been born against his will and controlled or imprisoned for most of his life. I couldn't begin to imagine what he had gone through.

"There you are," Em says, sticking her head out of the rock wall. "Sorry it took so long. I came out in the wrong place."

"No problem," I say, walking to meet her.

It turned out that once Em had gotten the hang of physically affecting objects, she'd read the copy of *Among the Eidola* by Lady Penelope Stanton. In it were the musings of a particularly freewheeling eidolon named Sister Della Strada, who'd figured out the key to moving through the Gloam freely. This, of course, had led Em to practice it. I'd tried it a few times with her to be sure it would work, but it certainly wasn't my favorite mode of transport.

For me to go with her, Em must possess me, which entails her walking into me and staying there. I relinquish all control over myself when she does because if we both try to move my body at the same time, we fall over. So, as Em approaches, I straighten up and wait. Truth be told, it makes me nauseous every time, but I don't plan on doing this ever again. I feel her enter me, and I let my muscles go slack. Then I watch as she pilots me forward and through the glimmering curtain home.

* * *

A week has passed since Em and I returned. Everything creaks: the stairs, the banister as I hold onto it for balance, and my bones as I slowly make my way downstairs. Reaching the bottom, I head to the kitchen. Passing the living room, I quickly glance in. It's like a dream—Em, mixing with the morning light, laughing and dancing about the room, the stereo playing. Poly, following Em like she's a fly to be caught, appears to be dancing too.

Arbuckle lounges on the warm hardwood before the door to the deck. Saoirse and Alexander are curled together in my reading chair, Saoirse giving Alexander's head a good cleaning. Em sees me and smiles, beckoning me over to join in. I smile and shake my head. She knows I don't dance.

Turning on the kettle, I grab a tea bag. Tearing it from its envelope, I slip it into the cup, letting the string hang over the side. As the water comes to a boil, I flip the kettle off and fill the mug, then move it to the edge of the counter to steep.

Something brushes my leg, and I look down. Augustus is there. He moves around my legs and walks to the door. Picking up the mug, I follow. Arbuckle barely moves as I open the door and close it back.

Augustus walks to the edge of the deck and sits on the stairs. Looking over the grass of a lawn in dire need of mowing, I follow him out and sit down next to him. He head-butts my arm. Putting the tea down, I look at him. Our eyes meet, and I know he's leaving.

I start to say something and then stop. The words are lost as quickly as they had formed. Augustus takes a step down, and I stand up as he descends the rest of the way. He walks across the back lawn, collecting dew on his fur that glitters like diamonds in the morning sun. At the edge of the yard, where large, unkempt hedges sit, he pauses for a second. From this vantage point, where he can easily take in the entirety of home and me, he looks as though he's deciding whether to stay.

"Johnathan never told me what a Gorwrath was," I yell, knowing he can't answer and that this is probably the last time I'll ever see him.

Tears blur my vision, and when I wipe them away, Augustus is gone— through the hedges and out into the world again. I'm not surprised, but a part of me wishes he had stayed a little longer. Johnathan had become a resource over the past week. I'd learned a lot from him.

No reason to linger here. I walk into the house and close the door behind me. I step over Arbuckle, who still hasn't moved, and throw the tea bag in the trash before walking to the living room where Poly and Em dance to Nick Drake's *Time Has Told Me.*

* * *

After taking a flight from TYS to ECP, I get an Uber to the storage facility to retrieve my car. Luckily, it cranks up after sitting for a few weeks. I cancel the rental unit and grab a few things, like an old metal toolbox with my uncle's initials. I fill it with the best tools I can find. I'm no handyman, but I like to be prepared. I gave the rest of the contents to the manager.

I drive by the park where my uncle's trailer used to be, and there's already another one parked on his old lot. Probably didn't take too long to shovel up the ash, although I suspect the park owner raked it level and sifted out any chunky bits to make the turnaround as quick as possible.

The Bay County Clerk of the Court and Comptroller's office had contacted me about my uncle's estate. Turns out he had a will and some assets, but no debt. I'd be dropping by there on my way out of town to sign a couple of forms to transfer it to me. His death is still being investigated, as it took them time to identify what little remained of him.

Luckily, most of his skull survived. It matched his dental records. I'm not sure if he did it on purpose or if it was a fluke, but a few years ago, he had all his amalgam fillings replaced with ceramic, so nothing had melted out. Ceramic fillings are harder to see on an X-ray, but since he was the registered occupant of the trailer, they found his updated dental file quickly.

The police officer who had called me before the court had reached out liked to talk and appreciated the speed at which the identification had been made. My uncle's lawyer had my number on file with a standing order to call it four times a year to verify it was me. He apologized for all the years of crank calls, but it was his job, he said, and my uncle had wished for me not to know it was him. I wondered if he'd also kept my uncle informed about where the members of the order had been. I didn't ask.

This time, when I leave, I take the drive slowly through Montgomery, Birmingham, and Chattanooga. Every road has a story, and every story has someone to tell it, so I listen as I drive, the wind whispering secrets. I feel different now. I'm not sure why. I feel more confident and more energetic. Maybe having all those other lives inside me finally made mine make sense. I guess I'll never know. But I know one thing for sure:

I miss Em and the cats. For the first time in a long time,
I belong somewhere.

∞

Author's Note

I'VE BEEN TRYING TO FIND the time to write a novel for thirty years. Along the way, there were plenty of starts and stops. In the case of this novel, it began as 40,000 words of blog posts—each post a chapter, each chapter under 1,000 words. People seemed to like it—at least, my friends did. The first post on that blog was published on April 14, 2008. I'm writing this on April 3, 2025.

A lot has changed from that story to this one, but one thing remains the same: the photograph that inspired it. As young Aubrey did in the story, I took a photograph of my uncle in January of 1978. It's the photograph I describe in the first paragraph of this novel. That description is where any resemblance to my uncle ends, and William Cockcroft takes over.

That particular photo is important because when I rediscovered it nearly thirty years later, the first thought that came to mind was, *My uncle was a wizard in the '70s.* That thought started everything. It made me imagine a polyester-wearing, sportscar-driving private investigator who also knew magic. Since I was born in the '70s, it made sense to create a character I could relate to. That's why this is Aubrey Cockcroft's story—not William's.

Sometimes an idea gets stuck in your head. And while it may take a while—in my case, nearly sixteen years—to finally sit down and execute it, if you keep at it, one day you'll create something you're proud of. I feel like I have. Some of you who read it will hopefully agree and enjoy the ride. Some of you won't—and that's okay, too.

Why did it take me so long? Life. Work often left me too tired or too stressed to come home and write. But, luckily—or maybe unluckily—I found myself largely unemployed in early 2023. After a year of doing nothing but trying to find a job and failing, I'd had enough. I sat down to write. It was Saturday, June 29, 2024. I was 54, with nothing to lose but my pride.

I wrote four rough drafts over the next month before sending it off to a friend. My ask was simple: "Do I have a book here?" Luckily, he said yes. That was all the boost I needed. I wrote an official first draft over the next two weeks and sent it to friends who had agreed to read it. From their notes, I wrote two more drafts and sent it again to a few new readers who hadn't been able to read the earlier version. With their feedback, I wrote this draft. Then I did a line edit—

just as I had done with the third draft. The free version of Grammarly was my copy editor. I'm sure there are still a few typos, but I did my best.

I already have the ideas for Aubrey's second kerfuffle—and his third. The fact that you're reading this means I might get the chance to write them. For that, dear reader, I am eternally grateful.

A few quick notes on the content: The poem Em recites in subbasement six to summon Aubrey is, of course, The Test by Emily Dickinson. I used it from the following book:

The Test: *Poems by Emily Dickinson*, edited by T. W. Higginson and Mabel Loomis Todd, Second Series, Roberts Brothers, 1891.

I kept the punctuation true to the original printing, which is why some punctuation may appear to be missing in that scene.

The idea to include her in the novel came from an article titled An English Doctor's First Tour of the Old Country by Jack Neely, published circa 1997 in his "Secret History" column for *The Metro Pulse*, a once ubiquitous and vital independent magazine in Knoxville. Sadly, it is no more. The article can be found here: HTTPS://MONKEYFIRE.COM/MPOL/DIR_ZINE/DIR_1997/740/T_SECRET.HTML

Acknowledgments

First, I would like to thank those gracious first readers who took the time to read and comment on early drafts. Special acknowledgment goes to Stuart Perkins, who kindly affirmed that I did, in fact, have a book—and that it was enjoyable to read. He was the ultimate reader of this first novel, and I am forever grateful, as is my self-esteem.

The second acknowledgment goes to Alan Gratz, the first to cross the finish line with notes. His insight was invaluable in shaping the story. I should also point out that Gratz Street is real and was named after Alan's ancestor, Louis Alexander Gratz—the first and only mayor of the short-lived town of North Knoxville.

Another first reader who provided a wealth of constructive—and, to be honest, excellent—feedback was Heather Zehring. Never underestimate the willingness of someone you've barely spoken to in twenty years to lend a hand—especially if you endured the rigors of graduate school together.

Kevin Kerwin was instrumental with the third draft. This spared him from copious run-on sentences—and who knows what other ravages of the English language I thrust upon everyone else. His detailed notes and sharp editorial eye were indispensable as I rounded out the final edits.

I'd also like to thank other readers who provided feedback, including Sandi Tan, whose forthrightness convinced me to throw away the first eighteen pages. I am forever in her debt for this. Thanks also to Steve Doughty and Rob Williams for their notes, observations, encouragement, and friendship.

To all the first readers who wanted to help but got distracted by life—trust me, I get it. You can read the next one.

Last, but certainly not least, I want to thank DIVCON for taking my cover sketch, ignoring it, and instead creating a stunning cover. I put them through a trial of indecision and threw many wrenches their way during the process. They dodged them all. They also designed the interior layout of the printed book, and for that, I am immensely grateful.

THE AUTHOR has been a concession stand worker, dishwasher, deli worker, bagboy, theater usher, projectionist, graphic designer, art director, technical surveyor, project manager, factotum in an immigration law firm, produce clerk, customer service manager, and consultant.

In college, he ran an art gallery, designed numerous underground magazines, and had a short-lived radio show. While there, he also ran for student body president and lost—*twice.*

He once worked on numerous films, both student and professional, in capacities as far-ranging as caterer, writer, art director, videographer, post PA, and assistant to producers.

He holds a Master's in Screenwriting from Columbia University and a BFA in Graphic Design from the University of Tennessee.

He currently resides in Knoxville, Tennessee, with his two indoor cats, Mishka and Dr. Twinkie; a porch cat he hasn't named yet, whose food often attracts a raccoon named Karl and a possum named Franklin.

**IN HIS SPARE TIME,
HE WRITES.**